The Golden Tide

John Guy

First published on Kindle and CreateSpace in 2014 by John Guy

ISBN-13: 978-1494714246

ISBN-10: 1494714248

DEDICATION

For Monica

Who's who?

Anna	Bank account manager
Antonio Cusumano	Bar and hotel owner
Bianca	Michiel's wife
Cesare Disario	Professor of Oceanography
David Chillingworth	P&I Club Associate Director
Dino Cervetto	Coastguard Captain
Eleni and Leta Kalargyrou	Salvage tug owners
Enrico Spinelli	Shipowner
Fortunato Redivo	Fishing boat owner
George Anand	Captain of the *Barbara S*
Giovanni Paci	Lawyer from New Orleans
Giuseppe Mammino	Regional Manager ENOL
Guido Recagno	Mafia family head
Kate Jones	ITOPF Director
Laura Filippone	Mayor of Siracusa
Linus Eerlandsson	IOPC Funds Director
Luca Consentini	Lawyer in Siracusa
Maria	Dino Cervetto's wife
Marlena Dozio	Bank account manager
Michiel van Roosmalen	Freelance journalist
Osman Mohamoud	Illegal immigrant
Paola di Bartolo	Mayor of Noto
Roberto Fraille	Coastguard Lieutenant/Ugo Vinciullo's nephew
Simone Boisson	Environmental activist
Ugo Vinciullo	Regional President of Siracusa Province
Yves	Simone's lover

CHAPTER ONE

The ship lurched heavily as the Captain stepped through the chartroom door into the bridge. In the grey dawn light he could see heavy seas punching the ship on the port bow, making it roll then stagger as its eighty-three thousand tonnes of steel and oil shouldered the waves aside.

"Good morning, Third Officer," he said, courteously. "A long day ahead before we get to Augusta, I think."

"Maybe more than a long day, Captain," replied the young Third Officer. "We have five miles more of this, then when we round Cape Passero these seas are going to be awful, and the forecast is getting worse."

After a lifetime at sea Captain George Anand was not unduly worried by bad weather or nervous Third Officers and he knew that oil companies took little account of either.

"ENOL wants us in Augusta tonight," he replied mildly. "They need to get the cargo out and us away before the New Year's Day shutdown. They don't want us getting a day off in port. They will be afraid of you youngsters going ashore and chasing the Sicilian girls, eh?"

"Here's the forecast, Captain," said the Third Officer, staggering slightly as the ship hit another hole in the sea, seeming to stop suddenly then shake itself free and throw the green water aside. "I just printed it out. We have been making this run for three years now. Last winter we had a storm like this in December, right around here, and we had ten metre waves and more. We were in ballast then, on our way back to Libya. We thought we were going to be blown ashore passing Siracusa. One ship did end up on the beach."

Captain Anand held the forecast under the chart table lamp. A deep low pressure system to the east of Sicily was intensifying. On the synoptic chart the isobars were packed together with complex fronts radiating out like spiders' legs. The deadpan text of the forecast promised 60 knot winds from the north-northeast. That would be right on the nose when they altered course around the southern tip of Sicily to head up to the refinery complex at Augusta. Heavy seas right on the bow, a tired ship, a full cargo of seventy-eight thousand tonnes of Libyan crude oil and a pushy Italian oil company wanting to save a day's hire for the ship by getting it in and out before the New Year gave the crew a day off in port.

"Not much of a Christmas present, Third," he grumbled. "But let's keep full speed while we can, and we will deal with what we find when we round the cape. I don't want to make my last voyage before I retire the first one where I arrive late."

****

The rain was catching at the sleeve of her blouse each time she lifted her arm to suck on the cigarette. She was shivering slightly. One layer of ethical hand-woven cotton was not enough to keep out the cold wind which pushed into the porch where she was standing. She should go back into the meeting.

She looked through the rain at the three tall masts of the *Duchess Anne*, the square-rigger moored in front of where she stood in the doorway of Dunkirk's Maritime Museum. Simone Boisson loved the purity of the sailing ship. No oil, no pollution, a ship in harmony with its environment. That's why I fight for clean seas, she thought. That's why I left Greenpeace to help set up Marine Bleu. Greenpeace has become a tool of governments, they work with shipowners, part of the system. Marine Bleu will never be that, we will fight for clean seas, as we have fought before.

She stubbed out the cigarette and felt her lips tighten with irritation as she pushed open the museum door. This was a lovely place, full of the history of the sea. Marine Bleu was a good cause, one worth fighting for. But Yves did not need to call a meeting today.

There were no leaders in Marine Bleu, every activist had an equal voice. That was how they had set it up, after the *Erika* oil spill had polluted the Bay of Biscay. Simone had fought to clean those beaches, fought to save the birds struggling in the filthy black oil and fought to make Total, the greedy oil company, pay compensation. That was twelve years ago, and she had been fighting since then to keep the seas clean.

Sometimes, like today, Simone felt she was fighting to keep her group focused. They did not need meetings to go and save the birds when the *Erika* broke up. They had not needed any meetings when they hitched down to Spain to join the clean-up after the *Prestige* sank and polluted Galicia. Now we are getting middle-aged, she thought. We have meetings instead of action. All voices are equal, but Yves seemed to like to hear his more than the others.

****

"You are forty-eight, Michiel. It is time to grow up."

Michiel van Roosmalen could hear his wife but he did not look up at her. He knew she had more to say and nothing he could reply would stop the bitter words.

"You follow these dream stories that no-one wants to buy. Your neighbours get up in the morning and put on a suit and tie and ride their bikes across the Willemsbrug to work. You chase around the world looking for fantasies and spending our money. Then you get up and put on a suit and tie to make a phone call which produces nothing. Nothing."

Michiel could see himself reflected in the long mirror, lit from the winter light which flooded through tall curtainless windows into their modern brick terraced house on Rotterdam's Noordereiland. Bianca is right, he thought. I put on a suit and tie before I make an important call. I work from home, I am a freelance journalist, I can dress as I want. But I'm not a sloppy journalist turning out pieces on the latest fashion. I'm a serious writer who tackles serious issues. Sometimes they sell, sometimes they don't, but they all matter to me. And I want to feel smart and sharp when I'm working.

Behind him he heard the front door open.

"I am going to work," he heard. "You could try it sometime." Then the door slammed and he sat in silence.

Bianca had not been like that when they married. The beautiful dark Dutch Sumatran girl had seemed to share his crusading concern for social justice. She had cheered and danced in the kitchen when he came home with the copy of the International Herald Tribune which published his exposé of child abuse scandals in Belgium. She had kissed and hugged him and almost torn his suit off when The Wall Street Journal took his articles skewering the reckless lending of Dutch mortgage banks. But over twenty years newspapers had become more timid and now had little space for crusading journalism. He could sell less and less, and Bianca had become angry and scornful.

She wants children, Michiel told himself. It is getting late for that and we cannot talk about it anymore. Through his thick-framed glasses he could see himself in the mirror, cropped brown hair, a few grey touches appearing, a neat white shirt and red tie. She wants a guy who looks like me but who has a steady job and who is home at six o'clock every day. Not a man who still wants to put the world right. Who wants to expose fraud and shine a light into dark corners. Who follows a story wherever it goes, whenever he has to.

Not that this one is going anywhere at the moment, he admitted to himself ruefully. He had made three calls that morning, trying to interest editors in his latest project. A total blank. "I don't care if the Spanish made millions of dollars from the *Prestige* oil spill ten years ago, I don't care if they are about to jail a Greek Captain for something he didn't do, I don't care if corruption follows oil spills as sure as night follows day and my readers don't want to spoil their New Year worrying about Americans ripping off BP for compensation for the Gulf oil spill," was the summary of what the three editors said. The last one put it most clearly. "Listen, Michiel. You are a good writer, but you care too much about things other people don't know and care about. An oil spill and pollution is a story when it happens, because it looks awful. If people do bad things because of the oil spill that might be a story too if you can prove it while the oil is still there to see. But I can't put a history of bad things behind oil spills in my paper, however much greed and corruption is involved. Do me a story on the latest diet. That always runs well in the New Year."

****

Capitano de Vascello Dino Cervetto could feel the weather coming. He could not have explained how. His father and his father before him were seamen, so he had the weather in his DNA. He had grown up watching the winter waves lashing over the tiny fishing port of Camogli, feeling the wind coming in over the Gulf of Genoa and searching for weaknesses in the old stone flats overlooking the fishing boats.

He had seen the women of the village watching the seas building and waiting for their husbands to bring the fishing boats surfing back in through the port entrance. He could remember the dark clothes and silence at the funerals of those who did not make it back. He knew the weather, he knew the sea and he respected it.

His career in the Italian Navy and Coastguard had taught him how to read weather maps. But he relied more on looking at the sea and sky and the feeling inside him than he did on forecasters and computer print-outs. Here in Sicily the weather was better than along his colder northern coast, but he knew that in winter it could deliver some nasty surprises.

He was a decisive man, but now he hesitated. With this storm coming he should be here, at his post as head of the Coastguard in Augusta, Sicily's main oil port. Only last year he had overseen the rescue of the crew of a cargo ship blown ashore just to the south at Siracusa. He should be here, but he could not say no to Maria. He could never say no to her, because when he tried she laughed and lit him up with that huge smile and made him feel dizzy looking into her eyes. She wanted them to spend a few days over the New Year with her family in their village west of Palermo. "The whole family will be there and I want them to enjoy my grizzly old sailor as much as I do," she said. "You can walk to the top of the hill where there is a mobile signal and you can call your officers every day and you will be happy. And so will I."

He could not believe that this beautiful, lively young Sicilian girl would love and marry a dry bachelor naval officer. A buttoned up disciplined Genovese naval officer from the uptight north of Italy which Sicilians laughed at. But she had and he could not say no to her, so now he reached for the phone, pushing his weather feeling to the back of his mind.

"Giuseppe," he said. "Dino here. I want to check on the tanker movements coming up for the next few days. What are you expecting at the outer terminal?"

He was calling Giuseppe Mammino, the regional manager for ENOL, Italy's major oil company and the main importer of oil into Augusta. He did not like talking to him. He is just too clever, thought Dino. Too Sicilian. I will never get used to these people.

"Just the *Barbara S*?" he confirmed. "She is a regular, so I suppose the master knows the area well. And the ship has been looked at recently by your people?"

He accepted Giuseppe's assurances, only half believing them. She's a tough old ship on a regular run, and regularly scrutinised by ENOL's people, he convinced himself. It will be OK. Maria will be happy and her father will get out his oldest wine and anyway I can be back here in three hours if anything happens.

CHAPTER TWO

"I think we should be slowing her down, Captain," said the Second Officer, tensely. He was looking hard at the Captain, moving his head from side to side to emphasise the point. "She will not take this for much longer and the seas are only building, Sir."

Captain Anand did not answer. He was bracing his short body against the side of the bridge instrument console, looking forward and down through the sloping bridge windows to the two hundred and twenty metres of red-painted steel deck which stretched ahead. He could see the deck flexing and feel the ship vibrating as it pitched forward into the waves. He had seen many storms and his thoughts went back over his fifty years at sea. How did these young men learn to speak like that to their superiors? When I was at sea school in Calcutta we were taught that the officers knew best and the Captain knew everything. Now I should be retired and I agreed to one last voyage and these boys I have never met before think they know more than me.

He felt the deck under his feet shudder and he gripped the handrail in front of him more tightly as the ship plunged forward into a trough. Green water exploded over the flare of the bows, there was a pause which seemed to last for a long time, then the ship shook herself like a dog coming out of a river and slowly began to lift again to the next wave. A torrent of foam ran down the deck and then sprayed up into curtains that momentarily obscured the bridge windows as the wind caught the water shedding from the sides of the deck.

The worst thing is that he is right, thought Anand. We should slow down. But they want us in Augusta by tomorrow morning latest and I don't want to let them down.

The habit of obedience was strong in Captain Anand. Since he had left his home in Calcutta at the age of sixteen to go to sea school he had learnt that obedience was the right way, even if sometimes you knew better. As a deck hand he had obeyed the Bosun. As a young officer he had obeyed the Chief Mate. Obedience had worked and he had risen up the ladder. For thirty years sailing as master he had obeyed the ship's owner and charterer.

He could see the Second Officer waiting for an answer. The ship had rounded Cape Passero and was now heading northeast to pass Siracusa and make for Augusta. The Third Officer had gratefully handed the watch over to the Second Officer and gone below, hoping to snatch some lunch and an afternoon sleep despite the ship's violent motion. The engines were still running at full ahead, although Anand reckoned the speed over the ground had probably dropped to ten knots. Slowing the engine would make the ship ride more easily but would drop the speed further. I think this boy must come from Bombay, he thought. They teach them to be so cocky there. Too clever, sometimes.

He looked up.

"I am going to speak to the owner and charterer, Second," he said. "Then we will decide what to do about her speed, eh."

****

He looked out through the window at the rain sweeping across the square. Antonio Cusumano's bar was the pride of Ortigia. Set right across the wide piazza opposite the Duomo, Ortigia's yellow stone cathedral, it was a magnet for tourists. Even the locals liked to sit in the shade of the umbrellas and drink an *aperitivo*.

The snacks I give them with the drinks are what make them talk about the bar, he thought. Shavings of fennel, sliced orange with chilli flakes, salty local cheese, they love it. He rubbed his hands together. It costs money, but it makes money. But now in December there are no tourists. Before the financial crisis they came to our beautiful jewel of a city even in winter. But now they come only in summer, they spend less when they do come, and the ones who come in the winter, the English who don't like to spend money, they don't come out in this weather anyway.

The weather does not keep some people away though, he thought. The door banged open. There was a pause, then a squat, heavily muscled man stepped in, turning sideways to avoid his shoulders touching the door posts. He thinks he is in a Hollywood movie, Antonio smiled to himself, as the man paused again, then slowly removed his soaking fedora.

"Good morning, Signor," Antonio said politely. "You are punctual as always."

For twenty years this man had pushed his way into the bar at the same time each week. Antonio had never asked his name. He knew from his accent that he came from the Iblei mountains. And he knew that he had to pay him ten per cent of his takings each week. Not because he was afraid of this man. He paid because he and his father before him had always paid *pizzo*, the Mafia protection tax. The *pizzo* was a way of life. They paid, like all the small businesses paid, and they were able to work in peace.

He had never considered not paying, but he knew of those foolish enough to defy the Mafia. The government had done much to tame the Mafia, and he knew the crime family head was a fugitive, forced to live underground, hidden in a bunker. But those who thought its power was broken soon found out the error of their thinking. Problems for anyone not paying the *pizzo* began with small things. Garbage not collected. Garbage dumped on the doorstep. Graffiti. Noisy, drunk customers. Articles in the local paper alleging hygiene problems. Intrusive inspections from government officials who insisted they were only doing their job. Police dropping in with unwelcome questions. The tax man looking where he had never looked before.

For those brave or foolish enough to continue to refuse to pay there were older, more direct methods. A child abducted on the way to school brought most business owners to heel. A car swerving into their wife on the way to market was quite effective. Antonio shivered. He paid, but times were hard now.

"Here are the accounts for this week, Signor," he said. "And I have a request. A reasonable one. For your family to consider. This is a good business, and we are loyal supporters. But the crisis has hit us hard. Our takings are down thirty per cent this year, and this winter we are running at only half the normal rate. This weather makes things worse. My costs are fixed. Can we discuss a change to our...arrangement? Can you consider a charge based on our profits, not our takings? Please, ask the family, I am afraid the business will not survive the winter otherwise."

The enforcer looked at him without expression. "Until next week," he growled, slipping the envelope into his coat pocket. "Have a good week, Signor Cusumano."

Antonio watched him replace his hat and turn to leave, playing out his own Hollywood fantasy of the Mafia. It's a joke, he thought. A joke to be a Sicilian. He smiled to himself. I don't think he can read those joke accounts anyway.

****

"Captain Anand here, on the *Barbara S*. Can I speak with the fleet manager please?"

He did not know this company, Armatori Fratelli Spinelli SpA, but it was not the first time he had sailed for Italian owners. Many Italian ships are crewed by Indian officers, and he had always found Italian shipowners good to work for, supportive of their seafarers. They are family companies, he said to himself while he was waiting with the satellite phone in his hand. The owners take a real interest, not like some of those big corporations.

He was surprised when he heard the voice barking down the phone at him.

"Enrico Spinelli here, Captain. Are you making good time for Augusta? ENOL is holding the berth for you."

Anand had not expected to get the owner himself on the phone. He was hoping to talk with a fleet manager, share with him the responsibility of slowing the ship down. He did not want to argue with an angry shipowner.

"Good day, Sir, good day, I am very happy to speak to you, Sir," said Anand. "I wanted to speak to the fleet manager, Sir. We have a little problem with the weather. Perhaps it will make it difficult for us to get to Augusta tonight, Sir. I think we may be looking at changing the ETA."

"We are a Neapolitan company, Captain," he heard. "In this company I manage my ships, and my Captains make sure the ships keep to their schedules."

There was a pause. Anand was having difficulty keeping the phone to his ear while holding on to the communications desk as the ship pitched heavily.

"Captain," said Spinelli forcefully. "We have a five year charter with ENOL to carry oil from Libya to Sicily. We will be due to renew that charter soon and I want to keep it, do you understand? We don't arrive late, we don't make ENOL wait and the ship does not sit idle because it is a public holiday."

"The weather…" Anand had begun to reply when he was cut off by Spinelli.

"Captain, I know this is your first voyage with us. You are in charge on the ship. You have to do what you think is best. But think carefully what is best, because it is best not to be late when an oil company is waiting for your cargo."

The phone went dead before Anand could reply. He had to steady the receiver with both hands to get it back into its rest as the ship pitched heavily again. He could not decide what to do. Oh dear, he thought, now I am thinking what is best, but what is best, that is the question?

****

She ran her fingers through her short, dark hair. In the mirror she could see Yves. He was naked, lounging against the half open window. He flicked the ash from his half-smoked cigarette out into the street.

She felt a stab of irritation. I wish he wouldn't do that, she thought. This is my home town. The neighbours know me. They know my mother and my father. They don't approve of me having a young lover here. They don't need to see him in the window. He does it on purpose. He is so vain. He wants them all to know he is the lover of an older woman. Of Simone Boisson, the local girl, the special needs teacher, the girl brought up in this lovely old town of Bergues, the girl who cares about children and birds who is becoming a spinster whom no-one will care about because she cares too much about things most men don't care about.

Simone tugged viciously at a grey hair. She did not want to nag, but she could not help herself.

"That English girl from Greenpeace had plenty to say yesterday," she said. "You found her very interesting, Yves."

She saw Yves smile. The bastard thinks he is quite something, she thought. I let him come to live with me because I wanted that young body. Because I wanted his commitment. His energy. Now I don't know what I want.

"Come away from the window, the neighbours don't want to see you like that," she said sharply. She hated herself for sounding middle-aged. "You could dress and go outside if you want to smoke."

"You don't want me to dress," he said, closing the window and stepping over the clothes on the floor as he came towards her. "And it is raining again. It is always raining here. You *Ch'ti's* like the rain. And you like me like this," he said as he touched himself against her back.

Simone was stiff and angry but her body was betraying her. She knew he could see her nipples hardening. She knew he would reach down and touch them now. He was a bastard, but she did not want him thinking of the English girl. She wanted to be loved. She leant her head back against him.

CHAPTER THREE

This can't be happening, he said to himself. It is a rough sea but the ship is not so old. He knew the *Barbara S* had been built in 1995 in Korea, one of the very first double-hull tankers. She was an Aframax, optimised for the oil freight trade and an ocean workhorse. Seventeen years old was not a great age for a modern ship.

"Tell me again," he said to the overall-clad engineer who stood next to him at the bridge front, holding on to the handrail with one hand and swaying as the ship plunged into the growing seas. "You say water is coming into the pump room. But the pump room is sealed. Have you checked the hatches are closed, eh? Have you checked you engineers have not left a valve open?"

The engineer was not afraid of the Captain.

"Captain, I could see the water coming down the bulkhead from the deck area. I tasted it. It is salt water and it must be coming from a crack in the deck. I told the Chief and he and the Second Engineer are in there now, looking for the crack. They sent me up to tell you."

He did not repeat what the Chief Engineer had said next, which was, "Tell that pompous old fool to slow the ship down before he drowns us all." Instead he looked at the Captain and said, "The Chief requests you slow down, Sir, enough to allow us to get some people out on deck to check there."

Captain Anand did not answer. He was thinking fast. So they are all on this slowing down thing now, the Chief is also a young guy, they are all on slowing down, they see the chance of a day off over New Year and they think they can pull the wool over my eyes. But maybe he is right. Maybe there is a crack. The ship is flexing a lot, maybe we should be going slower. I will call their bluff, they will not catch me out. They will not make an old fool out of me.

He turned away from the engineer and addressed the Second Officer, who was waiting expectantly by the engine telegraph. "Second, call the duty engineer and tell him we are going to manoeuvring speed for a short while. When he is ready reduce to half speed and alter course a little to starboard so she rides easily. Also call the Bosun and have him ready to go on deck with some sailors and lifelines."

He looked back at the engineer, who had not moved except to brace himself against the ship's motion. "Tell the Chief Engineer we will have a look for his crack. Yes, I am coming myself to see this important crack. Then we will get back on course for Augusta, where they do not believe in cracks and are waiting for us."

****

In the gloom of the old wine press he paced up and down, not looking at the thin, bespectacled man who stood just inside the closed door. He did not like what he was hearing.

"Tell my cousin not to put up with any crap from Cusumano," he said. "That parasite has more bars and hotels and *pensiones* than even we know, and he cooks his books more than he ever cooks in his kitchens. Tell my cousin to stop acting like a Hollywood Mafia enforcer and instead act like a real one. Twist Cusumano's nose and twist his wallet."

Guido Recagno was frustrated. He wanted to go to Ortigia. To walk down the middle of the road. To see the people draw back as he passed. To slap fat Cusumano in the face in front of everyone. But he could not. He was the head of Sicily's major Mafia family, but he was forced to hide from the police in this bunker.

The village tour guide nodded. He tried not to talk with Recagno more than he had to. He took the calls from the enforcer in Ortigia on the town hall telephone, where he worked as a guide to the village's living museum. He relayed the news from Ortigia to Recagno and the instructions from Recagno to his enforcers, and he made sure his most important living exhibit was properly looked after. But he never felt comfortable with him.

He shivered slightly. It was cold standing still in the old stone building. They were in the village of Buscemi, 800 metres up in the Iblei mountains. It is so remote, he thought, quiet, everyone knows everyone. No-one speaks of strangers coming and going at night. But the genius of this is that one hundred thousand tourists come here every summer. They all walk into U Parmientu, the old wine press. They know they are in the presence of history. They don't know that three metres below them is a living space built into the old wine tank. They would not be happy if they learnt that the old tank was home to Sicily's most wanted man.

Buscemi has kept its traditions, he thought. We kept the last carpenter's shop intact when he died. We kept the winemaker's place, the tinker's shop, the shoemaker and plate fixer's shop, the blacksmith's shop, the labourer's house. And we made a living museum of them which thousands of people come to visit. They come to walk around our village. But they don't know we also preserve another Sicilian tradition, the last of the Mafia family heads.

The guide knew what was coming next. After a month Recagno could no longer hide his agitation. "Bring Annabella to the old farm manager's place tonight," he said. "The usual precautions. The village roads watched. No lights. And no-one out after ten o'clock. I will be there at eleven. Pick her up again at midnight."

The guide nodded and left. What a life, he thought. Your whore brought to a museum bed once a month. Your wife watched twenty-four hours a day in case she goes near you. Your food delivered in a basket. No sunshine, no pretty girls, no wine and no bed to share all three in the afternoon. Power in Sicily comes at a high price.

****

"Come down to slow speed, Second," ordered Captain Anand. "And alter course to steer north. Let's put the sea on the starboard bow a little and see if we can tuck in behind Capo Murro di Porco."

He was giving the orders as he stepped into the bridge, shaking seawater from his heavy weather jacket. He could see the Second Officer standing by the control console and waited for his acknowledgement. There was a pause. He wants an explanation as well, Anand sensed. These boys want everything spelt out for them, they question too much.

"Do what I am telling you, Second," he said sharply. "There is a crack. A small crack. The deck is opening a little by the pump room cofferdam bulkhead. We will shelter until the weather eases. Now move sharply."

He reached for the VHF radio handset. The ship was moving more easily now. The seas were still growing bigger, and spray was whipping from the tops of them as the wind increased in force. But a loaded Aframax tanker has plenty of buoyancy and the bow was rising to the waves comfortably as the ship slowed to walking speed. The seas will be easier in the shelter of the cape, he told himself. So many times I have run for shelter in the old days. When we had small ships and old ships. The owners understood we had to do that. But it is many years since then, I can't remember when I last had to shelter.

Modern big ships can ride out most things. That's good, he thought, because oil company charterers are less understanding now than the owners used to be.

Better safe than sorry, he decided, and pressed the transmit switch on the VHF.

"Augusta Coastguard, Augusta Coastguard, this is the *Barbara S*, *Barbara S*," he said. When the crackling voice of the Coastguard answered he gave his position and a quick summary of the situation.

"This is the *Barbara S*, loaded tanker bound for Augusta. We are ten miles south-southeast of Capo Murro di Porco. We are in heavy seas and have a small crack in the deck, so we are moving closer to the cape to seek shelter. When the weather moderates we will return to our course for Augusta. We do NOT require assistance, I repeat we do NOT require assistance. This call is for information only."

The Coastguard asked for confirmation of the vessel's name and call sign and asked the Captain to stand by.

The rules about what tanker captains have to report to shore authorities vary around the world, and Captain Anand did not know if he was obliged to report his change of course towards shelter to the Italian Coastguard or not. But he supposed the Sicilians might be a little touchy about a loaded tanker closing into the shore just south of a historic city without any explanation. He was not worried about the crack. It was small and did not appear to be spreading, so as long as he could keep the ship in shelter it would be safe and could easily be repaired later after discharging the cargo. But always better safe than sorry, he repeated to himself.

"Keep the watch and listen out for the Coastguard, Second," he said, more sharply than he meant. "I am going to tell the owner we will be delayed."

That's not going to be an easy call, he thought.

****

The young Coastguard officer was close to panic. His English was not as good as it should have been, and he had struggled to understand the Indian accent of the Captain of the *Barbara S* whom he had just spoken to on the VHF. He knew the *Barbara S*, she was the regular crude oil tanker due in later that day to the ENOL berth. He half understood the Captain had told him that the ship was cracked. A big loaded tanker like that cracking up? He did not know if it was possible, and he did not know what he should be doing about it.

In fact Lieutenant Roberto Fraille did not know enough to be left in charge of a Coastguard station. At his age he should have been at sea learning his trade in the Italian Navy, then serving in different Italian ports to gain experience and get used to dealing with foreign ship masters. But this was Sicily, he was a local boy, his mother wanted him at home and her brother was Ugo Vinciullo, the Regional President. So he had a rank he did not deserve and a comfy job close to Mama.

He reached for the phone. It was the post-Christmas holiday period and he knew Capitano Cervetto was away with his wife. He had strict orders to call the Capitano if he needed help, but he did not want to lose face if there was nothing wrong. He was afraid to call him, but more afraid not to call him. What if the ship got into trouble now and he had not sought assistance? He felt his pulse racing as the call went straight through to his senior officer's answerphone. He left a quick message and put the phone down with relief. He did not like talking to Capitano Cervetto, because he knew that the Capitano did not think much of young men who got their jobs because of their powerful uncles rather than through hard work and discipline.

He did not know what to do next. Should he call the ship to try and get more information? There was no-one else on duty whom he could ask to do that because he was the designated English speaker of the watch. He would not call the ship back, he did not want to make himself look silly.

He fidgeted in his chair, then reached for the phone again. He knew how to solve his problem. He would call his uncle. His uncle always knew what to do, and always seemed to have the power to do it.

CHAPTER FOUR

Captain Anand could not believe what he was hearing. He waited for the Coastguard officer to finish talking then pressed the transmit button on the VHF. He spoke slowly and as clearly as he could.

"I do not understand, Sir," he said. "I have just reported to you that the ship is getting safely into shelter now. We are in shelter from Capo Murro di Porco, the waves here are smaller and we are monitoring the crack in the deck. It is very small and is not growing. So why are you saying we must go out to sea again? That is not the way for the ship to be safe, Sir."

If the Captain had known he was speaking to a young Lieutenant with no seagoing experience who was taking his orders from a local politician with no connection with the sea he might have been more forceful. But he did not know that. He knew only that he was talking to the authorities ashore, and he heard the order repeated.

"Captain, you must move the ship away from the coast. You cannot stay where you are. I am ordering you to move the ship at least 12 miles from the nearest shore. Do you understand? You must move the ship at least 12 miles offshore. That is an order from the Italian Coastguard."

The Captain hesitated. The ship was still rising and falling over the waves and even at dead slow ahead was taking water over the bow each time it plunged into a wave trough. If he took her out to sea again the full force of the storm would hit them.

Respect for the authorities battled with fear that the ship would not stand any more pounding. He tried again.

"Sir, our ship is safe here. We can ride out the storm and then come in for repair. I will call my owner and they can send out a classification society expert. You will see the crack is safe and we will be able to come to port safely when the storm is over."

In the warm operations room of the Augusta Coastguard, Lieutenant Roberto Fraille was getting annoyed. His uncle was the Regional President, and his uncle had been very clear what he should do. He should not allow a tanker full of oil to come close to the coast if he suspected that it was in trouble. Tell him to go out of our territorial waters, his uncle had ordered, and he repeated the order again to the Captain.

On the bridge of the *Barbara S* Captain Anand acknowledged the order and looked at the Chief Mate, who had taken over the watch from the Second Mate at 1600. They had both heard the order to go to sea repeated. They both looked out through the bridge windows at the lumpy grey seas and flying spray, and they both looked seaward at the huge waves building up outside the lee of the point ahead of them. Captain Anand knew what the Chief Mate was thinking. They should stay here, in safety. He thought of the masters who had been jailed for disobeying orders from the shore, even when those orders were clearly wrong.

He shook his head, then looked up.

"Alter course to 045 degrees True, Mate," he said, avoiding the Mate's accusing stare. "Push the engine up to slow speed and we will see how she goes. We will go twelve miles offshore. Tell the Chief Engineer to keep an eye on the pump room. I have not been able to call the owner yet. I will speak to him now and then we will see."

****

He clicked on Google. He had three tabs open, researching what US blogs were saying about the Winter Cabbage Diet. He clicked back to his Word file. He had written three hundred words and he had a quote from a top Dutch model to give authenticity to the piece. He had to pump it up to eight hundred words. If the editor wanted a topical diet article, he could write a topical diet article. Michiel was forming the words in his head as he typed.

Only half his brain was engaged. The other half was drifting. It doesn't take much to write this dross, he was thinking. But they'll pay me for it, and pay well to hear what some neurotic super-thin woman eats for breakfast. I could use the cash to buy presents for children at Sinterklaas. That's what Bianca wants. Children, presents, a family around her. I want that too. I'll tell her, he decided. I'll tell her we should try for a baby. It will be her best Christmas present.

Rain was fingering the windows and the light shifted as the wind gusted through the young trees that lined the street. Michiel was closing out the diet article now, how to use the cabbage water, the vitamins, the g-factor. He could send it off today, send an invoice, get some wine in the fridge for Bianca when she came in, tell her about the baby.

He was looking at Google again now. The tabs open were about recent oil spills. He was checking out the results of the investigation into the *Sea Empress* spill. Seventy-two thousand tonnes of crude oil spilt in West Wales. How many millions of pounds had been spent on cleaning up seabirds which then died? How much spent on research after the event? How much spent to establish that the seabird colonies were thriving the year after? How much spent on loss of earnings for hotels and tourist facilities, even though the whole area was clean and open the summer after the spill? How much spent on the beach clean-up even though beaches not cleaned were exactly the same as those cleaned one year after the event?

He was working steadily, brain engaged. He could feel the story building. The *Prestige* disaster. Seventy-seven thousand tonnes of heavy fuel oil spilt off Galicia, North Spain, because an idiot in the Spanish government had forced the ship to go to sea when it needed shelter. How many millions spent on compensation? But Galicia had more Blue Flag beaches that summer than ever in history, because the millions spent on clean-up had cleaned up all the muck that was on the beaches before the oil spill.

He looked up, startled. Hours had passed. The front door was open and Bianca was coming in, shaking the rain from her coat. She stepped across the open plan hallway and looked over his shoulder.

"Busy doing something useful, I see," she said. Her tone was flat. No sarcasm in her voice, but the words cut like a whip.

No wine, no article sent off, no welcome and no way to talk about babies. Michiel wanted to stand up and hug her but it was too late.

"I am going to my sister's," he heard. "She has the family round. It will be nice to play with the children."

The front door closed behind her. Michiel shut his eyes.

****

It was not a good time to call Enrico Spinelli. He was a short, tough man and the oldest brother in a hard Neapolitan family. He did not like being threatened and humiliated, but that was the only way he could understand the call he had just taken. His father had left the shipping company to him and his two brothers. His father and his uncle had built a sound, small company run on a tight budget from an old office in an ornate but crumbling building overlooking the Port of Naples. It was too sound, too small and too tight for Enrico and his brothers. They wanted capital to expand. Everywhere shipping was mushrooming as China's economy sucked in imports and spurted out exports. Why should they miss out?

There is always a willing investor in Naples if you don't ask too many questions. So their small shipping company, Armatori Fratelli Spinelli SpA, had made good use of the money that the local crime families, the Camorra, needed to launder. They had used the money to back an order for a long line of new bulk carriers and tankers to be built for them in Chinese shipyards. That was when the shipping markets were booming, and new ships paid for themselves in a year of trading. When they had begun to take the dirty money it looked a one way bet. Enrico convinced his brothers that they were not in debt to the Camorra because they would return the cash quickly, clean and with interest, leaving AFS as a leading family shipowner.

Enrico thumped the heavy old wooden desk with his thick, hairy fist. The one way bet had turned sour when the markets crashed in 2008. Now the shipyards were delivering the new ships and the Camorra was paying for them. But there was no payback because the shipping markets were at the lowest rates for thirty years and getting worse. The ships were bleeding cash, not making it. The caller had got straight to the point. The Camorra families did not mind being kept waiting to get their money back, but while they were waiting Enrico should remember who owned his ships, and who now also owned him.

The phone rang again. His secretary put through the satellite phone call from the *Barbara S.*

"Captain, are you any closer to Augusta," he shouted into the phone. "I need this charter and you need to get the ship in."

That fool of a Captain was almost babbling with fear. Enrico liked that, he liked to dominate. But he did not like what he was hearing from the Captain.

"You have cracked the ship, Captain?" he queried. "What sort of a crack? How do you know? Where is the ship now?"

The line was poor and he struggled to understand the master.

"You told the Coastguard? Are you mad, Captain? Is there any oil leaking?"

His thick forearm bulged as he squeezed the phone receiver in his fist.

"Captain, you must get the ship into port. We will be overrun by those Coastguard idiots but that cannot be helped. If there is no oil then there is no crack worth worrying about and you do not need to tell them anything. Try to get to Augusta. A superintendent will meet you there and we will sort this out. We will sort you out, Captain. I need that ship and I need the ENOL charter."

****

There is no doubt, thought Dino. Maria's mother is the best cook on earth. He loved the austere and simple food of his Ligurian home province. He had grown used to the food in the naval messes. He ate to function. Then he had met Maria. Here in Sicily he had discovered that food could be something deeper and more complex. Not just for survival, something hotter and more sensual. He looked up across the scrubbed wooden table and saw Maria was smiling at him. She has guessed what I am thinking, he thought. How does she do it?

Maria winked at him and mouthed one word - later - and got up to clear away the plates. Her father picked up the bottle of Nero d'Avola to pour him some more wine but Dino covered his glass. He was warm in this old stone farmhouse sheltered by the mountains west of Palermo. He could not hear any wind. The octopus pressed with pistachio nuts had been superb, the baby milk lamb chops cooked with pine kernels melted off the bone and the *caponata* was every flavour of Sicily's history in one dish. But he could not relax.

"Maria," he said. "I will go to call the office. I need to check, and then after the walk up the hill I will be able to eat some of your mother's *panna cotta*. And take some more of your father's good wine."

At the top of the steep cobbled stone alleyway Dino came out of the village onto the open hillside. In the five minutes climbing up the path until his mobile began to pick up a signal he felt the wind growing stronger. He saw the missed call icon and dialled up the message. The words were like a punch in the stomach. He had left that pampered idiot in charge with a storm coming and now there was a tanker in trouble.

He stabbed the quick dial icon for his office.

"Fraille, Cervetto here," he said, and heard the Lieutenant draw in his breath at the other end of the phone. "What is the situation with the *Barbara S*? Where is she?"

The wind was gusting around him and making it hard to hear the soft tones of the so-called watch officer. If it is like this here, what must it be like off the east coast? He shivered slightly as he imagined the waves building in the wind.

"So the ship has a crack in the deck, it is not leaking, and the Captain has told you the ship is in shelter behind Capo Murro di Porco," he repeated. He was thinking fast. The master was a regular, he knew that, and he was sensible and knew the coast. The ship would be safe there, and he had time to get to Augusta and take over from Fraille before he did any damage.

"Do nothing and say nothing to anyone, Fraille," ordered Cervetto, grimly. "I will be there as quickly as I can."

In Augusta Lieutenant Fraille hung up the phone. His hand was shaking. He had ordered the ship to go to sea, but Capitano Cervetto had not asked him if he had given any orders to the ship, so he had not told him. Capitano Cervetto had not asked him if it was the regular master on the ship, so he had not told him that it was a new Captain they did not know. And Capitano Cervetto had told him to tell no-one now, but he had told his uncle before that. He sat back in the chair. The ship would be fine, it was a massive vessel. And his uncle would look after him. Capitano Cervetto was a very scary man, but his uncle was a very well-connected man. In Sicily connections are protection, even against angry senior Coastguard officers.

CHAPTER FIVE

He was standing athwartships looking forward through the bridge windows. His legs were braced and he held tightly on to the rail along the front of the instrument console. His body jerked sideways each time the ship slammed into a wave, then his weight came down on his knee joints as the ship lifted and rolled away from the crest. You feel your knees, he said to himself. When you get old things wear out. I never felt storms when I was young.

It was dark now, but he could make out the white curling tops of the waves. They were big, and getting bigger. So far she is riding OK like this, he thought. How big can these seas get?

The Chief Mate was bending over the chart table. He did not look up when he spoke. "We are five miles due south of the point now, Captain," he said, raising his voice slightly to compete with the noise of the wind outside the open lee door. "It is not too late to turn now and get back into shelter. I do not think we will be able to turn so easily if we go further out, Sir. I have been on this run for three years now and the seas get very big here."

Captain Anand did not answer. The sensible thing to do was to turn now and stay in shelter. The ship would be safe there. But ships are not built to stay in shelter, and sensible Captains do not disobey a direct order from the Coastguard or disappoint their owners. I do not want to end up in a Sicilian jail, he thought, or fighting for my wages.

Ashore the man who could have countermanded that order and kept the ship in safety was in his car, scaring even Sicilian drivers in his rush to get back to Augusta. Dino did not know the ship was not safe in shelter. But he did know one of the two things Captain Anand did not know, and which might have made him change course. Dino knew what the Chief Mate was trying to tell the Captain. Where the old city of Siracusa pushes the coast of Sicily out eastwards into the Messina current huge waves build up during northerly winds. The shore resists the sea moving south, and the sea resists the wind blowing over it. Together they pile up their energy into short, ugly and steep waves.

The other thing that Captain Anand did not know, and Dino could not have foreseen, was that in 1995 a Korean naval architect had made a small miscalculation. He was on the rack, pushed by his yard managers to complete the design approval for the new double-hull tankers that the market needed. The US government had reacted to the oil spill from the *Exxon Valdez* by insisting that only double-hull tankers could trade to the USA and the rest of the world had followed suit. Double-hull tankers are not safer than single-hull tankers, they have the same strength spread over more structure. But a double-hull is something politicians and the public can understand, and after an oil spill everyone wants to see action.

The US Oil Pollution Act 1990 led directly from the *Exxon Valdez* spill and that led directly to the whole world suddenly needing to operate double-hull ships. That led in turn to the shipyards of Korea and Japan, where most ships were built then, coming under intense pressure to bring out new designs. And that led inevitably to a tired naval architect making a small mistake on fatigue calculations for the hull structure.

There were no powerful software programs to model the ship's structure then, and the tiny mistake passed unnoticed by the ship's classification society plan review, and was rubber stamped by the government which lent its nationality to the ship, Panama. The yard welders faithfully followed the plans. And if the ship had led a normal, varied working life then it might never have mattered.

The *Barbara S* had led a harder life. Repeated short voyages from North African to Italian ports meant cyclic stresses always in the same place. Six decks below where the Captain was bracing his feet were the transverse steel frames which supported the ship's side plating around the engine room. If he had leant forward and looked down he would have been looking at the top of the pump room, where the transverse ship's side frames switched to longitudinal and then ran forward as girders the length of the cargo tanks. Between the two sets of frames stresses build up, high tensile steel gets tired and small structural failures begin.

Surveyors know this, shipyards know this and ship inspectors know this. Captain Anand knew it too. Everyone at sea knew the fate of the similar tanker *Prestige,* which had broken in two off Spain ten years before. But he did not know that he was facing the same problem this time. He believed that the small deck crack was the problem, not the symptom. If you have been at sea for fifty years and sailed on old ships you have seen a deck crack before. In bad seas the crack may grow a little. But it can usually be fixed in the next port. Captain Anand weighed up the risk of the deck cracking a little further against the risk of a jail sentence when the ship docked. He could still turn back to shelter. But he did not.

"Keep her on this course, Mate," he said. "We are making ground towards Augusta, that is what matters."

****

Eleni and Leta Kalargyrou had not been blessed with beauty. But the twin sisters had been blessed with sharp business brains, a character stronger than any man in Greece, and a father who had the good sense to leave them a growing tug and salvage company. He had died when the girls were only eighteen, killed by a broken tow wire whipping across the deck of one of his tugs. His cousins and brothers had come to the funeral, shedding tears for Yianni, but rubbing their hands at the thought of getting their share of his business. Yianni was sharper than they knew. His will left no room for doubt, the tug business went to his daughters. And they had done him proud.

Kalargyrou was a global name now in salvage. Anywhere a ship was in trouble, there was a Kalargyrou tug nearby to offer a line. To offer a salvage contract. No cure, no pay. Or as the sisters saw it, cure what you could, and then get paid a lot.

They had built their global empire by understanding how men worked. They knew when to push their salvage masters. When to charm their bankers. When to send in their lawyers. And how to make men want what they had – money and tugs.

Coastguard Lieutenant Roberto Fraille was no match for them. Eleni had met him at a shipping conference and slipped him a business card. Call us if there is anything that would interest us. You will be well rewarded. A smile and an understanding.

Eleni was not surprised when she answered the phone. She knew each Coastguard officer in her network. She knew which had tipped her off so her tugs could be first on a lucrative job and she knew how much she had paid them.

"Lieutenant Fraille, how nice to hear from you again," she said. "Of course you are not disturbing me. How can I help you?"

Leta was with her in the office, listening to the phone on a headset. The sisters always manned the office together when storms hit the area. That was when salvors had to be ready. When they got lucky. When they got rich.

She listened to Eleni charming the stupid young Italian and plotted the position of the ship on the chart open in front of her. The *Barbara S*, a loaded tanker, deck cracking, ordered out to sea in this storm. She was already on the radio to their largest salvage tug as Eleni completed the call. It was on standby in Kalamata, ready to cover any emergencies in the eastern Mediterranean.

"Thank you so much, Lieutenant Fraille. Very professional of you to alert us. Yes, I have your bank details. A little present for Epiphany will be on its way. Of course, Lieutenant, no trace of this call. Thank you and Happy New Year," she said.

She put the phone down and laughed.

"Idiot. His commander would kill him if he knew. How long to mobilise and get to the scene?"

Leta was tapping instructions into the email she was sending to the tug to confirm the radio message.

"Maybe twelve hours in this," she said. "But no-one else will be out there, and no-one else will know. So we will be there when she breaks up. They have all the necessary equipment but I'll order up some extra oil spill containment equipment."

She paused.

"Eleni," she laughed. "As you are so good at charming these Italian men, why don't you make a couple of calls? You know what the Sicilians are like. As soon as the emergency starts they will want a piece of the action. Make sure we have the local tug company subcontracted to us before they know what is going on. In fact, get the tug companies in both Siracusa and in Augusta. Stitch them up now, so when they find out we have the prize they will be on our side."

****

"Repeat what you have just told me, Lieutenant Fraille," ordered Dino. He was tense and his voice was quiet but very firm. "Repeat it, because I do not want to believe what I am hearing."

Dino had felt the shock of the wind as he had run from the car to the Coastguard control tower. Through the darkness he could sense the spray flying over the outer breakwater. The seas must be building to ten metres or more, he thought.

Fraille was brushing sleep from his eyes when Dino pushed through the door and demanded a situation report.

"Sir, I am not sure of the position of the ship now, because you told me not to call anyone, Sir," repeated Fraille, standing to attention now and wishing his uncle was with him. "But I know it is going out to sea because my uncle ordered it to go twelve miles offshore, Sir. And I know he has been in touch with the Ministry of Defence and they have confirmed the order, Sir, because they are very worried that we have a cracked loaded tanker close to the coast, Sir."

"Your uncle?" said Dino. He could only just keep the anger out of his voice. "Your uncle is now a maritime expert, is he? Your uncle can send men to drown, can he? The ship was safe in shelter. Can you not hear the wind out there? Can you not read the weather forecast? Do you know what those seas will do to the ship? I cannot believe the Captain took any notice of such a stupid order."

"It is a new Captain, Sir," Fraille was standing rigidly to attention, not daring to move. "He seems very cooperative. I told him what my uncle wanted and he agreed, Sir. It is a big ship, Sir. I am sure it will be alright."

Holy God, thought Dino. I have let these people down. I have let myself down. For a good meal and my wife's smile I left this idiot in charge.

"Get the *Barbara S* on the radio, right now," he ordered sharply.

"Let's at least find out where she is and what is happening."

"Yes, Sir," responded Fraille. Dino could hear a little strength coming back into his voice. "But you also need to see these signals from HQ, Sir. They confirm the orders, we are to keep the ship at least twelve miles away from the coast....Sir."

His uncle, calling his friends in Rome. Calling his greedy, lazy, thieving, double-dealing bloated little friends who run the powerful ministries. They are safe in Rome, they will not get wet or cold or dirty or afraid but they can tell us all what to do.

"Get me the ship, Fraille." Dino was not shouting, but his voice had the power that only naval officers who are very angry indeed can put into every syllable. "Then get out of my sight. Get out, go home to Mama. You have done enough damage."

****

The seas were sweeping right over the foredeck now. The white foam was lifting into towers of spray as it hit the pipes and valves and tank entrance hatches that cluttered the deck. Each wave shook the ship and the shock travelled through the structure. The ship flexed and the six storey accommodation block toppled forward then snapped back into the vertical. High up on the bridge each wave felt like the dip at the bottom of a roller coaster ride. But this was no fun day out.

The Third Officer was now back on the bridge for his evening watch, but Captain Anand noticed that the Chief Mate had not gone below. He could feel the tension in the two officers.

"We'll take a look at the deck, Mate," he said. "Third, put the deck lights on please."

The ship was slowly making headway out to sea, and also towards the north. On the port beam he could see the lights of Siracusa. From here it was not so far to Augusta. He was obeying the Coastguard but he was not twelve miles off shore yet, and he was obeying the owner, trying to get to port. He was sure that if he could make it there then they would let him into a safe berth.

The seas were more than ten metres high now and getting shorter and steeper. The engine was back to dead slow ahead, but the speed at which the ship crashed into each wave was increasing. We can ride seas as big as this, he told himself. But it is not good for the ship if the seas are steep. She is punching through them, not rising to the waves.

The deck lights showed the white water lashing the deck. Peering down towards the pump room deck Captain Anand could not see the crack.

"Ask the Chief Engineer if there is any change," he said. "Let's see, I think maybe a little pumping is all they need to do."

He tried to sound confident.

CHAPTER SIX

The Chief Engineer was in the engine room control room, right at the forward end of the cavernous machinery space. His back was to the pump room aft bulkhead. He was bracing himself as he anxiously scanned the dials set into the control panel. Just forward of where he stood, out of sight and sound behind the two cm thick steel bulkhead, the small steel tripping bracket which secured frame 68 to the side plating gave up the unequal task. It had flexed once too often and now the steel cracked and then tore.

The stresses carried by the side plating into the longitudinal structure increased by the tiny amount which had been taken by the torn bracket. As the ship came down into the wave trough it punched into the almost vertical wall of solid angry water of the next wave face. A shock wave travelled back through the ship. At frame 68 the forces being pushed through the steel had nowhere to go. The tiny miscalculation by the tired Korean naval architect became a hammer blow which tore into the next bracket.

The ship slowly shook itself free of the green sea and laboured to rise as the wave moved aft. The complex forces on the structure spread out through the intricate web of steel that was the ship. But now there were two fewer routes for the brutal force to travel through. An uneven and increased stress fell on the remaining structure.

When a ship is designed and built, thousands and thousands of pieces of steel are welded into a spider's web structure which is sheathed in the side plates. The weight and size of every piece of steel is carefully calculated. Every tonne of steel in the structure is one tonne less of cargo the ship can carry. So the shipyard wants to build the ship as light as possible while still meeting the minimum strength requirements set down by the International Maritime Organisation.

When a ship is redesigned as a double hull instead of a single hull, the shipyard does not add more steel to build the outer hull. It takes the same total amount of steel for the ship and builds a thinner and finer and more intricate spider's web structure with room for a double hull. It weighs the same as the single hull tanker it replaces. In theory, it is just as strong. Which is fine, as long as no-one gets their sums wrong.

The two phones in front of the Chief Engineer rang at the same time. He reached for the bridge phone, while the watch engineer beside him picked up the phone from the pump room.

"Yes, Captain, Chief Engineer here," he began, then hesitated as he heard in his other ear the watch engineer repeating what he was hearing down the pump room phone. The engineer monitoring the crack was reporting oil in the seawater entering the pump room.

"Wait, Captain," he said sharply, reaching for the pump room phone.

"You are sure, there is oil? Can you see where it is coming from?" he asked.

He listened then slowly put the phone back into its cradle. He picked up the bridge phone.

"Captain," he said. He was trying to speak calmly, but the stress made his voice rise at the end of each sentence. "I am getting my report from the Second Engineer, he is in the pump room. There is more water now, and there is oil in it. This is not a question of a little pumping. I am afraid we will be breaking up soon if we cannot get out of this."

****

To the Captain listening at the other end of the radio link Dino sounded calm and controlled. He held his voice steady and pushed the authority of years of service into each sentence.

"Repeat your position please, Captain," said Dino. "Repeat your position."

In his mind Dino was whispering to himself. "Jesus, Mary and Joseph, he can't have got the ship there. The one place where there is no shelter and the sea will be worst. How the hell has he driven the ship there?"

There was no mistake. The Indian voice coming over the radio repeated that the *Barbara S* was now eight miles east-northeast of Siracusa and trying to make for Augusta.

"What is the situation with the crack?" asked Dino. "A situation report please, Captain."

Sweet Jesus, how did I get this lunatic here on this night of all nights, he asked himself as heard the Captain. Why did he leave the shelter of the cape? His conscience answered him. He left the shelter because your officer ordered him to. He was sent out to sea because you were not there to stop him.

"The crack is getting a little worse, Sir," he heard. "My Chief Engineer is reporting some oil in the seawater in the pump room. But I think we can make it to Augusta, Sir."

Dino looked at the papers on his desk. The weather chart told the story. This storm was going nowhere and would be worse before it was better. There was no way a loaded tanker could enter Augusta port in sixty knot winds, even if she could make it to the port entrance. With oil already leaking Dino did not think that she would make it anyway.

It was clear to him that the ship was already in bad trouble. In calm waters it could survive. The oil leaks could be contained. The ship could be pumped out. Experts could assess the damage. Repairs could be done. But there were no calm waters in this weather. The only option was for the ship to go back south and west of Capo Murro di Porco. The seas would be much easier there, the wind had no purchase and no current to fight. If he could get the ship there it could survive.

Beside the weather chart was the daily signal log. It contained all the messages to and from headquarters in Rome. On top of the pile was the clear instruction to ensure the *Barbara S* remained twelve miles offshore until the crack could be investigated.

Dino was thinking quickly. In one part of his mind he was calculating the chances of the ship turning safely and making it back into shelter. He was working out how long it would take in this weather. What orders would he have to give? What precautions were necessary? He was putting himself out there in the storm. He could feel the ship lifting and falling under his feet, staggering with each wave. He knew what should be done.

At the back of his mind a relentless voice was telling a different story. You are close to the peak of your career, said the voice. You have a beautiful young wife. You have a good life here in Sicily. A life you never expected to live. If you obey the orders then you will be safe. It is a big ship, a strong ship. The Captain thinks he can make it. If you disobey the orders then they will investigate. When they investigate then you will always be wrong. The men behind the desks in Rome will always be right.

He hesitated, then pressed the transmit switch.

"Captain," he ordered firmly. "I am Capitano Cervetto, the senior Coastguard officer. Listen carefully. You will not be able to enter Augusta in this weather, and where you are now the seas will get worse. You were ordered to go twelve miles offshore. The seas will be even worse there. I am giving you a new order. You should turn the ship now Captain, while you can, and make for shelter south of Capo Murro di Porco. Do you understand, Captain, you must make for shelter until the storm passes."

He heard the Captain acknowledge the order. That's it, he thought. I hope he can turn. I hope he can get back into shelter. There is no going back for me now, anyway.

Dino spoke politely to the young signalman who was manning the watch. "Log the time and the order I have just given," he ordered. "Note it carefully, then call headquarters in Rome and get me the duty national commander."

****

"You have some powerful connections, Cervetto, powerful connections. Vinciullo himself has been on the line. The Secretary of Marine has been on the line. Shall I get a call from Signor Berlusconi also to tell me that I must back your order to send a cracked tanker offshore into a major storm?"

Dino Cervetto was on the line to the national Coastguard commander. He thinks I gave the order and got the local politicians to back me up by calling their friends in Rome, he thought.

"Well, Cervetto? Have you gone native? We sent you to Sicily to clean up that nest of nepotism. They got to you with a girl, I hear. I hope she is worth it."

Dino squared his shoulders.

"*Almirante*," he said forcefully. "The order to take the ship to sea was given under my authority by a junior officer who could not contact me. I have called to report to you that I have now ordered the ship to return to shelter. The ship is already reporting an oil leak internally. I am preparing for a major incident."

"I have every politician in Palermo and Rome and Siracusa breathing down my neck to back up what I thought was your stupid order to send a damaged tanker out to sea," replied the Coastguard Admiral. "So I backed you up. And now you tell me you have ordered it back to the coast. I think, Cervetto, that it must be good wine, or a very good woman. Something has got to you. You are on your own with this little Christmas present. I cannot countermand these orders now."

There was a pause. "And Cervetto," continued the Admiral. "Good luck. Call in some favours. You are a good man, but you are going to need all your friends if this goes tits up."

****

Captain Anand was tired. He had been on the bridge now for more than twelve hours. The slamming of the ship made standing still an effort. He was trying to force his mind to a decision.

I have the Coastguard who wants me to go for shelter, he thought. I have all these boys on the ship who think I should take the ship to shelter. I have the owner who wants the ship in Augusta. What can I do?

Deference to authority was bred deep into the Captain. In fifty years of sea service he had tried never to take a decision unless he knew it was what his superiors wanted. He looked forward through the bridge windows. The deck lights were off now, but in the glow of the foremast navigation light he could see a heavy sea coming over the bow. He felt the ship trembling. She feels more sluggish, he thought. Perhaps the Chief Engineer is right? Perhaps the Coastguard is right?

I should not have agreed to this voyage. I have been a good servant. I am due my pension now. I have a bungalow in a place where I can see the coast. They asked me to come because the regular Captain was ill so I took his place. One voyage only, they said. Now I don't know what to do.

He did not look at the two officers who were watching him. They are waiting for the order to turn, he said to himself. But if I turn now then the ship will not reach Augusta for at least two days more. That is not what the owner wants.

CHAPTER SEVEN

Dino was on the phone to the Italian Air Force base at Catania. He had served with the Search and Rescue Co-ordinator there. They had spent twelve months at military academy together. We were young then, thought Dino, good times.

"Beppe," he said. "Ciao. It is not a good night to call you."

Beppe was happy to agree that a filthy night between Christmas and New Year with sixty knot winds and driving rain was not a good night for a call. "Unless you are going to invite me over to meet that lovely young wife I hear you have married?" he queried. "How did you manage that? Never too old to learn hypnotism, I suppose?"

Dino did not respond to the teasing. He knew he was going to be asking a lot from Beppe and his crews. They operated a flight of Augusta Westland AW139 helicopters for search and rescue over Sicily and the eastern Mediterranean. They were tough, competent pilots and aircrew. They knew that when others ran for shelter, that was their time to work. But tonight would not be easy.

"Beppe," he said. "There is no specific order yet, and we might still get away with this. But tell your boys to get some rest. Get the mechanics to give the aircraft an extra check. They may have a tough night ahead. I have a loaded tanker which may be breaking up close to Siracusa. There are twenty-three men on board, Indians I think, and maybe Filipinos. I am not confident in the Captain. This could be very nasty."

****

"Captain, we should turn and go for shelter."

Captain Anand heard the Chief Mate but did not answer. He is right, he thought. We should go to shelter. But perhaps it is too late. I do not think I can turn the ship in this sea.

"Captain," the Chief Mate's voice was urgent. "Captain, Sir, you have the order from the Coastguard. And the engineers say we have oil coming in now. The ship cannot take this."

The Captain looked forward and tried to peer down at the aft part of the foredeck. In the darkness and flying spray he could see nothing.

If he had been able to see through the swirling water and the deck plating he would have seen the domino effect on the structure accelerating. When the first bracket tore it put a little more stress on all the others. When the second one tore it doubled the extra stress on the next bracket along. That one gave up quicker than the first two. As the ship hit each wave the shuddering power of over eighty thousand tonnes of steel and oil hitting the solid waves came through the structure, frame by frame, tank by tank until it reached the damaged area. When it came to the broken frames it had nowhere to go, so it broke up the next brackets. And as each bracket went the extra force on the next one multiplied, tearing open the welding between the ship's frames and the side plating.

He felt the touch on his arm. The Chief Mate was trying to get his attention. He felt tired. How to choose? The owner, the ship, these boys, the Coastguard. Can I turn the ship in these waves? I am so tired. But I am the Captain. I have to act.

"Mate," he roused himself. "Yes, we will try to turn. But it will not be easy. First get all hands to muster in the crew mess, by the poop deck entrance. Make sure they have their lifejackets with them but they stay in shelter. And call the Chief Engineer. Tell him to bring all his boys out of the engine room to join the others. After the turn they can go back, but just in case they need to be close to the deck."

****

"Everyone is ready, Mate?" asked Captain Anand. His voice was stronger now. He had found some strength. The habit of command straightened his back. "We will turn to starboard. I do not want to push her into the seas. Third Officer, take the wheel and wait for my order. Mate, I want you by the engine control, please."

He braced himself, feeling the ship as it lifted slowly to another wave. He waited, holding tight to the handrail as the wave travelled aft and the stern began to lift. The seas were very fine on the port bow now. He would try to turn her right through the wave train as a wave came through, avoiding the trough.

Now, he said to himself. Now we have a chance. The ship was falling forward and soon a wave would begin to lift the bow. "Starboard twenty," he ordered. "Half ahead, Mate. Let's get her round."

The bows began to swing quickly to starboard. The rudder was forcing the ship to turn. The extra engine power pushed against the rudder and forced the stern to port, making the ship swing to starboard. Instead of pushing into the wave, the port bow was swinging away from it, and the wave was pushing the ship, helping it to turn. We will do it, willed Captain Anand. She will turn.

The motion under his feet changed. Instead of the shock of hitting the wave, the ship lifted and twisted, then lurched heavily to port, slamming downwards into the trough behind the wave. Water exploded up the side of the bridge. A full green sea swept over the port side as the ship rolled into the face of the next wave. The wave went through too quickly, he thought. We cannot stay across the seas like this. "Hard to starboard," he ordered sharply. "Full ahead." She must turn now. He was willing her to make the turn. We will power her round over the next wave.

He held on tight as the ship rolled heavily to starboard. He could see the inclinometer in the middle of the bridge. The roll went on for ever. More than forty degrees, we cannot come back, he thought. Then the wave was past but the ship was thrust by the force of its passing back into the trough. The heading had not changed. The ship slid down the wave, the massive buoyancy forces conquering the turning power of the rudder and engine. She will roll again, thought Captain Anand. Then we will kill the engine or flood something.

"Come to port, Third," he said urgently. "Port twenty. We come back to head the seas."

The ship corkscrewed over the next wave, but the force of the engine was enough to push the bow out of the trough and bring the ship back towards her original course. "Dead slow, Mate," he ordered.

The ship slammed into the wave, but after the wild rolling the motion felt almost comfortable, familiar. "Steer that, Third," he said. "Keep the waves just to port. We can only ride this out now. There is no turning in this sea. Mate, tell the engineers they can go below again and stand the crew down."

We can survive this, he convinced himself. Storms do not last so long in this area. Just tonight, and tomorrow it will calm down and we will head for Augusta. We will be alright.

****

That's what I need now, thought Cervetto. That fat parasite politician calling me to put the pressure on. He took the phone from the duty signalman.

"Capitano Cervetto here," he said politely. "What can I do for you, Presidente Vinciullo?"

"I was simply calling to enquire about the safety of the tanker," came the soft, oily voice. "I am sure we are under control, Capitano. My nephew mentioned you had sent him home?"

Dino's thoughts were running like a soundtrack behind the phone call. I hate this man. I hate all he stands for. All the corruption and back scratching and all the incompetent little fools who have jobs they cannot do because they have uncles like this.

"Presidente," Dino replied politely but firmly. "Thanks to the order you gave the *Barbara S* is now in a very dangerous situation. Twenty or more innocent seamen have been put at risk because you sent them to sea. The ship is now cracking. Perhaps brave men from our air sea rescue units will risk their lives tonight to save them. You will be warm in your bed. I hope you sleep well.... Sir."

He kept his tone even but there was a momentary emphasis on the last word.

"Capitano," came the subtle, insidious reply, "if the ship is in trouble and cracking then the further it is from the coast of my province the better. You come here from Genova, perhaps you do not value our historic cities and coastline."

The voice at the other end of the line was calm, not showing any reaction to Dino's hostility. "And perhaps you should remember who gave the order. Not me, Capitano. You are mistaken. An officer under your command who could not contact you gave the order. I do not give orders to ships, Capitano. Orders to ships are given by the Coastguard. If we end up with oil on our beautiful beaches I think you will have occasion to remember that....Capitano."

The emphasis on the last word matched exactly the weight Dino had given to his insult. Dino was drawing in his breath to reply. He was on the verge of losing his temper. Oil, not people, he thought. That is what he cares about. Then he realised the phone had gone dead. Bastard, he said. *Figlio di puttana.*

CHAPTER EIGHT

It was surprisingly quiet inside the bridge now. With both bridge wing doors closed before the turn the noise of the storm was more distant. Rain was hammering at the windows, but the bridge windows of a tanker are made of thick, toughened glass. They muted the noise of the rain. They muted the noise of the spray hitting the accommodation. They muted the noise of the waves crashing down the foredeck.

The quiet was calming. Perhaps we can make it, thought Captain Anand. She can ride this out.

The shrill engine room phone sounded. He did not move. The Chief Mate lifted the phone from the control panel.

"You are sure?" he heard. "OK, evacuate the engine room. I will inform the master."

The Chief Mate put the phone down slowly and turned to face him.

"Captain," he said formally. "The Chief Engineer reports that the forward engine room bulkhead is buckling. Water is already entering the engine room. He believes the pump room is already flooded and the side shell is breached. He is running the bilge pump on the engine room bilges, Sir. And I have ordered him to evacuate the space."

In the quiet of the bridge it seemed no-one breathed. So it has come to this, he thought. My last command, and now we will lose her. God pity these young men.

A quiet dignity flooded through the Captain. He spoke clearly and calmly.

"Mate," he ordered. "Go below, rouse all hands and muster them on the poop deck. Make sure you account for everyone. If you can, swing the boats out and clear away the liferafts. I know we cannot launch a boat in this sea but if she sinks they will float free and give some of you a chance. I will make the Mayday call now, but it may take some time for helicopters to reach us. Make sure everyone waits calmly. There is no point in trying to abandon ship in this. We must wait and hope for a helicopter rescue. Third, I will take the wheel and remain here to keep her head to sea. You go with the rest of the crew. You will have more chance if you are in the open if she sinks suddenly."

The Third Mate did not move. The Captain made a shooing motion. It would have been funny but with the ship breaking up under them no-one was laughing.

"Go," he repeated. "You are young and I am old. Give me the wheel and I will call now while I steer."

He took the small electronic steering control in his left hand and looked forward at the seas. In his right hand he held the VHF transceiver. He took a deep breath. In fifty years at sea he had only heard these words in training.

"Mayday, Mayday, Mayday." His voice was strong and clear. "This is the *Barbara S*, *Barbara S*, *Barbara S*. We are eight miles east-northeast of Siracusa and we require urgent assistance. The vessel is breaking up and we need to abandon ship."

The Coastguard must have been waiting. They knew what would

happen. The reply was immediate. In a short, professional and undramatic conversation he made them understand that the ship was going to crack in two. In response he understood that helicopters were being scrambled from Catania and would take half an hour to reach them.

Half an hour, he pleaded. Give me that. Half an hour to save these boys. I thought they were rude, but I was stupid and did not make the right decisions. Trying to turn the ship was the last straw. The crack must have spread and the twisting of the ship has pushed it too far. Half an hour. Thirty minutes. Maybe sixty waves. He looked ahead where the bow was rising sluggishly to the next wave crest. If the engine keeps going and the seas stay like this, perhaps we can make it.

****

There are three circles of hell, he thought. There is the hell of this storm beating my ship to death. There is the hell of the noise and downdraft from the helicopters trying to save my crew. And there is the hell I shall always be in for bringing the ship here.

Captain Anand was calm. Time seemed elastic. He was on the bridge, holding the ship up to the seas. The engine was still running dead slow ahead, and with the steering control he could keep the seas just on the port bow. The ship was visibly flexing now, bending as it passed over each wave. He knew the end was inevitable, but he felt relieved. She will break in two, but we have done it. The helicopters are here and the crew will be saved.

Aft of the bridge three helicopters were hovering, leaning into the driving wind and rain. Powerful searchlights lit up the desperate scene on the deck. One helicopter was in closer, winching the crew one by one up from the deck. The Captain was using the walk-about control, so from the bridge side he could count them while he was steering. Ten times the wire with its rescue harness came down, swinging wildly as the wind caught it and the ship rose and fell sharply as it passed over the seas. Ten times he saw the frightened face of one of his crew as they were winched up and into the helicopter.

The first helicopter closed its door and inched away, crabbing to one side and shouldering the wind. Its searchlight came on and lit up the deck as the second helicopter powered in to take its place. Captain Anand could feel the ship's motion changing now. It was almost two ships already. The forepart will float, he thought. There is buoyancy there. But the aft part, with the engine room and accommodation, will sink quickly. I hope the engine gives us another five minutes. Long enough to get the rest of my boys off that deck.

He saw three more crew winched up, or was it four? He could not be sure. It was getting harder to hold the ship in position. He did not want it to fall off the seas now. If the ship came into the trough it would roll so heavily that it would be impossible to get into the harness and be lifted clear. He saw more figures being winched up. The second helicopter was inching clear of the ship now. Had it taken ten, or eleven? They would all be safe, thank God. Who is left?

"Captain," he heard. "Captain, you must come now. We are the only two left. Come now and we will make it."

The Third Officer was pulling at his arm. "Captain," he was yelling now. "You have saved us, now save yourself. Come on."

He dropped the control and started to move aft to climb down the accommodation ladders to the poop. The Third Officer was already ahead of him, sliding down quickly to get to the harness. Below his feet he felt the engine stop. Without power the ship began to fall off to starboard. The deck lurched under his feet, almost throwing him into the sea. He found the strength to cling on and was able to pull himself onto the aft deck. The ship wallowed sideways. He looked to the port side and saw the forepart of the ship right beside him. It cannot be there, his mind told him. But it was. The ship had broken into two pieces just forward of the engine room.

The noise of the helicopter was deafening him. I should go down with the ship, he thought. This is all my fault. Then two wiry hands grabbed him and the Italian Search and Rescue diver pulled him into a fierce embrace. The wire tightened and they were going up quickly. They were over the sea now, the helicopter moving quickly sideways to clear the sinking ship.

Four arms reached out and pulled him roughly into the helicopter. He saw the winch man pull the diver in and turn to give the thumbs up to the pilot.

The diver was beside him on the floor, laughing with relief.

"Welcome to Sicily, Capitano," he said. "Not a good time for an 'oliday, but 'ere we go."

****

"We did it, Dino. We did it. Twenty-three of them are safe in the helos. They'll be at the base in forty-five minutes."

Dino took a deep breath. The helicopters had been in the air for almost an hour. He felt he had not breathed in all that time. He had been dreading the phone call. Whatever came now did not matter. The crew were safe.

"Beppe, you are all stars," he said. "When this is all over I will invite you to Siracusa for lunch. Maria will be happy to cook for you. And you will be happy to eat what she cooks, because she is a very good cook indeed."

"It will be a little while before this is all over, Dino," replied Beppe seriously. "The crew are safe but the ship is not. My aircraft commander reports that the ship broke in two as he lifted the master clear. When they left the scene the aft part of the ship was already sinking quickly. It looked as if the whole forepart, with all the cargo tanks, was afloat and lying across the seas. There is oil everywhere, but in the visibility he could not see where it was coming from. Tell Maria not to buy the fish just yet."

Dino knew it would be a mess. A mess for the coast and a mess for his career. But with the crew safe he felt relieved. He spoke firmly.

"Beppe," he said. "You've got the Red Cross and ship's agents ready to care for the crew when they arrive? Good. Then I leave the crew to you. Can you get me a full report from the aircrew as soon as possible, with the exact position of the rescue? And task a helo for first light tomorrow to return to the scene. We will need eyes on this. Wake up the Long Range Maritime Patrol people too. I am going to activate the full oil pollution Emergency Response Plan."

"And Beppe," he added. "Thank you and thank your crews for a great job. Maria will cook you your best lunch ever. Ciao."

****

The turbine whined into silence and the helicopter rotor blades sagged and were still. The winchman unlatched the door and motioned to Captain Anand.

"Last in, first out," he said. "The medical people are waiting for you there. They will take you all to a hospital for a check, then to a hotel. You are a brave man, Captain. Be happy."

Captain Anand could not speak. He clasped the hand of the winchman, and then the diver who had plucked him from the deck. Through the helicopter door he could see the flashing red lights of the waiting ambulances. Blue lights of other emergency vehicles flickered alongside. He stepped down from the aircraft and pulled himself upright. Across the tarmac he could see the other two helicopters. As each crewman stepped down they were wrapped in a blanket and led to an ambulance.

He looked down at himself. Blood wept from skinned knuckles. His back and arms ached. Water dripped from his uniform, filling his shoes.

"Captain? Commandante? Capitano?" he heard. "Who Capitano?"

He took a step forward. He squinted into the lights. He could not see who was calling.

A paramedic came towards him, holding a blanket. Then two tall Carabinieri pushed the paramedic aside.

"Capitano?" demanded one.

He nodded. Their crisp white shirts, neat blue uniforms and hard peaked caps almost covering their eyes looked out of place in the crowd of urgent paramedics and blanket-wrapped survivors.

He felt a strong hand grasp his right arm, then a handcuff snapped shut on his wrist. His left arm was forced behind him and snapped into the other handcuff.

"*Lei è in arresto*," he heard. He was too tired, what was going on?

A paramedic was shouting at the Carabinieri. The paramedic pushed one of them, trying to get to the Captain and provide a blanket. He saw one of the Carabinieri reach out. His hand was a whiplash. The black glove caught the paramedic across the face, knocking her backwards.

He could not understand what the Carabiniere growled in Italian to the paramedic, but she stepped back fearfully. They were pulling at him now and one was shouting at him, trying to get him to walk towards the blue lights.

"Capitano, you arrest. Presidente Vinciullo say you arrest for pollution. Move to car. Now."

CHAPTER NINE

Dino was sitting very upright and very still. He had been home, showered, changed into a clean uniform and was freshly shaven. No-one would know he had been at his desk most of the night. In front of him the Major Environmental Emergency Manual was open on the desk. To the left of it was a computer plot showing the position of the sunken aft part of the *Barbara S* and the position of the drifting forepart of the tanker. It was overlaid by a plot of the oil patches on the surface, sent back from the helicopter which had reached the sinking position at first light. Opposite him sat a uniformed secretary. She knew better than to disturb him when he was thinking.

He was running through the checklist in his mind. He had put in place the emergency plan, calling each local authority emergency incident controller individually to ensure they understood the situation. He had alerted the state's contracted oil spill clean-up contractor, Castalia Mareazul. They were already mobilising booms and protection equipment and bringing personnel into the area. The Air Force and Navy had units ready. His secretary was working through the alert list, sending the formal e-mail orders out to each and every organ of the state that would respond to a major oil spill.

His call to the local towage companies had received an odd response. A salvage tug owned by the Greek company Kalargyrou was already almost at the scene, he was told. The local companies were subcontracting and would mobilise further tugs as requested by Kalargyrou. How the hell did they know, he thought? He filed the question for later. Right now he was happy to have experienced salvors with a very large tug right where it was needed. If they could get a line on the forepart and hold it away from the shore the damage might be limited yet.

There was one person on the list he had not rung. The plan called for the Regional President and his staff to be alerted. Dino was careful to make sure his secretary had alerted them by e-mail. But instead of calling Vinciullo he had called the Ministry of Defence and the Ministry of the Environment in Rome. He had spoken to people he knew there. This is not yet a national emergency, he had warned them. But it probably will be, and when it is I will need your backing. He was doing as the Admiral had advised him. He was getting his friends ready to help him.

I will need them and more, he reasoned, as he listened to the secretary answering the phone then holding it out to him.

"Good morning, Presidente Vinciullo," he said, keeping his voice flat. "I trust you slept well? Twenty-three men saved in a terrible night is a good result under the circumstances."

"Listen, and listen well, Capitano Cervetto," he heard. "You have activated the regional emergency plan…. but you have not called me. You have called your friends in Rome… but you have not called me. There is going to be a mess on this coast now. A big mess. A big mess means a big clean-up. So understand one thing, Capitano. You are in Sicily now, and in Sicily we clean up our own messes. You can make decisions and play the big man, but when it comes to my region, you are not the big man. There is only one big man in this region and it is not you. So be careful, Capitano, be very careful when you try to organise your oil spill protection and clean-up. Remember that work in Sicily goes to Sicilians. …And Capitano, if you don't want to be careful for yourself, be careful for your wife. She is a Sicilian, I believe. She will understand."

****

Michiel squeezed the juice from another orange and carefully picked the pips from the pulp before pouring it into the glass. Beside him the coffee was filtering quietly. Bianca had come home late last night. Late and angry. She had slept beside him, tense and closed. Michiel had slept badly and risen early. He had made up his mind. He would take Bianca breakfast in bed. Good strong coffee, orange juice the way she liked it and warm bread rolls. There was the best old Gouda cheese to slice finely. They would eat the breakfast. Touch each other. He would tell her that it was time for babies. They would make love as the winter morning sun slowly lit up the small plain white bedroom. He would make this marriage work. He knew he could get a regular job writing for a local magazine group. There would be no crusading there, he thought. But I have to grow up sometime and Bianca deserves the husband she wants and the children she was born to love.

The radio was murmuring beside him with the rolling morning news. He opened the oven where he was warming the rolls then jumped backwards as he burnt his arm on the oven door. He was straining to hear the announcer. A loaded tanker broken up in a storm off the coast of Sicily. He reached over and turned up the volume. Reports said part of the ship had sunk and oil was already threatening the historic coasts and city of Siracusa. He dropped his oven gloves and reached across the breakfast bar for his laptop. He was Googling up the reports of the ship. *Barbara S*, crude oil tanker, Italian-owned, not so old, double-hull. It all sounded like a repeat of the *Prestige*.

Behind him he heard Bianca's slippers slapping across the kitchen. "Can't you smell the bread burning?" she said. "Is there nothing you can concentrate on for more than one second? What is so important now?"

Michiel looked up. On one side of the small kitchen was the fresh orange juice, the coffee pot and the tray with neatly folded serviettes, the cheese slice and a pat of rich yellow Dutch butter on the plate ready for the rolls. Right beside him was the beautiful wife he had been preparing them for. A beautiful but very angry wife. And in front of him was his laptop offering him the opportunity he needed to tell his big story. The *Barbara S* would be the platform for him to sell his research, sell his exposé, sell the story of corruption and greed and incompetence which follows every oil spill. It would make money, it would be like it had always been, Michiel as the journalist who tells the stories which others don't.

"Bianca," he said. "Listen. I was making breakfast for us. I wanted to tell you. We can make this work. We can make babies. But there is a tanker in trouble. I just heard it on the news. It is what I need to make my big story sell. I can convince the editors that I should go there and report the spill and on the back of that I can report all that is wrong with the clean-up and compensation. It will be like the old days."

"A pity you had the radio on then, Michiel," answered Bianca coldly. "A pity. Go where you want to go. But do not be sure you will find me here when you come back."

****

"A meeting? We don't need a meeting, we need to get moving."

Simone could hear the shrillness in her voice. She hated that. She did not want Yves to see her angry, but she could not help herself.

"We have heard on the radio that there is another *Erika* spill happening off Sicily. We know that the most important bird reserve in Europe at this time of year is Vendicari, just south of the spill site. We know there will be massive pollution and birds that will need our help." She was spitting out the words. "And you want to stay here and hold meetings? We are Marine Bleu, we are activists. The clue is in the name, we are active. We act, not talk."

Simone could see Yves was not listening to her. He had that smug look on his face again. It made her even angrier.

"Calm down, Simone," she heard. Patronising bastard, she thought. He was still talking.

"I will be leading an important meeting with Greenpeace next week. We are making strategic plans for the future. Together we will have more funding, and we can do more. Rushing off to turn up at every oil spill is small beer. Working with Greenpeace we can change the system."

"Birds are already struggling with the oil in the sea and you talk of meetings," she said. "You are more interested in that English girl from Greenpeace than in saving those poor birds. You are young but you are becoming old before your time. Let's call the group, pack and we can be on the way to Sicily today."

She saw him reaching out and smacked his hand away. She did not trust herself. If he began to caress her then she would end up losing the argument, letting him win, letting him into her.

His words hit her hard.

"Perhaps it is you who are a little old for rushing about Europe to save birds," said Yves spitefully. "I have already called around the group and no-one wants to go running to Sicily now. We are agreed that if we can help we will do that after the New Year. For now the group will stay here, with us."

Simone felt impotent. This arrogant man was taking her for granted. He doesn't care about birds or the sea. He only cares about himself. She was afraid to lose him. Afraid to go alone. But anger drove her on.

"Stay and play with your words and your English girl and your strategies," she heard her shrill voice screeching. "I will do it without you. I am going to Sicily, where I can do something real."

****

Outside the offices of the Provincia Regionale di Siracusa the EU flag scattered raindrops as gusts of wind tore up the Foro Siracusano. Inside it was quiet and stuffy in the big meeting room. Looking down the long heavy dark wooden table Ugo Vinciullo saw each ornate chair occupied by a middle-aged man in a suit. Except one, he thought. Trust Laura to wear red.

They were all looking at him, waiting for his lead. All apart from Laura, he noticed. She is busy with her smartphone. She doesn't depend on me like the others. I never know what she is thinking.

Ugo was the Regional President, and confident in his power. He had worked his way up in the Forza Italia party, spent time in Brussels for them, served his masters well in Rome, and now he had been sent back to Sicily, to his home island, to milk the EU for grants for roads that were never built and traffic lights that were not installed and sewage systems that were not dug because the funds went to the party and to the pockets of the politicians. Which is why all these deputies and councillors are looking at me now, he thought. Because I have the money and I have them in my pocket. Except Laura.

Laura Filippone was Mayor of Siracusa. She was the ugly duckling when we were at school together in Ragusa, mused Ugo. I did not notice her then. A career in law and politics has changed her. Red suits her, and so does her age. It is not right that she will never accept my invitations or my little gifts. We could be good for each other. But sometimes I think she is laughing at me.

He pulled his attention away from Laura's red suit and drew in his breath, pulling himself more upright.

"Colleagues," he began importantly. "We are facing a grave emergency. My wishes have been ignored and thanks to the incompetent Coastguard we now have a tanker sinking close to our coast. We can expect up to eighty thousand tonnes of crude oil to hit our coastline. I am going to form an emergency cabinet to handle the situation, but first I wanted you all here to ensure you are taking all the right precautions in your respective areas."

One by one the deputies spoke, each trying to ingratiate himself, each asking for money to mobilise local resources. Ugo was only half listening, he was watching Laura. She was ignoring the meeting, tapping at her smartphone.

Laura looked up and caught his eye. "Signor Presidente, may I make a suggestion?" she asked formally.

The men stopped talking and looked at her. They all knew Laura. Some feared her. Some respected her. All of them knew that when she spoke quietly and formally she was about to throw a bomb into the meeting.

"Signor Presidente," she continued. "It is of course very right and correct that you are all organising the protection of the coastline. We have to protect our maritime heritage, our birds, our beaches. Yes, but there is another thing. This is our first experience of a big oil spill. So we should look at what others have done. I have done that. What I have found is perhaps worth your consideration."

She paused. She is playing with us, thought Ugo. I would like to spank her. Perhaps she would like that. He knew he would never dare to suggest it.

"What I have learnt is that local and regional authorities in the areas of oil spills can get very rich indeed if they act sensibly," she said. She had their attention now. "We can look at the figures later but local authorities can claim from the central government, the oil company that owns the oil and the insurers of the shipowner for the clean-up and loss of business in the area. These claims are many times more than the real costs. Especially if the costs can be put on the central government while the compensation comes to the regions. All the parties will pay out when the oil is there if the right pressure is brought to bear, and they can never ask for their money back. So here is a suggestion, gentlemen. Instead of doling out our local funds to set up oil pollution defences, instead of each of you trying to milk a little from the money you are given to protect the coast, we should instead do two things. Firstly we should keep our regional and municipal money in our pockets. We can insist that the precautions are taken by the government contractors, and in that way the government in Rome gets the bill. Secondly we put some good lawyers to work right away to bring pressure on ENOL, which owns the oil, and on the shipowner, who I think is based in Naples. That way we start to get money coming in to Sicily, rather than going out. And if the precautions are a little slow and a little oil does make a mess of some of the coast, well, that only helps our claim for compensation."

She paused again. No-one spoke.

"Only a suggestion, of course, Signor Presidente," she ended with a sweet smile.

CHAPTER TEN

Giuseppe Mammino did not think of himself as a man who obeyed rules. Obeying rules set by others was a concept he would not have understood. But he did set one rule for himself, and he tried very hard to live by it. It was a simple rule. Never call head office if you can avoid it.

As Regional Manager for ENOL in Sicily he had a reasonable degree of autonomy in the oil company's operations on the island. As a boy who had gone to school in Ragusa with Ugo Vinciullo, the Regional President, and Laura Filippone, the Mayor of Siracusa, he had the local political backing to stretch that autonomy as far as he could. As far as was convenient for meeting the special needs of a company operating in a special region. Sicily did things the Sicilian way, and ENOL's headquarters in Rome were happy to check the bottom line rather than the fine detail of how it was achieved.

He knew he would have to break his rule now. He had taken two calls that day, one from Laura and one from Ugo. They had put it in different ways, but the message was the same. They were going to take ENOL to the cleaners. He had a choice. He could be part of the golden opportunity, or he could be swept away by the golden tide.

Giuseppe had done a little internet search after the calls. He read that

BP had paid out forty-two billion dollars in clean-up costs and compensation for the *Deepwater Horizon* spill. France's TOTAL had paid out over four hundred million euros in compensation for the *Erika* spill in the Bay of Biscay twelve years before that. He looked at the figures. With the best part of eighty thousand tonnes of our oil about to hit the coast, ENOL is going to be in this for at least a billion euros, he estimated. Maybe more. At Sicilian kickback rates that will net us about a million euro if I can keep control of the cash, he thought.

There was no way he could authorise that sort of spending from his own resources, and he did not want to. New money coming into Sicily was the best kind of money, and Rome was where ENOL had the money he needed.

He was reaching for the phone, planning to call the general manager for Italy to spell out what was needed, but he hesitated. They are not going to give me an open call on that sort of cash. And I don't want those snotty Rome types getting on the next plane down here to poke their nose into our business.

There is a better way, he thought. He could see the way to do it now. I'll let the heat build up on ENOL a little. Perhaps a fuel boycott, a petrol station or two in flames and then an angry crowd trapping me in my office. They'll agree to anything then, and they will surely find they are too busy to fly down here to take charge themselves. Giuseppe laughed to himself. Those Roman pansies would piss their pants if they thought they were going to be attacked by a crowd of angry Sicilians.

****

Enrico Spinelli had very little respect for any of his insurers. They were all English, and he didn't like any of them. All his ships were insured through London-based brokers, and all his public liabilities were insured by the East of England P&I Club. Between them they provided Armatori Fratelli Spinelli SpA with a very high level of insurance cover at very good rates. That wasn't what Enrico didn't like. What he did not like was the people who ran the insurance companies and mutual societies. They were a lot of very polite Englishmen who went out of their way to agree with anything he said. I know they look down on me but I can never quite get them to show it, he thought. They are nice to me because I have ships and money and they want my business, but they think they are better than me.

It is a bad day for them today, he said to himself grimly. A bad day for me too. All morning he had been liaising with the Coastguard, with his operations people, with the ENOL chartering team, with his insurers, with his lawyers, with those Kalargyrou sisters, how the hell did they get there first, and shouting at his agent in Catania to get the Captain out of jail and the crew off the island of Sicily and back to India before they cost me any more money. It was not a morning to improve the temper of anyone. A ship broken in two, a charter lost, a tricky salvage to come and the possibility of a huge oil spill in a sensitive area. It is a time for blunt speaking, not this crap.

"Mr Chillingworth," he said forcefully. "I have not called you to discuss the weather or to give an opinion on the Italian rugby team's chances in the Six Nations matches. I have called you because you are my liability insurers, you are my P&I Club, and I am facing a mess. I do not want fine words, I want simply to know what you are doing about it. Right now."

From his office window Enrico could see across the old harbour in Naples. The weather is easing a little, he thought. The tug may yet save most of the oil. But I need these people to wake up and move. He could see in his mind the man he was speaking to. He wants to go off for a nice London lunch. He will talk about cricket with some other failed lawyer he went to school with and who now has a cushy job in marine insurance. David Chillingworth was everything Enrico did not like in the English, and that was a lot. He was tall, well-built and had a breezy confidence and an air of superiority. When he came to Naples he always wore pink cotton trousers and a blue blazer. He always defers to me, whatever I say. Perhaps he is gay, Enrico smiled grimly to himself. A lot of those English private schoolboys are.

He listened to the courteous voice on the phone. He is doing it again. He is patronising me.

"Waiting for a report is not enough, Mr Chillingworth," he broke in. "Waiting for anything is not enough now. We know oil is going to hit the coast anytime soon. Sicily is part of Italy, in case you did not know. And I am an Italian shipowner, with one of my ships spilling Italian oil onto an Italian coast. Hell is going to break out. I already have half the media in Italy camped outside my office and the other half on the telephone every two minutes. I have the Ministry of the Environment ranting at me. Every crook in Sicily has their hands out already. When I brought my ships into your insurance club you told me about your club spirit. About mutual support. Now is the time for that support. Tell me, Mr Chillingworth, that you are going to send someone senior to Sicily, and send them quickly. Tell me, Mr Chillingworth, that you are mobilising all your oil spill experts. I have heard before what you say when an owner wants something – it is their club, you say. Now it is my club, my need for help. I do not want to hear about waiting for reports. I want to hear about action."

His voice had been getting louder as he spoke and he could feel his anger building.

"Yes of course, Mr Spinelli," he heard as he paused for breath. "Yes of course."

They know just how to make me even more angry, he thought as he smashed the telephone down onto the desk.

****

David Chillingworth gently replaced his phone receiver. Emotional lot, the Neapolitans, he thought. But I think he is right. This is going to be a nasty one.

He tapped his finger on the table then pulled forward a notepad. His schooling at Charterhouse and law degree at Oxford had given him a methodical mind but not the drive and aggression to succeed in his chosen career as a barrister. On the rugby field he had played a useful number eight, but off the field he was just too lazy and too deferent to establish himself at the Bar.

Now he was Associate Director of the East of England P&I Club. It was one of the most traditional of old London-based marine liability insurers. David was responsible for their Italian clients, and all points eastwards from there to Dubai, except for the key Greek market. The Levant without the glory of Greece, as he joked with his friends.

A major oil spill hits a P&I Club only once a decade, so David had no experience to draw on. Where should he start? Perhaps we should have a manual, he thought. Oh well, I'll get the usual suspects rolling in the meantime.

He listed who he would call. Captain Allen Brink, he is a good old salt and will be the right Special Casualty Representative for us. I saw him last night at the wine tasting, so I know he is available. I'll get him out there right now, keep an eye on Kalargyrou's antics and keep their hands out of our pockets a bit.

Then IOPC and ITOPF. They'll know the drill. This won't be new to them.

The International Oil Pollution Compensation Funds (IOPC Funds) is a London-based body funded by a levy on oil shipments that provides financial compensation for pollution damage resulting from oil spills from tankers. It is run by international lawyers in a very precise way. And precision is very important because it pays out a lot of money during oil spill clean-ups. David put a call through to Linus Eerlandsson, the Swedish Deputy Director.

"I think we may be needing you soon," said David, once he was through to Linus.

"May and will are not the same thing, David," came the precise reply. "The exact terms of our engagement are very clear on our website. I thank you for the warning but it is clear that IOPC involvement is not yet an issue in this case. Please call me when those conditions are met. I wish you a Happy New Year."

Not much help there, he thought. He will thank me for the warning when he has to get over to Sicily. I can feel this is going to be a big one. I'll be glad to have Kate on my side then. He dialled up the ITOPF London office.

David did not usually feel comfortable with women. He found them rather difficult creatures. But he had real respect for Kate Jones. A blunt Welsh woman with a degree in marine biology and hard-won experience of oil spills around the world, she was one of the directors at the International Tanker Owners Pollution Federation. ITOPF is the world-recognised expert on oil pollution response, and within it Kate was known for her toughness and her knowledge. The first call a P&I Club insurer faced with an oil spill should make is to ITOPF, and the lucky ones got Kate to help them. To David she sounded like his school matron. It was always comforting to talk to her.

He got through to Kate and explained the situation. "Right, David," she replied cheerfully. "Sounds like a right mess coming. We'll get organised, get a team down to Syracuse and we'll be in touch. And David, don't make any plans for New Year. The way this sounds you will be in Syracuse too, buying me a beer after a tough day."

****

Capitano Dino Cervetto was managing three conversations at the same time. Around him in the Coastguard's emergency control room his staff were busy co-ordinating the first stages of the oil spill protection plan. The computer plot of the oil spilling to the surface and spreading out from the sunken aft part of the *Barbara S* was updated every ten minutes with information relayed from the Long Range Maritime Patrol aircraft that was now circling the scene. The prediction software responded to each update, showing where the oil would spread to in the next hours as the wind and current carried it towards the coast. The green and yellow areas on the plot screen were growing quickly. They would turn red when the oil hit the coastline.

That's only the fuel oil from the tanks by the engine room, thought Dino. It looks bad but with this weather it will disperse quickly. If we can only get the forepart under control we can save most of this mess.

In his headset he was listening to the Coastguard watch officer talking to the master of the Kalargyrou salvage tug. The *Krilov* was old, but it was a big tug, very strong and obtained very cheaply from the Ukrainian Navy by the Kalargyrou sisters when the Soviet Union fell apart. The Ukrainian master was calm. He was speaking in clear, sharp and simple English to the watch officer. By flipping the switch on his headset Dino could swap to the air controller channel and listen to the live feed from the eye in the sky, the patrol aircraft high up, and below that, the Air Sea Rescue helicopter that was working with the salvage tug. The controller and pilots worked in Italian, using crisp military phrases to keep each other continually in the picture.

The third conversation sounded softer, but Dino knew the person he was speaking with was the hardest of the lot. On his speaker phone he had Eleni Kalargyrou. She was in her Athens office, and she was also patched into the tug radio channel.

"As you can hear, Capitano Cervetto," said Eleni. "We have a major unit on scene and we are doing our best to get a line onto the forepart. The *Krilov* has a bollard pull of two hundred and fifty tonnes, so we are confident that we can at least hold the forepart away from the coast once we have a good connection. But I cannot say when we will get that connection. Your helicopter is very helpful, but conditions are terrible and my people are not able to board the forepart as yet. My naval architects think it will stay afloat for a while if the weather does not worsen, so maybe later today or tomorrow we will get the line across."

"Can the *Krilov* manage alone?" asked Dino. "What other resources do you have in the area?"

"Capitano, as I am sure you know, Kalargyrou is a most co-operative company," answered Eleni smoothly. "Both the harbour tug companies in Augusta and in Siracusa are working with us. They are currently provisioning their most seaworthy tugs and loading oil spill containment equipment."

Dino heard her pause. Here it comes, he thought.

"But I am sure you agree, Capitano, it would be foolish to send harbour tugs out to sea in these conditions. It is far too risky. So we will keep those units ready and deploy them as soon as we can. For now the *Krilov* is the only vessel on the scene and capable of doing anything." Eleni was speaking calmly and softly. "We are working on Lloyd's Open Form for now, and I am sure SCOPIC will kick in. Unless of course you want to change the financial arrangements?"

Dino knew he was over a barrel. Kalargyrou had the kit he needed and had stitched up the local tugs. But they would work, and work hard, he was sure of that. When it is all over they will make a big public fuss about how costly it all was but they will be well paid. He smiled to himself. These are real professionals, he thought.

"Miss Kalargyrou," he said politely. "We are delighted to have you and the *Krilov* on our side. Let's do all we can to get the forepart under control. Then we will think about containing the flow from the sunken part. And of course we will sort out the compensation in the normal way following the incident. As you say, you are providing the main asset. That is well noted."

CHAPTER ELEVEN

The tour guide took a step back and tried not to show his fear. He is like a caged dog, he thought. When a Mafia don gets angry it is best to give him some room.

"My cousin is an idiot," said Guido Recagno, thumping his fist down on the old wood of the heavy wine press beam. "He sends you here with a message that the coast is about to be flooded by a massive oil spill, and he wants me to know that perhaps *pizzo* will be less because business in the town will be bad! I am stuck in this place without windows but I can see much better than him."

The guide nodded a wary agreement. He did not know what Recagno could see that his cousin could not. He had never met this man's cousin and he did not want to meet him. He wanted only to live his quiet life in the small village, tending to his vegetable plot, taking tour groups around the living museum in summer, and taking the occasional amenable female tourist to see his own bedroom when the chance arose.

"Tell my cousin that the oil will bring us many benefits. There will be contractors needed to clean it up, contractors needed to dispose of the waste. Who controls the contractors? We do. There will be government functionaries and businessman and inspectors and journalists and every imp and pimp and banjo player in Italy descending on Siracusa for the oil circus. All those men will be on expenses. They will need to drink, and they will drink good wine. They will want women. Who controls the wine and women? We do."

Recagno had resumed his furious pacing, three paces each way, with a vicious turn as he came to the white plaster walls at each end of the wine press room.

"Tell my cousin to get all the boys he can find ready to help. We will need our people to be ready. New money will come into Sicily, new money will come to Siracusa, and we have to get a grip on that money," he continued urgently. "And tonight when it gets dark you will take me out of here and up to the mountain. Make sure the village is quiet. Bring a new mobile phone, one no-one has used. This is too important to leave to my cousin. I will need to make some calls myself."

****

For Presidente Ugo Vinciullo it was the best time of the day. The maid had cleared away the dinner plates, his wife had gone to do whatever wives do in the evening and he was free to stroll on the lawn with his cigar. It was cold and windy but the rain had stopped and he was glad to be alone and glad to be outside. Darkness was softening the edges of the old villa, and the lawn was springy under his feet. It was his special pride and joy, an English lawn maintained meticulously by his gardener through the long hot Sicilian summers with huge amounts of water. It was hidden from prying eyes behind the tall concrete walls topped by rampant bougainvillea which separated his villa from the coastal road south of Siracusa.

He took a deep draw on the cigar and thought about Laura. She is clever. She sees things we do not see, but she is clever enough not to make us look stupid. Somehow we always end up doing what she wants. She is married to that artist. I wonder who takes the lead in the bedroom?

It was a good cigar, and he thought today had gone well. The Coastguard had got those oil spill people mobilised and they would start hiring labour to build defences tomorrow. He had spoken to the Ministry of the Environment and insisted it was a national emergency so they had to pay. He had spoken to that old fox Giuseppe at ENOL and put him on notice that they would be coming to him for money. The lawyer had been dusted off and set to file claims against the shipowner and his insurers, just as soon as he could find out who they were. Some fool from the Vendicari bird reserve had rung up to bleat about the slowness of the reaction, panicking that the oil would get there before the defences were ready. His assistant had deflected that one. God knows, we have enough birds, he said to himself, especially now those EU idiots don't want us to shoot them anymore.

His thoughts went back to Laura. I wonder if Giuseppe had her when we were at school? He has always been a wily man, perhaps he could see she would become hot stuff. I was too busy, he smiled to himself, and there were plenty of prettier girls who knew it would be good to be close to a man who would inherit power.

His mobile phone was switched to silent but he could not ignore the insistent vibration in his pocket. He did not recognise the number. But he did recognise the voice.

"Vinciullo, Recagno here." All the self-congratulation spluttered out of Ugo like air from a balloon. He braced himself.

"What can I do for you, my dear Guido," he said. "I did not expect a call from you."

"You can stop dear Guidoing me," Recagno spat. "You weren't expecting a tanker to dump a load of liquid gold into your pockets either. Tomorrow the contracting starts, to build oil spill defences, am I right? Tomorrow the contracting for clean-up begins, am I right? Tomorrow there will be contracts let for waste disposal, getting rid of oily sand from beaches, am I right? The province and the puffed up president of the province will have fingers in all those juicy pies, am I right?"

The questions were staccato, Recagno was not waiting for an answer. How does he know what is going on out here when he lives in a hole under a farmyard somewhere in the mountains, thought Ugo? He looked around his private garden. In Sicily there is nowhere to hide from these people.

He dragged his attention back to the phone.

Recagno was speaking again. He could hear the sarcasm in the voice of the Mafia don. "Just in case you were thinking of trying to do this alone, my Presidente. I wanted you to know that you are not alone. My boys will be with you. Every step of the way. If you need people, they will provide them. If you need anyone encouraged, they will do the encouraging. And they will help to check the contracts and speed up the payments. For our regular fee."

There was a pause.

"Enjoy your cigar, Signor Presidente," heard Ugo, and the call was cut.

****

Seen from the sea the island of Ortigia is a rocky teardrop falling from Sicily into the Mediterranean. On the tip a castle towers over the huge broken rocks of the foreshore. The south side of the city is a sheltered port. A tree-lined promenade runs alongside the imposing Foro Vittorio Emanuele II, the main quay. In summer it is crowded with massive white super yachts.

The north side of the peninsula has been blighted by the Parcheggio Talete, an ugly rectangular concrete multi-storey car park built at sea level. Ortigia may be a historical jewel but visitors have to park somewhere, or so the council said when it awarded the contract to build it to a friend of the Regional President. Rubbish collects here, and prostitutes use the overhead walkway as a handy rendezvous. Used condoms and empty plastic bottles fill the spaces between the tumbled concrete blocks that protect the car park from the waves.

Next to it, just where the island is joined to the mainland by the first of three bridges, is the narrow entrance to the Porto Piccolo. This is a marina, home to the sleek yachts of the merely rich. The super-rich own the yachts that use the southern quayside in the Porto Grande on the other side of Ortigia, out of sight of the car park.

Seen from ashore Ortigia is a paradise of ornate Baroque buildings. The wide Corso Matteotti, lined with expensive designer shops, runs the length of the island, connecting it via a wide bridge to the modern city of Siracusa on the mainland. Each side of the Corso tall yellow stone buildings crowd in on each other, separated by cobbled alleyways. Here in summer crowds of tourists find welcome shade, friendly restaurants and shops willing to help them spend their euros in return for paintings of the tall yellow buildings they have been admiring.

The glory of Ortigia is the Piazza Duomo. Narrow streets open out suddenly into the long stone square dominated by the cathedral. In summer it is crowded with tourists, many walking sideways as they squint up against the sun's glare to admire the Baroque decorations of the buildings which line the square. Just across from the cathedral is the Municipio, the town hall. It attracts tourists into its cobbled courtyard to look up at the ornate wrought iron balconies.

Today there were no tourists. There was no sun either and no-one in the crowd jostling at the Muncipio entrance was squinting up at the balconies. Gusts of wind pushed spits of rain round the corners of the alleyways and into the doorway of the Municipio. There it ran off the oilskins of the fishermen who were blocking the entrance, and soaked into the old tracksuit tops worn by the crowd of African men trying to push past them.

Looking down on the crowd, Laura Filippone was regretting giving an office in the building to Castalia Mareazul. I wanted those clean-up people under my roof and under my eye. I wanted to keep the money close to the city administration. But I didn't think of the numbers of people they would need to hire. They should be hiring the fishermen first, they are our people and they are losing out already.

She could see that the fishermen were angry, but they were not stopping the Africans from pushing through them to the office she had lent to Castalia Mareazul. Each man went into the office and came out with a ticket in his hand. A job card for every illegal immigrant we have here to plague us, she thought. But nothing for the local men. What the hell is going on?

****

Dino looked down the table as people were taking their seats. Three men from the government oil spill response contractors, Castalia Mareazul. Two of them look like they know what they are doing, Dino reckoned. The other looks like a corporate type who has got lost. I bet he is the boss, fresh off the plane from Rome. A friendly-looking woman from ITOPF, Kate Jones, and her bag carrier, a young earnest-looking man. I know what they are going to say, thought Dino, and they know that they won't get what they want. Next to her was a puppet from the regional government. Here to spy for Vinciullo. Then the P&I Club Special Casualty Representative. He's a Captain, Dino guessed, he looks as if he has done this a few times. Two tough Greeks from Kalargyrou, salvage masters. No nonsense from them. Two of his own people, smart in their uniforms. And at the last minute, the Mayor of Siracusa. I did not expect her to drop in. Why does she always wear red?

"Ladies and gentlemen," he said, bringing the meeting to order. "Thank you for joining this meeting. We will work in English today, because we are an international group. I hope you are all comfortable with that?"

He looked around then continued.

"As you know, we are facing a potentially severe oil spill incident. The response will be co-ordinated by the Coastguard, and as the regional commander I have that overall responsibility. The response will work better if we all co-operate and use our respective strengths wisely. So I thank you again for joining this group, and I ask you all to work with me and together with each other so we can mitigate the damage to our seas and our coastline."

He had their attention, and he saw respectful nods from the salvage professionals and the P&I SCR. The others will all do what they think is best for them, thought Dino. But I'm going to do my best to make them toe the line.

Dino asked one of his officers to go through the situation report and to show the latest oil spill estimates and predictions on the large screen at the end of the room. So far the screen was showing streaks and bands of green and yellow spreading down the coast from the site of the sunken ship. A smaller patch of oil surrounded the plotted position of the floating tank section. No red yet, but it was obvious to everyone that the oil from the aft part would soon impact the coastline around the Ortigia peninsula.

Laura Filippone was the first to speak when the update finished.

"Very clear, Capitano," she said, softly. "Very clear. Very clear that my beautiful city will soon be coated with thick black oil. Can I ask what you are planning to do about it?"

The fresh-faced manager from Castalia Mareazul did not wait for Dino to answer.

"Signora, we are the Italian government oil spill containment and clean-up contractors. So we are already in action. As we sit here my people are deploying booms to prevent oil entering the Siracusa marina or any of the tourist site grottos to the north. We can also protect the port and berths to the south, and hopefully the nature reserve on the south side of the bay." He was speaking pedantically. "You do not have to worry."

Dino almost felt sorry for him when Laura leaned forward to reply. Still speaking softly she looked right at the manager. He began to squirm uncomfortably.

"You are so kind, Signor," she said, "to explain to this poor woman so clearly. Perhaps you could help me a little more. Perhaps you can explain how you will rig booms to protect the south harbour when there is nowhere to moor them in the deep water there? How you will protect the nature reserve at Salinas when there is no breakwater and no way to rig offshore booms either, especially in waves which are still over six metres high?"

The young manager wriggled and Dino let him suffer for a moment before saving him.

"We have Mrs Jones, from ITOPF, here, so perhaps before we go to specifics of the coastal defence we can ask her for her recommendations? Signora Filippone, you should know that ITOPF are the world leaders in oil spill response. Mrs Jones, perhaps you could outline the first stage response you would advocate at this point?"

"You know what the answer is, Captain Cervetto," was the robust reply from Kate Jones. "The wind is now dropping offshore. If you begin dispersant spraying right now, preferably from aircraft, you will break up the fuel oil spill and it will disperse before it fouls the coast. By all means let's get moving with booms and physical barriers, but you know it's dispersant that does the job so the oil doesn't make it to the shore."

He doesn't learn quickly, Dino said to himself, as the Castalia manager spoke out again.

"No, that is not possible," he said, pompously. "We are the official contractors here and in Italy we have a clear policy of not using dispersants. We do not want to create more damage with dispersants than the oil might do alone."

Unspoken but implied was that women had no business making suggestions in this case anyway.

"Captain Cervetto did not ask me what your policy is or what you are going to do," replied Kate Jones evenly. "He asked me what the best practice was and what should be done. That is what I have told you. Now if you want to work from an outdated manual with a policy that doesn't work I can't stop you. But I'm sure the minutes of this meeting and our report will clearly note that we recommended dispersant use at this stage. If you take that advice you will save thousands of man-hours of very dirty and unpleasant work cleaning up later."

It's going to be a long meeting, Dino said to himself. And in the end my hands will be tied by this pompous little fool in a smart suit and the official government policy.

CHAPTER TWELVE

Eleni Kalargyrou was at her most charming. Dino had never met her but thought as he listened to her on the phone from Athens that she knew how to make a man do what she wanted. It's a pity it is a wasted effort, he said to himself. I want to do what she wants me to do, but I cannot.

"Miss Kalargyrou," he replied evenly, when she stopped speaking. "It is indeed good news that your people are on board the forepart of the *Barbara S* and that the *Krilov* has a line attached. And I understand perfectly that with the weather moderating you now have the opportunity to tow the hulk into sheltered waters where perhaps the oil can be offloaded."

Dino paused. He did not want to be disloyal. He was a career naval officer and orders are there to be obeyed. But he hated being put in this position when his judgement as a professional, and the sensible thing to do, were overruled by politicians. He went on, carefully keeping his voice neutral.

"Our orders have been passed already to your salvage master. You are required to do two things. Firstly you must tow the tank section directly out to sea away from the Sicilian coast. Secondly you must mobilise the local tugs from Augusta and Siracusa to perform the tow and to assist in oil spill containment. That is our policy and it comes with all the authority of the Italian government. While I appreciate your call to me to endeavour to assist with another point of view, I cannot, and I will not, change these orders."

She knows it is crazy, he thought. I know it is crazy. We both know that interfering politicians are going to create a massive oil spill because that hulk cannot stay afloat out at sea for long. Her people are risking their lives out there to get a line onto the wreck to save it while that fat pig Vinciullo is pulling strings in Rome and making me dance to them like a puppet.

"Yes of course, Miss Kalargyrou," he said. She had acknowledged his reply and she clearly understood the situation. "It will help if your people produce a clear plan and situation report which shows how the shelter and discharge option could work. I can hope to use that in my discussions with the Ministry of the Environment. In any case I have no doubt that we will talk again tomorrow. For now we hope for settled weather and time to sort this out. Thank you, until tomorrow."

Dino replaced the phone handset and sat back in his hard upright chair. The orders from Rome were clear, keep the ship away from the coast. It cannot work, he thought. This will finish my career. Maria, I gave in to her and went to her parents' house to eat when I should have been here. This could have been avoided. Will she still smile at me when I am dismissed from the Coastguard?

He had not seen her since the mad dash from her parents' house. She had called and he had told her to stay there while he was dealing with this crisis. He felt sick. I let my guard down for her. Now I feel afraid of losing her. I need to focus on this mess, but I need her here with me. All the warmth of Sicily pulled me to her, and now all the tentacles of Sicily are wrapped around me and I am helpless.

****

Oily salt water dripped from the heavy plastic waterproof jacket of the fisherman. Laura could see it staining the wooden floor of her office. She did not flinch as he stepped forward, followed by two more men in oilskin trousers and jackets who shouldered their way into her office.

"There is oil on your clothing, Fortunato," she said calmly to the leader. "Perhaps we can have this meeting in the entrance where the stone will be easier to clean."

Laura stepped around her desk and walked directly towards the fishermen, who stepped back and let her pass, then followed her meekly outside.

"Now," Laura turned to face the fishermen. She was tall, but she had to look up at the leader. Fortunato is a big man for a Sicilian, she noticed. Big and hard, a fisherman all his life. "If there is oil on your clothing then can I assume there is oil already reaching the shores of Ortigia?"

"There is oil, Signora Filippone," replied Fortunato Redivo. "Oil in the waves on the north side. There is no fishing. My boat and all our boats have been forbidden to fish. The clean-up people are only hiring immigrants. How can this be? What will you do for us?"

As Mayor of Siracusa Laura made it her business to know the local leaders. She knew Fortunato Redivo as a quiet, tough man who spoke for the local fishing fleet. He had no title, but he had the respect of the other fishermen. He is not stupid, Laura calculated. He knows exactly why they are hiring the immigrants, and his people know too. That is why they are letting them pass. But neither of us can say it out loud.

Laura knew why they were hiring immigrants because she had spoken to the useless manager that Rome had sent to run the Castalia Mareazul government clean-up contractor operation. He was white and shaking, fresh from a brief but uncomfortable encounter with Guido Recagno's cousin. He had received the Mafia's instructions loud and clear. He would pay Sicilian wage rates, but he would pay those to the labour controller. And the labour controller would hire the labour, and pay what he could get away with to the immigrants.

Which also explained why the fishermen had not stopped the immigrants from pushing through them to get the work. They knew better than to argue with the third man in the office below where they stood now. Our life is run by these *Mafiosi*, she thought. There is a *bustarella*, a kick back, in everything. We all know it, and none of us do anything to stop it.

"Fortunato," she said with respect. "I understand your problem and sympathise with you. We have to protect Ortigia and we have to protect your livelihood. But the city is powerless in all this. The money comes from Rome, and we do not control how it is spent."

She paused. They were listening intently, but she knew she had to phrase this carefully. There were ways to get more money, but she could not be the one to suggest them directly.

"I will speak to the contractors. They will need boats to lay booms, and I will make sure they hire yours. As for the loss of fishing, you might like to think about who is responsible and who has money to spend," she said carefully. "The oil in the tanker is owned by ENOL, and it is the provincial government, led by Signor Vinciullo, which has the direct line to our friends in Rome."

****

The flurries of rain rattled the plastic windows of the awning surrounding the outside tables of the Ristorante Antico Porto. The noise did not interrupt the fishermen who were hunched together inside around the tables. The crowd of fishermen who could not get into the awning did not notice it either. They stood on the Via Trieste in their oilskins and heavy boots, looking out at the oily sea, smoking with their hands cupped over the cigarettes. Inside the awning the fishing boat owners were doing the talking. Those outside were the crews. They waited, not speaking. They would not fish today, and when they did not fish they did not get paid. But they were not yet angry. There are many days when a fisherman cannot fish. They were used to waiting.

Fortunato picked at the plate of fried baby squid which the middle-aged waitress had put beside him. Frozen, imported from China, he guessed. Soon everything will be imported from China. He was letting the torrent of complaints from the other owners wash over him. They have to talk, he thought. When they have spoken they will be ready to listen.

The inshore fishing fleet of Siracusa moors in the Darsena, the ancient dock between the new city and the island of Ortigia. From where they sat now in the small old fish restaurant their boats were hidden by a grey stone warehouse. They could not see the boats, but they were part of their lives. Like Fortunato, all of them had grown up as sons of fishing boat owners. Most of the boats were old, because there was not enough money in the fishing to build new ones.

"*Allora*," Fortunato spoke finally. He had given them all enough time to complain about the oily sea, the fishing ban, the immigrants who even now were on the foreshore moving bales of straw into position and swabbing at oil splashes. "Let us be clear. We want compensation for the closed fishery. If we cannot fish, we cannot eat. The tourists will not care, they will eat more of this imported frozen muck. But our families will not eat. We cannot go back to these oil spill people and ask for clean-up work. That work has gone to others. You know why. No-one wants their boat to be burnt in the night, their nets to be shredded, their children at risk. So we have to look elsewhere. We ask ourselves. Who owns this oil that has hurt us?

Should they not pay?"

"ENOL, ENOL." Fortunato sat back as the fishing boat owners shouted the name of the oil company. He paused, waiting for the exact moment, then lifted his hand.

"ENOL must pay, yes," he said. "But listen, my friends, ENOL is not alone."

He had their attention now. "ENOL owns the oil, so they must pay us. Yes, but that is not all. Who is spending all the money to pay these immigrants? The money does not come from those fools in the Municipio. It comes from Rome. Rome is where the money is coming from, through the provincial government. If they can pay these negroes who steal our bread, they can pay us. Rome has only ever hurt us, restricted our fishing, chased us for licences, sent idiots in uniform to inspect our boats. Now let them send us some money when we need it."

The boat owners roared back. "ENOL and Rome. ENOL and Rome."

Fortunato played the moment. He raised his hands again. They fell silent.

"My friends, we will make this work. First let us plan. We must agree what we want, and we must stick to it. Every one of us must agree the daily rate we want for loss of earnings while not fishing. Every one of us must agree the rate for chartering a fishing boat to help with the clean-up. Let us agree that, and then we will plan how we will lean on these people. Let us set a rate, and not a cheap one."

****

Antonio Cusumano was shouting at his wife. There was nothing unusual about that. He shouted at his wife every day. What was different this time was that he had a reason to shout.

"What do you mean, woman, you cannot open the *pensiones*?" he shouted. "What do you mean you cannot prepare more hotel rooms? The phone is ringing, the computer is running red hot with bookings, and you tell me you have no rooms ready?"

Signora Cusumano shouted back. There was nothing unusual about that either. She shouted back every day. Their teamwork was built on mutual antipathy. What was different this time was that she could see he was right.

"Listen, you donkey," she shouted. "You are a man so you shout when you want a room ready. You do not think that for every ready room a woman has cleaned it, a woman has made the bed, a woman has put out the towels. And when the guest comes a woman will meet them and take them to the room. If they are pigs like you then a woman will carry their luggage. Without women there are no rooms. You are shouting now for rooms. But what your Donkeyness does not remember is that it is wintertime. It is Christmas, it will be New Year tomorrow. All the women of Siracusa are busy making huge meals for pigs like you to eat. Our hotels and *pensiones* are shut for the winter. Do you remember, you shouted for us to clean the rooms and store the sheets and close the hotels and send the women home with no pay because there is no business in winter? Now you want to click your fingers and shout for rooms, but there are no women. No women, and no rooms ready."

They stared at each other. On the desk between them they could see the computer screen where the bookings were clicking up. In the winter they ran only the Bar Duomo and one hotel but in high summer they ran three hotels and four *pensiones* and let rooms all over Ortigia. They had good ratings on TripAdvisor. Antonio knew how to flatter tourists, how to guide them to the right restaurants and shops, how to help them park their cars in the narrow streets of Ortigia. His wife knew how to clean a room so it shone, how to marshal the summer girls who came from the villages inland to earn good money keeping the rooms clean and the restaurants working. They were an efficient team, united by a desire to make money. The summers were long and hot and busy. In winter they closed all the hotels except one, shut down the *pensiones*, sent the girls back to the villages. There was less to shout at each other about in the winter. Until now.

This had never happened before. Not at Christmas, in the dead, cold wet days of winter. Bookings were coming in from Italy, from London, from all over Europe. Some were seeking cheap rooms, some wanted the luxury suites, there was demand for all they could provide.

"Some are newspapers," said Antonio, quietly now. "Some are TV crews. They called me, they want good rooms. I suppose some are from Rome, come to work on this oil spill we are hearing of. I do not know who the rest are, but they are coming to Ortigia. Call everyone you can think of, offer them double money to come in to work, now. We will charge triple, so we will not lose. We will fill the hotels, fill the rooms, fill the bar. The Three Kings are bringing a present for all of us."

A rare thing happened. Antonio saw his wife smile.

"We pay double and we charge triple," she said. "It is the first time in twenty miserable years I have heard you talk sense."

****

"*Basta!* Enough!" Laura Filippone did not shout, but the men jostling each other in the courtyard of the Municipio heard her clearly. They stopped shouting and pushing and stood back, shamefaced like children caught fighting in the playground by the teacher. Her red suit stood out against the yellow and green slickers of the fishermen on one side of the yard. On the other side was a group of men in sailing jackets and blue trousers.

Laura picked out the leaders on both sides. They did not want to catch her eye.

"Fortunato," she said. "What is going on? Why are you turning my Municipio into a zoo?"

She looked at the other crowd. "And you, Andreu, I did not expect such behaviour from you. What is the problem?"

Fortunato spoke forcefully.

"These tour boat people want to steal our money," he said. "*Signora Sindaco*, you told us that the clean-up people would hire our boats. And they have begun to do that. Look, we are all here, the owners of the fishing fleet of Siracusa. Each of us has chartered our boat out to work on the protection and clean-up. We cannot fish but there is work for our boats. Then we find these people here too. The tour boat operators. They also want to charter their boats. They want to take money from the clean-up. But their boats do not work in winter anyway. They have lost nothing. If money goes to them, it means less money for us. You understand, we have to fight for our share."

Laura looked at Andreu and the men with him. She knew them well. They had small open boats that in summer took groups of tourists to the marine grottos north of Ortigia or for trips around the island. At this time of year the boats were tied up in the quietest corner of the Darsena, or being worked on ashore in preparation for the summer season to come. They are swift off the mark, she thought. The smell of money carries quickly on this wind.

"Our boats can be of use, Signora Filippone," said Andreu. "We want to protect the grottos or we will have no work in the summer. And these men are greedy. The charter rate they are demanding for their boats is double what they would earn from fishing. We all own boats here in Siracusa. We should have a share of this."

Laura looked from one man to the other. Behind each of them the other men were getting restless and beginning to mutter. Why are men so stupid, she thought? They get something and the first thing they do is try to stop others from getting the same thing.

She smiled and beckoned the two men closer.

"Listen, my friends," she said quietly. "I do not want to shout this out in front of the office I have given to Castalia Mareazul. So listen carefully. There is no need to fight each other. The sea is deep, and so are their pockets. They will get the money from the government, from the shipowner, from his insurers and from a fund of oil companies. You cannot imagine how much money they will have to spend if this oil spill gets worse. And they are not the only ones with money, Fortunato, I already told you that. So work together, my friends, and save the fighting for outsiders. Let Castalia Mareazul charter all the boats in the harbour, they will not run out of money because they are spending the money of Rome and because they will get it back. Trust me, I know how deep this sea can be. Fight together, and we will all gain more."

CHAPTER THIRTEEN

Through the windows of the Coastguard control room Dino could see the sun trying to break through the clouds. The weather was clearing, but he knew it was only a lull. The forecast for the next few days looked bleak again. Like this situation, he thought. A moment of quiet now, with hell to come and nowhere to hide.

He was waiting patiently while his secretary was assembling a conference call. He could hear them checking in on the line but he remained silent. Part of his mind was focused on what he was going to have to say in the call. Most of it should have been on that. Instead Maria was filling his head. He had told her to stay with her parents, but last night she had been waiting when he came home. Late, tired, unhappy and expecting to pour a small glass of wine alone he was crushed into her arms and pulled into the bedroom. He shook his head. I can never understand what she sees in me.

His secretary could have told him. She would have said that modest, honest and competent men are only too rare, but she was careful to keep her thoughts to herself. She placed the phone list in front of him and gave him a thumbs-up and a smile. He smiled back. If the men of Sicily were as hard working and efficient as the women this would be a rich country indeed, he thought.

"Miss Kalargyrou, Captain Brink, Mr Chillingworth, Mrs Jones, good morning to all of you and thank you for joining this call. Also on the line are representatives from the Ministry of the Environment in Rome, Castalia Mareazul here in Sicily and the harbour masters of Siracusa and Augusta, but they are listening for information only. One of my people will take a record of what is said and decided. I will speak for the Coastguard," he said. "The purpose of this call is to review the situation with the *Barbara S*, to review the options which Miss Kalargyrou's people have outlined concerning the forepart of the vessel and also the protection of the shoreline. Perhaps we can begin with a summary from the salvage master and Special Casualty Representative on scene."

He sat back, listening while Kalargyrou's salvage master reported what he already knew. The hulk was under tow, there were now lines attached to the powerful *Krilov,* and three smaller tugs from Siracusa and Augusta were also on the scene. Fuel oil spillage from the sunken part of the ship appeared to be increasing but minimal oil was leaking from the cargo tanks in the floating forepart. Kalargyrou's people were confident they could move the hulk into shelter in the weather window today, and had a plan to anchor it and discharge the oil into smaller tankers. It makes so much sense, his rational mind told him. It is a pity that sense does not apply in this case.

Captain Allen Brink, the experienced marine surveyor who was on the scene to represent the P&I Club, was speaking now. He has a strange accent, thought Dino, perhaps he is Australian. Anyway, he seems to know what he is doing. I wish I was able to agree with him.

Dino let them speak in turn. David Chillingworth said the P&I Club wanted the hulk moved to shelter, he supported the plan. Kate Jones, for ITOPF, said bluntly it was the only bloody sensible thing to do. And wasn't it time to start spraying the oil with dispersant before any more shoreline was polluted? Another good woman, recognised Dino, and more good ideas I have to say no to.

It would be a comedy if it was not such a tragedy, he thought. We have a meeting to decide something important, but the decision has already been made before we even start. In Italy there is always somebody behind everybody, and in Sicily there is always somebody behind them. Somebody no-one sees but we all know is there.

"Ladies and gentlemen," he said courteously. "Thank you for your input and ideas, which of course are coherent and correct. However in this situation I would ask you to bear in mind two issues. Firstly, we cannot deploy dispersants without direct permission from the Ministry of the Environment. That permission has not been given, so all oil spill containment efforts must focus on physical protection, using booms wherever possible. And for the hulk, we will not take the risk of bringing it closer to the coast. In our estimation the likelihood of it breaking up is too great. It must be towed directly out to sea, away from the Sicilian coast."

There was a moment of silence. They cannot believe what they are hearing, Dino said to himself. I cannot believe I am saying it. They do not know that I have no choice. Vinciullo has powerful connections in Rome, and Rome has power over me. That much I know. What I cannot be sure of is who is behind Vinciullo.

The call dragged on but finally it was over. The hulk would be moved further offshore. Into the coming storm. He knew what would happen tomorrow when the storm came. He was helpless to change that. He thanked each of the callers and switched off his speakerphone. I need a shower, he thought. I can feel the clammy hands of that bastard Vinciullo all over me.

****

They are getting in a flap, thought Giuseppe Mammino. That's good. I want them really scared before I put the screws on for cash. But not so scared they will get involved.

He was in ENOL's office overlooking the ugly refinery and tanker port complex of Augusta. He had taken special care to dress sharply that morning. I need to look as if I am a Sicilian, but a Sicilian they can trust, he had calculated. Any sign of panic or sloppiness and I get a planeload of pain in the arses piling down here. Too slick and they won't believe me. He had chosen a neat brown suit and a crisp white shirt. At the last moment he had taken his tie off. Those idiots think it is always summer down here. Let them see me dressed for good weather.

He smiled confidently at the cameras. ENOL had a very high tech video conference system linking its offices. On the screen in front of him he could see the General Manager for Italian operations and two of his bag carriers in the Rome headquarters. I can see they look worried, he thought. They need to see me looking in charge.

"Yes, of course," he said smoothly. "I am in constant touch with the Coastguard. The forepart of the ship is under tow and being pulled clear of the coast. There is some oil now coming ashore around Ortigia but it is not serious yet. There is a major operation to protect the coast and with the weather improving there is every chance we will not be hugely affected."

In the Rome office his boss was flourishing that day's Il Sole 24 Ore, Italy's main business paper. It was predicting an environmental catastrophe in Sicily, and ENOL's shares were already under pressure. ENOL should be doing something, but what?

"It is the silly season," said Giuseppe reassuringly. "Here on the ground there is no talk of catastrophe. We do not want to move too fast and end up spending money we did not need to. I have spoken with the authorities, they tell me the insurers for the ship are already active and the government oil spill contractors are in action. They will reclaim their spending from the insurers. If we do anything now we run the risk of spending money which we could have saved. That also would not be good for our share price, I think."

Any arguments which point to saving money always work well with that tight-arse, he said to himself. He could see on the screen that his boss had taken the point. Let him think he can save now, and I will bleed him all the more when the shit hits the fan. Or rather when the oil hits the coast, because only an idiot would believe that they can save that tanker hulk. It will be ENOL's New Year gift to Sicily, eighty thousand tonnes of sticky oil. Then you will be ready to pay out, and Sicily will be ready to help you spend the money. He smiled confidently as they closed the conversation.

"OK," said Giuseppe. "I quite agree. I will keep a good eye on events and the moment you are needed I will let you know and you can come down and take charge. In the meantime you will issue a statement to the press which emphasises that everything is under control."

He killed the video system and sat back. "Idiot," he said to the dead camera. "If you could read a weather forecast as well as you can read a share price you would know very well what is going to happen."

****

"May I speak with you frankly, Captain?" David Chillingworth asked. "I did not want to ask with all the others on the line, but I would appreciate a steer from you. No records, just between you and me?"

David was calling Dino Cervetto from his London office. He had a gut feeling that the *Barbara S* was going wrong, badly wrong, but he could not decide what to do. Should he be mobilising a team for a major incident and getting out there himself, or should he accept the assurances that the Italian authorities knew what they were doing, despite the advice from his own expert on the spot?

"Mr Chillingworth, I am willing to help, and I am alone here," replied Dino, courteously.

"It's just this, old fellow," said David. "You have told us that your orders are clear and that the hulk will be towed out to sea. My expert, Captain Brink, says this is madness and the hulk will certainly break up and create a massive spill. I find myself in a bit of a quandary, you know. Should I be getting a team ready locally, or not?"

Sweet Jesus, thought Dino. Here in Italy we have interfering politicians who don't understand anything and who only know how to make problems worse, then blame the mess on others. It seems that in England they have insurers who don't understand anything much either.

"Mr Chillingworth," he said evenly. "I will not comment on the advice from your expert, nor on the orders we have given. But if you ask my advice on what you should do, off the record, then I will tell you. I would not be making any plans to enjoy the New Year with my family. If I was in your position I would be mobilising a major team, I would have my local correspondent find me an office and hotel before the whole place is full, I would have local bank accounts set up and I would be on the next plane down here with my best people."

David sat back. Couldn't be clearer than that. Sounds like a good man who's rather having to toe a line he doesn't like.

"Oh, roger that," he said, "got the message, old boy. I'll look forward to meeting you. Heard Sicily is a lovely spot."

"Of course, Mr Chillingworth," replied Dino. "It will be a pleasure." He put the phone down and took a deep breath. "You are not going to find so much pleasure here," he said quietly to himself. "Vinciullo and his nasty friends are going to eat you for breakfast, and there is nothing I can do to stop them."

****

Simone was fighting to keep her voice steady. She would not let Yves know that her stomach was knotted tight. He would not get the satisfaction of knowing she was afraid. It would be so easy to give in, she thought. I could stay here with him. I'm not looking forward to twenty-six hours on trains and a ferry. I don't know what good I can do alone when I get there. But I have to go. He should be with me, but he is staying. And so is the English girl.

"I have researched carefully, Yves," she said as calmly as she could. "The whole of that coast around Siracusa and to the south is a haven for birds at this time of the year. The Riserva Naturale di Vendicari is where all our water birds are in the winter. December is the big month for waders, herons, storks, flamingos, mallards, gulls and cormorants and duck and terns, they are all there. And now there is oil hitting the coastline and more threatened. It is why we set up Marine Bleu, and I am going to fight for those birds."

Yves did not reply. He was leaning on the wall, gazing moodily out of the window. Simone wanted to stop talking but could not. Perhaps he is going to change his mind. He will turn, and pack, and we can go together.

"I will get the train from Dunkerque at 1215. I can go via Paris, Rome and then down to get the ferry across to the island," she said. "I will be there tomorrow and find some local activists to work with." Why am I telling him this, he is playing with me.

"At your age you would be better to get the plane, Simone," said Yves. His words cut into her. "That is if you want to be any use when you arrive."

He paused. She could not speak. If she opened her mouth she would scream at him, or burst into tears. She saw him peel himself upright and slouch over towards her. He is going to kiss me, she thought. He says that, then he comes to touch me, to hold me, he knows he has power over me.

She turned away, her body rigid. She hated him, but wanted him to touch her, to say he was wrong, to apologise. She felt him hesitate, then he was walking past her towards the door.

"Good luck," he said. "*Bon voyage.* I will let you know how the meetings go here." Then he was gone, and Simone could let herself cry.

CHAPTER FOURTEEN

David was uncomfortable. The business class seats on the BA flight
from London to Catania had felt cramped, but bearable. There was a
long wait for his luggage, but he was not in a hurry. But when he
strode confidently out through customs to look for the hire car desk
he was annoyed to find it was not in the terminal. The walk from the
terminal to the hire car building was where the discomfort had set in.
Catania airport is home to a drifting population of vagrants and illegal
immigrants. Most of them use the route from the terminal to the hire
cars for shelter. It was unpleasant to wheel his cases past them. He
felt them sizing him up. He pulled his blazer tighter, he did not want
his pocket picked.

The discomfort was worse now. They did not seem to understand
that he had a reservation. He repeated himself a little louder, and
pointed at the itinerary his secretary had typed out for him.

"Yes, Sir," said the hire car clerk. "I can hear you and I can
understand English. Let me tell you again. I understand you have a
reservation. You have a reservation, and so do those people behind
you. But I do not have any cars. So I cannot give you the car you
have reserved. You can try Hertz, you can try Avis, you can do as you
say, and call my boss in Rome, but there will still be no cars."

David had never been to an airport without hire cars before.

"Look, old boy," he tried bluff friendliness. "There must be a car somewhere. What is going on? How long do I have to wait?"

"Yes," replied the clerk. David could see from his badge that his name was Bruno. "There are cars somewhere. There are cars in Rome, there are cars in Brindisi, but there are no more hire cars available in Sicily. Something big and unexpected is happening in Siracusa. We do not have so many cars on Sicily in the wintertime, because we do not expect so many visitors. All the airport hire car companies have been swamped. The system has gone down and your reservation cannot be met. More cars will be brought on the ferry, but not today."

David noticed that Bruno did not say he was sorry. He is not sorry, he thought, he is just fed up.

"I have an important job to do in Siracusa, I have to get there," he said, feeling slightly foolish.

"Of course," replied Bruno, who was not looking up. He was busy closing down his terminal. "Perhaps you will find a taxi at the terminal? You will not be charged for the reservation."

David pushed his bags back towards the door, finding it hard going through the thickening angry crowd. They were in tight groups, pushing heavy metal suitcases. Some were lugging large TV cameras. He saw that one crew was filming the crush and the scenes at the counters as the drivers were turned away carless. They are all media, he noticed. They all want cars, I suppose they are all going to Syracuse. A crowd fighting for hire cars is already news. This is already bigger than I expected.

At the door of the hire car building he hesitated. Right in front of him was the exit barrier from the car park. If they are all going to Syracuse then all the cars coming out will be going there too, he reasoned.

Coming up to the barrier was a white Fiat 500 driven by a smart middle-aged man with thick-rimmed glasses. David flapped his hands to attract attention and left his cases while he walked over to the car.

"Any chance of a lift to Syracuse, old boy?" he asked.

"I guessed you were looking for that," replied the driver in a clipped Dutch accent. "Bring your bags. You will not get there now otherwise. Every news team in Europe is on its way. I am Michiel, a freelance journalist. We can all feel a big story coming."

****

"You are a good seaman, Cervetto," said the Coastguard Admiral. "I remember that. You were always in tune with the sea. But this is a storm of a different kind. I have one year more to serve in this post. Not navigating a ship, but steering a course for our Coastguard between all the politicians who want any excuse to cut our budgets. I have to know when to say yes to them even if I want to say no. It is a skill you have not yet learnt. I think that if you are not careful you will never have the chance to learn it. Of course, you might well have time to study. Five years in a military jail for disobeying orders will give you plenty of time, but your career will be over."

"Almirante," said Dino respectfully. "The politicians are wrong. We have one chance to stop this hulk from breaking up. If we turn it now and run for shelter with three tugs they can make it before the weather turns. It will be a bit of a mess locally, but we can contain the spillage. If we continue to force them out to sea we put the whole southeast coastline of Sicily at risk."

"If I go against the politicians then I put the whole Coastguard at risk, Cervetto," replied the Admiral. "Whatever we do now, someone is going to get covered in oil. That will not be me. And if you have any sense it will not be you, Capitano. Don't throw away a good career. Beaches can be cleaned, but the stains never come off your record if you disobey an order. I made the order to back you in the first place. You went against that once, and I am doing my best to act like the English Almirante Nelson, to turn a blind eye to that. Don't ask me to blind both my eyes."

Dino thanked the Admiral for his advice and put the phone down. He felt calm now. He knew that feeling. With chaos all around he knew how his body reacted. He felt himself slowing down. He could see clearly. He could see the duty officer waiting to talk to him. He could see his secretary holding a call for him. He could see the pile of messages on his desk needing his attention. He could see the plot of the oil spillage growing red. He could see the hulk, only a few precious miles from shelter behind the cape but being hauled slowly in the wrong direction. He could see the weather forecast, and the blow coming through. He could see the city and the beaches and bird sanctuary covered in oil. He could see the court martial, the judge advocate stripping him of his rank, his life. And he could see Maria. She likes me because I am honest, he thought. I can stop this pollution if I act now. I have to do it.

He spoke calmly and deliberately.

"Get me the on-scene salvage master on the radio and then line up a conference call with Kalargyrou and Castalia Mareazul. We will try to put the hulk into shelter, and contain the oil with booms until we can unload it."

He saw the duty watch officer hesitate.

"Do it, on my authority," he ordered sharply. "And note the order and time in the log before you call your uncle, Fraille. Sicily deserves better than you and your family."

****

Somewhere through the thick walls of his hotel room David could hear nuns singing. His secretary had booked him into the Hotel Domus Marae, which was built into an old chapel on the north side of Ortigia island and run by nuns. There was very little Christian about the way the grumpy desk clerk had been turning away people when he arrived, thought David. But they kept my room, so the Lord be thanked for that.

"Linus," he said. "Sorry to disturb you again but I really think you should be mobilising."

He was on his mobile phone to Linus Eerlandsson at the International Oil Pollution Compensation Funds in London.

"I am here in Ortigia. My correspondent is overwhelmed with claims, there is oil all over the place, the weather is getting worse and tomorrow everyone expects the main part of this tanker to break up and release the whole oil cargo. The place is crawling with media, I had to hitch a ride with a Dutch guy, Michiel someone or another. He is an old oil spill hand, says this is going to be huge."

He was bubbling over, feeling a little out his depth. Someone to share the claims handling with would make his life much easier.

"My dear David," replied Linus. The pompous bastard is laughing at me again, thought David. He is imitating me. "My dear fellow, you are running ahead of yourself. You are fully aware that the P&I Club cover will handle any claims up to $136 million. The funds do not become involved below that. Even if a Dutch journalist wants to see a bigger pay out. At this stage it must be a little early to suggest that the IOPC commits itself to considerable expenditure."

David wanted to murder this dried-up Swedish lawyer, but he held his temper back.

"Linus," he tried again. "I spoke with the Coastguard chief. He is certain there will be a disaster. The world's media are descending on us because this whole area is a Baroque UNESCO World Heritage Site. Even if it is not a disaster they will show it as one. I can see from my hotel window TV crews already filming the oil and clean-up gangs on the rocks in front of me. The Dutch guy told me how it works. The media send a crew, and the crew has to make the news to justify the trip. My local correspondent is already seeing claims stacking up from the fishermen, from the local councils, from the government, and he knows this place. We are going to have a mountain of claims whatever happens to the rest of the oil. We need to set up a joint office and agree a policy on interim payments."

"We need to remain calm and objective, David," replied Linus. "Calm and objective. We do not pay out on media storms. I suggest you set up your office and if we are needed then I will come to join you. Not before."

There was a pause. "And David," he continued, "let me take this opportunity to wish you a Happy New Year. I do not expect to talk with you again before the end of this less happy one. Goodbye."

CHAPTER FIFTEEN

The lumpy grey seas were breaking right over the deck of the hulk. It was only just afloat, almost submerged. The salvage master on the *Krilov* had already taken his men off. They had worked in surging water for three hours to connect lines to the two Sicilian tugs. It had taken another hour to turn the whole spread slowly through the gathering wind. Now the *Krilov* was stretched out ahead of the hulk, connected to it by eight hundred metres of heavy wire rope. They were making progress now, painful progress, but moving towards safety. On each side were the two harbour tugs, also with wires to the hulk, steadying the tow. They were rolling and pitching in the growing seas.

We can do it, calculated the salvage master. Eight miles, two and a half hours, and we are in shelter. We can do it if those local tugs stay with it and co-operate. Then we can hold the hulk in place until the weather goes through.

He spoke in Ukrainian to the watch officer. "I am going to try for an hour's sleep. Keep a good eye on those Italian tugs. It is a pity we need them, but they know this way we can save the big spill. Stay sharp, this is the last chance."

****

Ugo Vinciullo took the call at his villa. He could not believe it. His nephew told him that Cervetto had ordered the hulk into shelter. Three tugs were bringing the broken ship in now, and in less than three hours it would be anchored, leaking oil. Anchored right here, right on the sheltered coast where he so loved the view out to sea.

He paced the lawn. Its neat greenness gave him no pleasure. What if oil is blown on spray over the villa? This Coastguard Captain is mad. He does not know who is the boss. He cannot see that if a ship is leaking it should be away from the coast, not closer. Perhaps he wants money, he thought. He felt relief. He could understand now. He is doing this to get money from me. If I offer him money he will turn the hulk away.

He may have a Sicilian wife, Ugo said to himself, but he has not learnt to think like a Sicilian. I will never give him any money. I will ruin him, I will ruin his wife and I will ruin his family. I will ruin the Coastguard, they will be sorry they have attacked me like this. But first I will get this hulk away from here.

He fumbled in his pocket for his mobile phone and pressed the speed dial for his secretary.

"Get me the owners of the harbour tugs in Siracusa and Augusta, right now," he ordered.

"Yes, I know it is almost New Year and they will be at home. Just do it, and do it now."

****

The salvage master was on the bridge within seconds. He knew the watch officer would not call him unless there was trouble.

On normal ships the watch officer is always looking forward, and when the Captain comes to the bridge he instinctively looks that way too. That is where the danger is likely to be. On tugs the Captain

113

always looks aft first, because that is where the tow is, and that is where things go wrong.

His first quick glance told him that all was in order. The tow was connected, they were making headway, and he could see the two local tugs out each side, partly pulling and partly guiding.

"Something is going on, boss," said the watch officer. "The Italian tugs are sheering around all over the place. The weather is getting worse, sure, but they were coping fine. Then ten minutes ago I noticed a lot more weight on the towline, and they both began dancing around. Just watch, it looks as if they are deliberately getting themselves into trouble."

The salvage master had his binoculars up now, focussed on the port side tug. He saw it seesawing in the building seas. It was definitely steering badly. He saw it take green water over the aft deck as it swung sideways on its towline.

"Maybe they thought it was a good time to put an apprentice on the wheel," he grunted, swinging his binoculars to the other tug. As it came into focus he saw the tug surge to port, then snap up short on the towline and curtsey into a wave. "Not an apprentice on that one," he added. "Some sort of a suicide merchant. Maybe it is lunchtime in Sicily, they took a little too much wine."

Salvage tugs have excellent communication systems, and these are constantly monitored. The watch officer could hear the two tugs speaking to each other on the radio in Italian. Until now the traffic had sounded routine, but the voices were suddenly more urgent. What he could not monitor and had not heard were the mobile phone calls both masters of the local tugs had just received from their owners. The messages were identical and simple. They were not to help bring the hulk towards the coast, but they must not do anything to allow blame for the delay to fall on them.

The salvage master looked at the electronic chart. Progress had been slower than he hoped. At this speed they would still need an hour and a half to reach shelter. But their speed was dropping. The Italian tugs were no longer contributing to the tow.

Before he could reach for the VHF and call the local tugs the receiver sprang into life on the working channel.

"*Krilov*, we are dropping the tow portside," he heard. "It is too dangerous for us to tow in this seaway. We need to run for shelter ourselves."

One gone, he thought. The other will go also now. They make jokes about Italians being cowards, but this is not that. They could do this if they wanted to. But they don't want to, and they are going to leave me here with eighty thousand tonnes of oil in a broken ship hanging onto the towline and a storm coming. There is no way we can get the hulk to shelter without their help and no way we can turn now and try to pull it away from the shore. Not with the seas as they are.

"Well, Mate," he said calmly. "Wave our friends goodbye. Let's shorten in the tow so we don't lose too much wire when we have to cut it. We are fucked now, and in a few more hours that hulk will be fucked too, then the whole coast will be fucked. We can at least save as much fucking wire as we can, there is fuck all else we can do."

****

George Anand felt old. Old, tired, afraid and alone. It was a new feeling for him, and he did not like it. On a ship, cloaked in the authority of the Captain, he had sometimes felt tired. Sometimes afraid, and occasionally alone. But never old. At home he was surrounded by family and treated with respect. The grandchildren made him tired, but that was not this sort of tiredness.

With an effort he pulled himself back to the present. He was not at home. He was not on a ship. He was not cloaked in authority. He was not treated with respect. He looked down at himself. He was wearing grey prison clothes. They were the same energy-sapping grey as the peeling paint on the walls. He was seated on a hard chair, his hands linked in front of him by handcuffs. Beside him was a middle-aged man wearing a badge which identified him as an interpreter, and across the steel table in front of him were two men in suits he had never seen before. He felt a spark of hope. Perhaps they were from the owner's office, come to get him released.

He did not turn, but if he had he would have seen two tall Carabinieri standing rigidly close behind his chair, forbidding in their dark uniforms. He knew they were there, and he knew they were waiting for him to move, to give them an excuse to tighten the handcuffs further.

"This is the magistrate, he is here to examine you," he heard the interpreter speak, but the words made no sense.

"Explain to them that I saved my crew," he said quietly. "Tell them I want to go home. I saved my crew, but now I am in jail. I just want to go home."

The three men were talking in Italian. Captain Anand let the words wash over him. Since being picked up from the helicopter he had been hustled to a van, driven at speed to a jail, stripped and searched and then left in a cold stone cell. This is not right, he thought. Where is my owner, where is my lawyer, what do they want from me?

He touched the interpreter on his arm, breaking into the Italian conversation.

"Tell them to call Armatori Fratelli Spinelli SpA, they must send someone to arrange my flight home to India. Tell them to call the ship's agent in Augusta. You have no right to hold me here. Where is my owner?"

"Captain," replied the interpreter, speaking slowly and carefully, as if to a child. "These men are the authority. They will question you. Your ship has sunk and it is polluting the coast. You disobeyed orders, and now we all must suffer for that. So be quiet, and answer the questions they will ask now."

One of the men opened a pad in front of him and began to write, glancing up at the Captain from time to time. The older of the two men barked a question in Italian.

"Why did you disobey the Coastguard, Captain?" said the interpreter.

He did not answer. The first man wrote quickly. Another barked question.

"Why did you navigate without care and break the ship, Captain?" he heard.

"Why did you spill this oil on our coast, Captain?"

"Why did you not take the ship away from the coast, Captain?"

He could not answer, but the questions went on. The older man asked in Italian, the interpreter repeated the question in English. Each time he was silent the man opposite him wrote a sentence or two on his pad. After a long time he saw the two men look at each other and nod. The pad was turned around towards him and a pen offered.

"Here is your statement, Captain. Please sign it," said the interpreter.

He looked down at the scribble, all in Italian. What can it say? He searched for strength.

"Tell them I saved my crew. None of my boys were drowned. Tell them I want a lawyer and I want to speak to my owner."

Before the interpreter could speak the man who had been barking the questions in Italian leant forward. He tapped the pad and pushed his face towards the Captain.

"Sign it," he said, in clear English. "Sign it and you plead guilty, you go to jail for five years."

There was silence in the room. No-one moved.

"OK Captain," he went on. "You don't sign, you go to jail for five years to wait for a trial, then you get a sentence of ten years. In Palermo jail. You will not like it."

Before the Captain could speak he saw the older man give a slight nod. The hard gloved hands of the Carabinieri pulled him to his feet.

"*Arrivederci*, Captain," he heard someone say as he was pushed from the room. "Think hard, you will have time to think what is good for you, then you will ask for one more chance to sign."

****

It takes a lot to make a salvage master angry. When you spend your life going out in storms to pull ships off rocks or tow them to safety you expect things to go wrong. You expect wires to break and steel to rupture and waves to wipe out all your efforts. So you learn to be calm, to roll with the punches, to keep working away to save what you can.

The salvage master on the *Krilov* was calm now. But was also very, very angry. He could have saved the broken tanker and its cargo. But now he was cutting the tow wire and standing off to watch while it broke up and sank. A lost tow, a wasted wire and a low salvage award. Those bastard local tugs, he cursed inwardly.

He was braced in the corner of the tug's bridge, holding himself steady against the rolling and pitching. Outside the wind was changing up a gear, the whine strengthening to a full roar. He looked down at the aft deck of the tug where his men were struggling to secure the last of the line, then up and through the binoculars at the hulk. We could not have waited any longer, he told himself. The seas were six metres now, short and brutal. Each wave pushed part of the hulk out of the surface for a few seconds, then tumbled it over as it fell across the trough.

With one finger he signalled to the watch officer to turn the tug to face the hulk and the seas. The tug was free now and despite the heavy seas felt secure. He could watch the hulk break up, but there was nothing else he could do.

He punched the buttons on his mobile phone.

"Miss Kalargyrou? *Krilov* here. I am watching the hulk breaking up now. Oil is spreading, I think the first tanks have ruptured. We are seven miles off Siracusa. We could have made it but the locals messed us up. Yes, we saved as much line as possible. We will stay on station and I will call the Coastguard now. Yes, we will stay in touch."

The Coastguard can do nothing now, he thought, and neither can we. He could see the hulk turning right over now and broken steel emerging from the wave front. Then it was gone. He waited but it did not reappear. That's it. Broken, sunk, leaking oil and close to the coast.

"Log the position, Mate," he said. "Note tow sunk at this time. Hold the tug upwind of the position for now, keep us out of the worst of the oil. We wait for the storm to go through. I will finish my sleep."

I will finish some vodka when we get off this job, he promised himself. I'd finish off those bloody tug skippers if I could too.

CHAPTER SIXTEEN

Michiel stabbed at the TV remote control. He was trying to turn the volume up, but the TV did not react. The screen on the wall-mounted TV was flickering but Michiel could see the pictures of oiled seabirds, then the camera switched to a talking head.

"Predictable," he said out loud to the screen, although he was alone in the small hotel room. "Always the first to call the studios, always the first to offer photographs and opinions. But you had a lot less to say when I interviewed you about the aftermath of some of the spills you had made such a fuss about."

Michiel gave up on the TV and tossed the remote control down on the bed. At least they have a Wi-Fi signal, he thought, reaching for his laptop. He had managed to get a room in the hotel before the rush of media arrived in Ortigia. It was tucked away in a small side street, not far from the Piazza Duomo. Not too expensive, not very new, but clean and quiet. His hire car was safe in an ugly concrete multi-storey parking a few minutes' walk away.

On the laptop he quickly found the website of the satellite news channel that the TV was struggling with. The 24-hour rolling news presenters were spinning out the thin facts they had about the *Barbara S* and the Siracusa oil spill, supplementing their reports with still photographs of oiled seabirds and shorelines, and interviews with any experts they could find. Their camera crew and presenter are not yet in Sicily, guessed Michiel. I can see that. They don't have any material of their own. So they fill the time with what they have and what they can pull in from people who have an angle to push.

Andrew Horsland was still talking as Michiel clicked on the site. Across the bottom of the screen the strapline identified him as a bird expert for the RSPB and Greenpeace. He was talking for the *Vogelbescherming Nederland* when I last saw him in Rotterdam, remembered Michiel. He is rent-a-mouth for seabirds, and the TV stations love him almost as much as he loves himself.

Michiel listened with the disciplined ear of a professional journalist. He is good at it, he recognised. He sounds confident, and he never actually claims to have been here or seen anything with his own eyes. He just gives that impression, especially when he talks about the catastrophe facing the poor migratory birds of North Europe. The newspapers will really pick this one up, he told himself. Horsland will be on all the front pages tomorrow, and so will the photos he supplies them with. Not photos of actual birds oiled here, because so far there aren't any oiled birds and there aren't any photographers in action. But that never stops Horsland, thought Michiel, he has plenty of photos of birds of the type that might be found here, taken at previous incidents and happily recycled.

It was the usual story. Horsland was explaining earnestly that the ship should not have been there, it was old and unsafe, it was the biggest environmental disaster to hit the coast of Europe for decades, thousands of birds would die, the reserve at Vendicari was particularly environmentally sensitive. Then the call to action, European politicians should crack down on irresponsible shipowners and oil companies, action was needed now to keep our seas clean.

He has no facts, Michiel guessed. If he had he would use them. He doesn't know who the owner is, or anything about the ship or cargo or what happened, and I bet he has never been to Sicily. But most people listening will be convinced. Donations will come into the bird charities from concerned people, and Euro politicians with nothing better to do will dream up more laws about shipping. While he was thinking he was waiting. He knew what would come next. "There," he said. He laughed to himself. There was the clip of the pretty young girl cleaning the oiled seagull. It was used every time. "Someone should be getting royalties," he said out loud.

Michiel could recall clearly his own interview with Andrew Horsland. He had attended a public meeting in Rotterdam, called to discuss plans to extend the port with more reclaimed land. Horsland was there to speak for the Dutch bird protection charity, which claimed that the expansion would affect the feeding areas of thousands of seabirds. After the meeting Michiel had caught up with him and asked for an interview, mentioning the International Herald Tribune. Horsland bit my arm off to talk, recalled Michiel. Until I asked him about the studies which showed increased and healthier bird populations in places where there had been oil spills, places he had publicly declared that a disaster was occurring. The *Braer*, the *Sea Empress*, the *Erika,* all huge spills, all catastrophes according to Horsland, all showing good healthy bird populations one year after the spill. He just got up and walked off, remembered Michiel. If he can't spout his propaganda he is not interested.

He shut his laptop lid. I'm going to report this story accurately, he convinced himself. And I'm going to report the whole story. What happened, why it happened, who are the losers. But this time it will be different. I'm going to report the bit we never see. I'm going to report who the winners are as well.

He reached into the khaki canvas bag he used as a briefcase and pulled out his pad and a biro. He needed a plan of who to try and talk to tomorrow. The Coastguard, the shipowner, ENOL, the local authorities, whoever is organising the oil spill defences, the fishermen, he was jotting down targets. And lucky chance for me, he smiled to himself. That English bag of wind I gave a lift to from the airport is the insurance man who will be paying for all this. I'll give him a day to settle in then drop by the claims office and get a story there.

****

Michiel was on the phone to the editor of *Algemeen Dagblad*, Rotterdam's biggest daily paper. It was his fifth phone call to different editors that morning.

"Glad to have you on the spot with a disaster coming, Michiel," said the editor. "We can take eyewitness copy from you. Perhaps you can find a Dutch angle, maybe there is a tourist from Rotterdam who has had their holiday spoiled?"

"Look," said Michiel urgently. "I've done a lot of good work for you in the past, and you know I get behind the story and do it thoroughly. This isn't a disaster yet, but from what I see bungling by the authorities is making a small problem into a big one. That's a story, and then there will be a lot of profiteering here from cleaning up the mess. That will be a huge story."

"Michiel," he could hear the guarded note in the editor's voice. "Don't push your luck. We have a very small freelance budget. I'm going to buy some copy from you, but it has to be stories that our readers want to see. People expect to read about unhappy holiday makers, so that is what I want. People expect to see oiled birds in an oil spill, so that's what I want. Find me a fisherman who has lost his livelihood and I can run the story. But don't get too clever on me. We are not going out on a limb about incompetence and corruption in Sicily. Just like we wouldn't run a story about snow at Christmas, get me?"

Michiel did not protest. It's not worth it, he thought. At least I have enough commissions now to pay for the trip. I have the names of a few powerful papers which I am representing. That will open doors. I can do the stories they want now while I research the real big story, get the people and the places and the times and the dates and the money. Especially find out where the money goes. Then I will have a buyer for the real story.

"Ok chief," he said cheerfully. "You've got it. A grumpy fisherman, Cees and Ellen from Bergambacht and their ruined wedding anniversary holiday trip to Sicily, a cormorant with oil on it and a sense of disaster. Usual rates?"

****

Her bag seemed to be getting heavier. Simone had lugged it from the railway station to the hostel, but she had been turned away. It was already full. *Activists who got here before me,* she realised ruefully. *We said we would be the first at any oil spill and the last to leave. Yves has changed Marine Bleu, and not for the better.*

The hostel manager had pointed her the way to the tourist office on Ortigia island, told her they would find a room for her. It was a twenty minute walk with the duffel slung over her shoulder. Siracusa looked bleak in the thin winter light. She was tired and scratchy. She could feel the wind gusting, lifting litter and blowing it around the streets. *The architecture is grand enough,* she recognised, *I can see why tourists flock here. But they are obviously not expecting any now.* She felt a surge of annoyance. The tourist office door was clearly marked with opening hours from 10 am to 12 pm. It was 11.30, she had been travelling all night, and she needed a room and a shower. But the office was shut.

"*Merde,*" she said. *I feel my age, maybe Yves was right.* "The bastard," she said out loud. "The fucking bastard."

Swearing out loud made her feel a bit better. Further along the square she could see the awnings of a bar. I'll get a coffee and ask them about rooms, she decided. She felt better thinking about the coffee.

In the Bar Duomo it was gloomy. She felt rather than saw the tubby middle-aged owner eyeing her up from behind the bar. Dirty old man, she thought, but straightened her back automatically and looked at him with a smile. He can look all he wants if he knows of rooms to let.

French, thought Antonio Cusumano. Skinny and with a tight smile. He liked to win bets with his waiters guessing the nationality of the tourists. The French are the easiest to pick out, he laughed to himself. And the most difficult to please. This one looks as if she has no money. Maybe if I help her she'll be grateful.

"What can I do for you, *mam'selle*," he asked. "It is not a good day for tourism. Perhaps a nice *aperitivo*? Some good Sicilian pasta to warm you up?"

He makes my skin crawl, thought Simone, but her reply was friendly.

"I would like a large coffee, Americano, please," she said. "And can you help me, I am looking for a cheap room to stay a few days. Perhaps you know somewhere? The tourist office is closed and the hostel is full."

Antonio glanced behind him automatically. He wanted to be sure his wife was not watching. He looked back at Simone. She was wearing skinny jeans and an old sweater. Not much money, not so young, but no wedding ring and a great bottom. He was calculating. He had rooms, but he did not want to let them cheap. But he didn't want to let this little *bonbon* go either.

"The coffee is coming up," he said with his best smile. "And you are lucky. There is a big demand for rooms. That is why the tourist office closed early, too many people wanting help to find a place to stay. But we have some rooms and I can help you. They are not so cheap, but they are better than a hostel, with a good bathroom and a nice shower." And a big comfy bed, he continued to himself.

Simone felt as if she was caught in a bad film. The stereotype is too clear. I can read his mind exactly. So let me take his room, let him give me a good price because he thinks he is going to fuck me, and I will play him along. I can kick him in the balls if he tries anything on. Then I will tell his wife if he tries to put me out. That will stop him.

"Let me drink the coffee and see the room," she said, looking directly at Antonio. She could see him preening himself. "And tell me the cost. I am here to help the birds in the oil spill, I have not got a large budget. It is a charity, you understand."

****

The gloomy portraits of previous regional presidents stared down from within their heavy gilt frames. They lined one side of the meeting room in the offices of the Provincia Regionale di Siracusa. The other side of the room was dimly lit by a line of grimy windows partially obscured by thick curtains. Sitting at the dark wooden table which took up most of the room, Dino realised it was all part of an act.

They could smarten up their offices and have bright modern meeting rooms if they wanted to, he knew. But it suits them to look a little poor, a little old-fashioned, a little pessimistic. That way it is easier to get their hands on the grants from Rome and Brussels.

He was wearing his full uniform. Maria had brushed his jacket and tweaked his tie that morning before he left home. For a meeting with Vinciullo you need to look your best, she said. You did what you could to save them, and now they will try to sink you. If you look like a man who has taken a knock they will be on you like wolves. Stand proud, she said. Your wife is proud of you. She had hugged him. He could feel the strength from that. I'm going to need it, he thought.

Around Dino the secretaries were showing the others to their places. They have two kinds of help here, Dino said to himself. The middle-aged women in old cardigans who do the work and the glamorous girls with too much make up and short skirts who are too young even to be the daughters of most of these deputies. They have work of a sort, he reasoned grimly, they have to work hard at it too, making these old fools feel important.

"*Buongiorno,* Capitano," said a confident female voice. "I do not disturb you if I sit next to you?"

"You are welcome, Signora Filippone," said Dino. The Mayor in red beside me, Vinciullo in his expensive suit looking down the table at me, the rest all here, let's get on with it. In front of him he could see David Chillingworth and Kate Jones, and further down the table on this side were the two corporate types from Castalia Mareazul. The rest are all politicians, he thought, here to get their snouts into the trough and to blame me for their crocodile tears.

Ugo Vinciullo brought the meeting to order and set out the agenda.

"Ladies and gentlemen," he said seriously. "What we feared has happened. The main part of the tanker has now broken up and sunk very close to Siracusa. I do not intend to examine who was responsible for that. Today we must focus on what we do next. We are the heirs to a beautiful civilisation. This city goes back before the time of Archimedes. We are custodians of some of the most beautiful buildings and coastline in Europe. Indeed, in the world. It is vital that all parts of the regional, local and national government work together now to protect the coast, our fishermen and of course our birdlife. We are the guardians of the birds of Europe, it is an honour and a heavy responsibility. We must not let them down."

A very Sicilian speech, thought Dino. Full of fine sentiments, focussed on regional issues only, and the national government last in his priorities. He heard his name mentioned and straightened his back. Here it comes. They name the man who did it.

Ugo could not have been more courteous.

"Capitano Cervetto is head of the Coastguard, as most of you know. He is here today as the expert who is in charge of the protection and clean-up. Capitano, perhaps you could brief the meeting on the current status of the spill, the prognosis, and the actions you have taken and are planning."

Strange, he thought. No attack, and no blame. He looked around the room and spoke carefully.

"Signor Presidente, ladies and gentlemen," he began, engaging the delegates. He was conscious of Laura Filippone beside him, but he did not look at her. "We are indeed facing a severe situation. We have two pollution sites, where the two parts of the tanker sunk. Together we estimate that around eighty thousand tonnes of crude oil and some smaller tonnages of fuel oil will leak out over the coming days and weeks. We cannot be sure of the rate of release."

He stood and walked to the end of the room where his assistant had unrolled a large chart of the area from Augusta down the southeast coast of Sicily to Capo Passero.

"We have several vulnerable areas, they are highlighted here and I will be happy to talk about each of them in detail with you after the meeting. At risk are tourist areas and beaches, fisheries, fish farms and of course our bird reserves, especially Vendicari. Just here."

He looked around the room, he had their attention now.

"We have a lot of resources deployed already, in the form of labour already contracted, protective gear for them, booms, clean-up systems and tankers to move contaminated oil and beach sand away. We have dispersant if we can get permission from the Ministry of the Environment to use it. And we have a powerful friend and a powerful enemy."

He paused. They are probably thinking I will mention the Mafia, or the oil company.

He gestured at the chart, moving his hand parallel to the coast.

"Our enemy is the current. The wind is our friend. At the moment the wind is winning. It is very strong and it is whipping up a heavy sea which breaks up the oil. At the same time it is tending to push the oil to the north. However the current here sweeps down the coast, pushing the oil southwards. If the oil stays to the north we are looking at contaminating the already industrialised area around Augusta. Bad, but not so bad because much of the oil will disperse naturally and there are no fisheries or birds or fish farms here. If the wind dies then the current will spread the oil towards Vendicari, the main tourist beaches and the fish farms and our main fishing ports. And with no wind the oil will form a heavy slick on the surface of the sea. So I suggest we prepare as well as we can, then you say a little prayer to your favourite saint for the strong wind to continue."

No-one spoke. "That's not something a sailor would normally say," he said, breaking the tension. He could see the deputies smiling. Saints did not often get mentioned in the regional meeting room.

The meeting broke open and Dino resumed his seat while the deputies did their best to catch the attention of Ugo and ask questions about the resources in their own areas.

Dino saw Kate Jones pushing a piece of paper in front of David Chillingworth, who then raised his hand.

"If I may, Mr President," he asked. "Could I say that while we agree with the analysis by Captain Cervetto we are concerned that the opportunity is being missed to deal with this spill out at sea. The weather is moderating, and aircraft could spray dispersant over the spill sites in these conditions. There is no sense in letting the oil come ashore if we can break it up out at sea."

For a moment the room was quiet. Then David ploughed on.

"Look, I have the figures here," he said. "It will cost about seventy pounds, so I suppose eighty euros per tonne to disperse the oil at sea, about two thousand euros or more per tonne to recover oil mechanically from the sea surface if we catch it offshore, and probably ten thousand euros per tonne to recover the oil and clean it up once it hits the beach."

Dino could see the deputies looking at Ugo for a response. Out of the corner of his eye he saw Laura Filippone writing down the three estimates and drawing a ring around the figure of 10,000 euros.

That's it, he realised. We will never get them to agree to use dispersant now. That idiot has just given them the choice of seeing eighty euros per tonne of oil spent on aircraft hired outside Sicily, two thousand euros per tonne spent on hiring ships and equipment from outside Sicily to clean up at sea, or ten thousand euros per tonne which will be spent here on labour and local equipment and transport. If they didn't know the numbers before they do now, and they will not hesitate. Eighty euros in Rome's pocket or ten thousand in theirs. That is how they will see it. They don't care who gets dirty, as long as they get rich. I was planning to talk quietly to the environment people, get the dispersant ban lifted. No chance now. Vinciullo will be on the line to his minister friends in Rome before I can get back to my office and make the calls. They will find plenty of reasons for not using dispersant, none of them about money, but all of them blocking its use. The insurers have shot themselves in the foot, and the coast of Sicily will be the victim.

CHAPTER SEVENTEEN

Paci & Delaney had come up in the world since the BP *Deepwater Horizon* spill. Handling a tidal wave of compensation claims against the energy company had washed the small law firm from a modern office in an ugly block downtown to an elegant converted house in the French Quarter. In New Orleans going backwards in time with your offices is a way of showing you are going forward in wealth and status.

"We godda get a piece of this," growled Giovanni Paci. "I got good family right there in Syracuse. They're good people, but a little slow. Old style. With what we've done here we can show them how to put the heat on the oil company. Raise a claims storm, get some money moving."

He was stabbing his finger at the rolling news reports on the TV as he spoke. They showed oily waves breaking on the rocks around Ortigia, intercut with shots of the tanker sinking. The commentary was hyping up the disaster. It would be Europe's worst oil spill for decades, an environmentally and historically sensitive area, it would cost millions to clean up, there was no plan yet to contain the oil from the sunken tanker, the oil company ENOL was silent and seemed to be doing nothing.

Across the office Patrick Delaney was shaking his head. He had huge respect for his volatile partner. They made a good team. Giovanni would push his bullet neck and cropped red hair into anything, and rely on his wit and quick anger to work his way out of it at a profit. Patrick knew his role was different. He was the quiet guy who kept the law firm on track, who placated the clients and judges and opposing firms whom Giovanni had rubbed up the wrong way.

"This is Sicily, right?" he said. "US law doesn't apply, right? You don't know the place, you don't know the people, you don't know the law. Meanwhile we've got a stack of claims here still to process against BP, there is a bottomless pit of money we still have to try and empty and we've got the Louisiana courts forcing them to pay. What's the deal with shooting off halfway round the world to some Italian island when you still got work getting rich here?"

Paci brushed his partner's protests aside. He was out of his chair, pacing the office.

"BP is today, we got that in automatic. You can hire some bum right out of Tulane Law School to push the claims through. But one day we're gonna run out of businesses in Louisiana that have lost money this year, or BP's gonna convince the courts they've done enough. Whaddya gonna do then, Patrick?"

Patrick didn't flinch. He was used to the blaze of words and the psychotic stare that would have made most people sit back. But before he could reply Paci was speaking again.

"I'll tell you what we got out of this BP oil spill, Patrick, because I can see you can't see what we got. You think we got this office and the fancy secretaries and the new cars. But we got a lot more than that, we got expertise, my friend. Expertise. Before those goddam Brits forgot to put the stopper in the oil hole we didn't know that oil companies could take a hit like this. We didn't know that art galleries and recruitment agencies and goddam pole dancing joints could tick some boxes and get a bucket of cash out of an oily ocean. Now we know, and we know how to liberate that money. So when I see oil coming ashore in Sicily I see an opportunity to sell our expertise. Expertise, my friend, and a little aggression. Trust me, I'm gonna call Syracuse, I'm gonna call the lawyer we got in the family, what's the point of being a Sicilian-American if you can't share a little expertise with the old country when it needs it?"

****

Dino was listening intently to the briefing being given by one of his Lieutenants. He spoke concisely and carefully. The plot showed where oil was now hitting the shoreline, mostly north of Siracusa but also on the Ortigia peninsula itself. So far the fouling was moderate. It looks bad, he recognised, but this is easily containable. It's what comes next I am afraid of.

The officer ran through the precautions and clean-up teams in place, looking from time to time for confirmation from the Castalia Mareazul contractors across the table. He detailed the teams hired and in place, the scrapers and tanker trucks, the mops and buckets and swabs and protective clothing ready to use. He showed where booms were anchored. They had sealed off the marina to the north of Siracusa, and the tourist marine grottos up the coast from there were also protected.

Dino nodded in approval. The smug rich with their white yachts will not be able to complain, at least. They can stay safe behind the boom until we clean this lot up. He felt happy with the dispositions so far. Not much else they could do there. He looked around the small meeting. Just his people, the Castalia people, the salvors, David Chillingworth and Kate Jones. This is our mess and we have to clean it up, but they will get the bill. So it's right to invite them in to the daily planning meetings. The woman from ITOPF really knows her stuff too, I only hope we can learn from her.

The Lieutenant was waiting so Dino gestured to him to continue. He turned to the scenario planning for the days ahead. The weather forecast was for the wind to moderate and die away. The coastal current reports showed a stronger than normal south-southwest current coming down from the Messina Straits. All the water piles up in the neck of the straits with these storms, Dino reasoned. Now we get it back again, just when we don't need it.

The estimated oil spread for the next five days showed oil flowing south of Siracusa and fouling first the nature reserves at Fiume Ciane Saline then passing the Capo Murro di Porco and reaching down to the beach resorts at Fontane Bianche. It will take some days to reach Noto, he noted, then we have the problem of protecting Vendicari.

"Yes, Mrs Jones," he said courteously. "What is your question?"

"You can see where this is going, Captain," said Kate Jones. "What is the response from Rome on dispersant use? We have the storm now breaking up the oil, but tomorrow and the days afterwards we will have a real thick black slick and it will be ideal conditions for using dispersant."

"Yes, Mrs Jones," replied Dino evenly. He kept his voice neutral. "The issue of dispersant use has been considered in depth by our Ministry of the Environment. They feel that the sensitive fisheries to the southwest of the site will be affected by its use. We have strict orders not to use chemicals. We will deploy protection, and as you can see we are ahead of the oil with that, and we will deploy clean-up teams where we cannot protect. I can also tell you that four craft equipped with surface skimmers are on their way to recover what they can offshore, and EMSA, our friends at the European Maritime Safety Agency, have mobilised their oil spill recovery vessel which is presently in Malta."

You know and I know that these skimmers will hardly touch this oil, he thought. But what I know and you don't is that powerful people want this oil cleaned up by lots and lots of labour, and they want them employed right here. So my hands are tied, and this time there are no operational decisions I can take to change that.

"Let's finish with a summary of the press coverage so far," he asked the Lieutenant. "Let's see what sort of a disaster they are telling us we have, and what we have missed. Then we can plan a press response. I will have to give a statement later today. And Lieutenant, I have already seen the photos of the sinking ship one too many times. You don't need to show those clips again. But after this meeting you do need to get me in touch with the helicopter base. Someone there leaked the film of the rescue and sinking. I want to make sure they are found and punished, and no more bad news leaks out. We have enough to do without managing the world's hysterical media as well."

****

David Chillingworth was struggling to keep his temper. After a perfectly foul day trying and failing to set up a reasonable claims handling procedure with his local correspondent the last person he wanted to speak to was this pompous Swedish lawyer. On the other hand Linus Eerlandsson would bring some valuable experience and financial clout to the situation.

"My dear David," he heard. Linus succeeded in setting his teeth on edge with his first words. "It looks as if this whole Sicily thing is going to escalate and involve the IOPC Funds. So I'm putting together a team and we'll be there as soon as we can. Do you have an office we can share?"

Two days ago he was snottily telling me that nothing was going to involve him, thought David. Now he is making out it is his idea to get a team on the ground. I could murder him, but I need him and his people.

"Yes, Linus," David kept his voice even. "Indeed it is looking a little messy, so we'll be glad to have you on board. My correspondent has found us an office in Ortigia, close to the local authorities. We already face claims from fishermen and tourist boats, and of course there is a major clean-up and protection effort going on. Everything points to the situation getting worse, because the weather is getting better and we can expect more oil moving to the most sensitive areas. And I must say these Sicilians seem very quick to focus on the money."

He wanted to say that he really needed Linus there as a back-up but he didn't want to give him that satisfaction.

"Stick to the procedures, David," said Linus drily. "Procedure and precision protect us against excitable locals. I will bring some experienced assessors with me, and we'll get a grip on this. See you soon."

The line was cut. Dry Swedish stick, thought David. We'll see how he feels once he has to deal with this tricky lot.

****

From the windows of his third floor offices Luca Consentini could look down across the Viale Mazzini at the new yacht harbour and along the Foro Vittorio Emanuele II to where the super yachts were moored for the winter. Nothing was moving in the harbour, and under the overcast sky the quay in front of the super yachts was lifeless. He could not see any oil on the water.

"Giovanni," he said carefully, in formal Italian. "It is always a pleasure to hear from our American cousins. Of course in Sicily we are great admirers of the energy and enterprise that our families have shown in the United States. My sister told me last week that your law firm has prospered. I congratulate you. Here in Sicily we have also achieved a modest success. But the law works in a different way in Sicily to the way we see on American dramas. You can make a big splash in court and change a case. Here it is more about who you know, and the correct application of appropriate pressure. I cannot see any oil for now, and I think it will be some time before civil lawyers like me are involved with this matter."

He was holding the antique telephone receiver in his carefully manicured hand. In front of him on the leather-topped desk were three files, neatly ordered by his capable middle-aged secretary. He wanted to revise them before the lunch he was looking forward to at the Camera di Commercio, just along the road. There two or three of his long-established clients would stop by his table and enquire quietly about the cases he was handling for them, and he wanted to be prepared. He did not want his brother-in-law's arrogant American nephew shouting broken Italian down his telephone and trying to convince him to set out a market stall to drum up a crisis claims business.

It was hard to get a word in. The line from New Orleans seemed to carry the heat of Giovanni Paci's arguments. There was a big oil spill hitting Siracusa, right? The oil was from an Italian tanker and was owned by an Italian oil company, right? So there was work for lawyers, smart lawyers who could get the people who maybe didn't know they could claim compensation to step up and grab their share. They were doing it in New Orleans, right? So they could do it in Sicily. Luca had a law firm, he knew the local law, Giovanni knew how this oil thing worked, they could team up and clean up, right?

Luca waited for Giovanni to draw breath and then spoke firmly.

"Giovanni," he said. "If you want to come to Sicily to visit the family then you are always welcome. Can I recommend you come in the spring, when we have beautiful sunshine? My wife will cook the finest *caponata* you have ever tasted, and we can eat the lightest *arancini* while we take a little *aperitivo*. But I have to tell you that in Sicily we lawyers do not go out looking for business. We do not drum up business, we do not team up to clean up, as you so charmingly suggest. Please observe the sensitivities of your old country."

They exchanged cordial greetings and Luca carefully replaced the handset. I don't think he was listening, he thought. He smells money, and he will come, whatever I say. He pulled the files towards him and began to read. After lunch I will read up a little on oil spill compensation in Italian courts, he said to himself. Better to be ready, he is a hard young man to say no to.

CHAPTER EIGHTEEN

Osman Mohamoud did not like the winter in Sicily. In summer he sold sunglasses and fake designer handbags to tourists. There were the police to dodge, and most of the money went to the Sicilian gang boss who provided the goods and allocated the pitches. But the summer was hot and dry, he could eat every day and on the luckiest days there was a tourist girl who would find his laughing sales style funny enough to spend a little more time with him. A lot of these girls are curious about black men, he thought.

In the winter there were few tourists, no girls, nothing to sell, not enough to eat and the rain and cold made him hungry for his home village in Somalia. Not hungry enough to go back there, of course. Just hungry for the heat of the African sun and the taste of goat cooked with cardamoms and rice. He would not go back until he had earned some big money. Enough to protect himself. Enough to take a wife. He did not know when that would be. He was still paying off the traffickers who had brought him here in a rickety old fishing boat, crossing in the night from Tunisia.

At home Osman spoke Somali and a broken Italian passed down from the time of Italy's colony in Somalia. In Sicily that made him a natural leader among the thousands of African illegal immigrants. Most of them spoke a little English, most a little French, but they struggled to understand anything in Sicily. Trapped on the island, first stop from Africa, they all dreamt of reaching their friends and families in England and France. There were the real jobs, real money and police who did not beat you. It was a dream. This was reality. Sitting on a damp park bench in Siracusa, nothing to do except talk with other Africans, nothing to eat today, police looking for an excuse to move them on and the overcast skies depressing their spirits.

They were talking about the oil spill clean-up. Some illegal immigrants had been hired to work on the foreshore, but most of them had been turned away. Those who had found work had been paid a pittance, then set upon by fishermen on their way home and robbed of that.

He looked up. The Mafia enforcer was standing over him. He spoke in his Hollywood Mafia accent. Osman found it funny, but knew he could not laugh.

"There is work to be done. Work for all of you. No more sitting around frightening our women. It's time to get moving. Osman, go get all the blacks and tell them to come to the Municipio in Ortigia. We are going to get all of you working on the oil spill. Your pay will be safe. I will collect it for you and pay you every day at the end of the day. You will get home safely, no-one will bother you."

Osman asked how much they would be paid. Would this work also be set off against what they owed the people traffickers?

"Wise up, Osman," was the snarled reply. "This is summer in winter for you lot. You'll be paid what you'll be paid. It's real work, not waving your fat black dicks at German girls. Get moving and get all your people here today, *subito*. And for trafficking, if it was me I would traffic the lot of you off my island tomorrow. But since you are here you are going to work."

Osman wanted to hit him. He held back. He remembered what had happened to those who had defied the gang boss before. Left to crawl as cripples, they were a lesson in obedience to all the illegals. He nodded.

"OK, boss," he said. "We'll be there, coming now."

****

Simone was tired and dispirited, and she knew she looked it. She had spent all day trying to get a seabird cleaning station set up. All day organising young activists from the hostel. Keen but running around like puppies, she thought. It is more like a festival for them than a real cause. No help from the locals. The mayor's office would not provide any premises. Someone in the crowd of men milling around the Municipio had pinched her bottom as she pushed through them. She had not been able to locate the claims office of the P&I Club. She had sent activists to ask every waterfront business if they would host a cleaning centre, but they all came back with the same message. Not here and don't come back was the politest response, and in some places a dog had been loosed.

If Yves were here, she felt, if some of the others in Marine Bleu were with me, we would laugh this off. We would find a way. She shook herself. Fuck Yves, he is not here and I don't want him. It's worse that he is right, maybe I'm getting too old for this. I could be the mother of some of those kids I was trying to organise today. I have nothing in common with them anymore, which is why I'm here alone in this bar while they are all getting it on together in the hostel.

Not that my age seems to put this greaseball off. I don't need this now. She was sitting at a table in the Bar Duomo, drinking a small glass of red wine. Antonio Cusumano had slipped into the chair opposite.

"Your room is good, yes?" he asked, rubbing his hands together.

"But you look tired. You need to eat, we have good food here. A bowl of *bucatini alla Siracusana* will be good for you."

I don't want to encourage him but I need help, Simone told herself. Let's see how far I can take this before I have to handle the come on.

She smiled and straightened her back. She knew that pushed her breasts forward, and saw him glance down quickly at her sweater. Not much there for him really, she reasoned, but if he is such a fool he deserves to be led on a bit.

"You are right, I am hungry," she said, looking straight into his eyes. "But as much as food I need some help. I have been trying all day to get a place to set up a seabird cleaning station. We have to rescue some of these birds that are getting oiled. No-one will give us a place and I can't get near the local authorities. I guess you are an important man, perhaps you can help me?"

She could almost see his thoughts. A small bead of sweat had appeared on his forehead. God, he is disgusting, she said to herself, but maintained her gaze and a slight smile.

"I have it," he said. "I do not own any suitable property, but we can apply some public pressure. Why not organise a press conference to show off an oiled bird, show what you can do, and shame the authorities into some action?"

"We usually do a press conference once we have a place to work," she said. "It's a good idea but I have no place to hold a conference and no way of inviting the press along."

"No problem," Antonio was triumphant. He almost managed to swagger while sitting down. "Of course we can use this bar for the press conference. And I know every hotel in Siracusa and Ortigia, it will be easy to deliver a note to all of them to tell their press guests to be here at four pm tomorrow. You will need to prepare what you want to say and show. I can do the rest. How will that be?"

"I don't have the money to hire the bar," said Simone. "We are a charity, I told you."

"Hire the bar is no problem, *mam'selle*," said Antonio. "Journalists drink a lot. I will be happy to get them all here. Once they taste my *aperitivo* they will come back every day. They have expense accounts, I sell a lot of wine. And for charity, we give a little, take a little, what you say?"

I would like to say 'Fuck off you dirty old lecher', thought Simone. But I need this.

"You are kind," she replied. "I will write a note for you to give out to the hotels. And I would like to eat something. Perhaps some pizza?"

****

Fortunato Redivo was a big man, and in his heavy oilskins he knew he could intimidate most people. If there was an argument in the bars on the dock the other fishermen tended to agree with him once he stood up. Those who did not agree quickly agreed soon after, once they had seen his fists clenching. Now in the entrance to the office which the Municipio had set aside for the P&I Club he was backed by three other fishermen. Fortunato was not looking for trouble, but he wanted these Englishmen to know he meant business.

"We cannot fish. The Municipio says you are the insurance for the owner of this tanker that has stopped us fishing. Now you pay us what we have lost," he said. In front of him a very young Englishman and a young woman who looked as if she was from the Mediterranean were sitting at a table. They had a stack of forms in front of them. Behind them Fortunato could see six or seven other foreigners busy at desks.

"Please sit down, Sir," replied the young man politely. "We will be happy to explain the claims procedure and provide you with the correct forms to complete."

Fortunato leant forward. He almost smiled as he saw the two youngsters flinch and shuffle their chairs back.

"We are here for cash, not forms. Not procedures. My wife cannot make fish soup out of procedures," he growled.

As the boy began to answer he felt a presence next to him. He turned, straightening up, then had to look up again to meet the face of a tall well-built Englishman who was standing suddenly between him and the desk.

"You will not get cash by bullying my staff," said David Chillingworth mildly, but with purpose. Boarding school had taught him about bullies. Playing rugby had taught him when to stand up tall. And his sense of fair play would not let him see his young staff pushed around. "Now please sit down, your friends as well, and we will be happy to discuss your claims."

For a moment there was silence in the office. Fortunato took in the size and poise of the Englishman. He knew when force would work, and he knew this was one time when it would not. He smiled. A big smile.

"OK, my friend," he said. "We sit. You explain. Then you give cash."

David waited until the fishermen were sitting in front of the table then spoke across the office to Linus.

"Let's handle this one ourselves, Linus, shall we? I think it is time for a little precision and procedures to protect our staff, and our claims fund."

****

David smiled to himself. Linus had come back into the room. He was wiping his hand fastidiously with a biocide wet wipe. I'm sure he has washed his hands twice out in the toilet too, thought David. His likes his precision but he does not like having to deal with people. He is quite ready to be sarcastic to me, but he finds it a bit harder to look an angry Sicilian fisherman in the eye.

He felt quietly satisfied. I think I am getting the measure of this lot, he told himself. They won't push me around, and they face down quickly enough if you stand up to them.

Together with Linus he had explained to Fortunato and the other fishermen the way in which oil spill compensation works. First, you have to be able to show you have actually been affected by the oil spill and have actually suffered some damage, or lost some earnings, he had told them. Second, you need to be able to prove, with proper accounts and records, what your losses are. Third, you have to apply with full details of yourself and your business on these forms, or you can download the forms from the IOPC website.

Fourth, and he had numbered the steps off slowly on his fingers, conscious that he was pushing his luck a little with the patience of the fishermen. Conscious of making Linus move nervously in his seat. Fourth, he had said, we send an expert to assess the evidence and ensure the claim is genuine and is for the right amount. Fifth, he had said, if the expert agrees with the claim we can pay you an interim amount right away. Sixth, you must initiate a claim in court. And seventh and finally, when it is all over we will settle all the claims up to the total available. "Which may mean you will get some more money later, or it may not," he had finished.

Linus had spoken then. He had begun to explain in his prim Swedish accent about the relative role of the P&I Club and the IOPC Funds, and their applicability in Italy. A raised hand from Fortunato had cut him off.

"We fill the forms, you send a man, we get the money, yes?" he had asked David directly.

"More or less, old boy, you have the gist of it," David had replied with a smile. "Now if you promise to behave I'll ask my staff to come back to the table and help you with the forms. Shall we do that?"

David had gone back to his desk, and watched with amusement as Linus had almost run to the door leading to the toilet. Perhaps he will be a little less sarcastic when he comes back, he thought.

CHAPTER NINETEEN

"Goddamit, those guys at Woods Hole make gazillions from oil spills, we should have a piece of that action."

Cesare Disario, Professor of Oceanography, University of Savannah, was losing the argument, and he wasn't taking it well.

He looked around the table at the meeting of the University board. Most of them can't even look at me, he thought. These losers will screw me over when I have this big chance for once.

"Look," he said, trying to push authority into his voice. "This is the chance for the University of Savannah to get big on the world stage. We can get enough funding to double the size of our Oceanography department and sew up research grants to keep us going for years. That way we are positioned to exploit the next oil spill here in the US. Right now we are letting Woods Hole clean up. Just recently the courts fined Transocean a billion dollars, yes, one billion US, and directed it be spent on research and studies into the *Deepwater Horizon* spill. We didn't get jack shit of the cash, Woods Hole has most of the Horizon budget sewn up. This spill is in Italy, it's a big one, I got Italian, I got friends in Italy. We can tell them how to study the spill, how to show its effects, how to measure the ongoing impact, we can do anything goddam Woods Hole can do, and they will pay for that because they respect US expertise. All I'm asking is your blessing and a lousy few thousand bucks to get me over there. Do that and I'll come back with cash to keep you all in mint juleps."

He was getting excited, waving his hands, his voice rising. No-one looked up at him. He knew he had lost them. There was no way these dumb bookheads could see the bigger picture. Oceanography wasn't a high profile department in Savannah, and he didn't have the friends on the board he needed to back his idea.

When he stopped talking the room was silent. Cesare could see some of the professors whispering to each other. The Dean looked around the meeting and nodded at the head of the Liberal Arts school. He turned back to Cesare.

"I'm sorry, Professor Disario," he said. "We can recognise your enthusiasm for this project. But I guess the faculty doesn't want to be seen to profit from the misfortune of others. And this is a field where Woods Hole Oceanographic Institution is the global name. We could waste a lot of time and effort and find ourselves excluded. As happened when you persuaded us you could bid for some of the study funds from the *Deepwater Horizon*, as I recall. I think the board is with me on this one, we have to let it go."

****

The watery sun was reaching around the dull grey clouds and lighting up the ornate entrance to the Palazzo Ducezio. Walking carefully up the crumbling stone steps Paola di Bartolo did not notice the sunlight. Her mind was on the city council meeting ahead of her. Her family had been providing the mayors of Noto for generations and she had grown up knowing that this golden stone city would one day be hers to run. But that didn't make it easy.

Noto has always been a rich city, built on the bountiful produce of the fields around it and the seas in front of its coastline. Today most of its income comes from tourists, drawn to the Baroque churches, palaces and balconies which make Noto a UNESCO World Heritage Site. The tourists bring money, but they bring conflicts and headaches, thought Paola. She smiled at the receptionist and passed through the gilt doors into the Sala degli Specchi, the 17th-century meeting room where Noto's city council meet under the gaze of exquisite murals, reflected in multiple mirrors and beneath a trompe l'oeil ceiling.

"Well," she said brightly. "Good morning to you all." She greeted the councillors courteously, nodding to her old friends and her old enemies, who more or less alternated around the oval table. Her family had spent three centuries acquiring both friends and enemies, and the bonds that bound them together were strong in this ancient city. "Today we need to reach an agreement on protecting the Lido di Noto. Our coastline is only thirty kilometres south of the spill, and oil is already reaching down towards us. I have spoken with the Coastguard, who estimate that oil will hit our beaches in two days from now. The Romans have people in Siracusa who are willing to build defences for our resort. They have government money. They have labour, and booms, and will hire machinery locally." She paused and smiled at the two councillors who controlled the local road building companies. "So you can be happy that your bulldozers will get a good rate. But they want to use the labour they have contracted. They want to use the Africans."

Paolo stopped speaking and let the idea sink in. She knew that there were at least three councillors who ran the street sellers, the hawkers who mopped up the tourist money in the summer selling sunglasses to tourists and toys to the parties of school children. Two were the heads of local families, the third was from an inland village, and Paolo knew he was the voice of the Mafia. Her family was aristocratic, above street sellers, above arguments over pitches, above dealing directly with thugs who lived in bunkers. At least, that was the outward appearance. In fact Paola was a skilful politician who knew how to keep her family's interests aligned with those who had power on the streets and in the villages. Today she would need that skill, because she knew a conflict was coming.

"Not here. No negroes will work here." The outburst was from the old man who represented one of the street seller families. "We have worked hard to keep those black bastards out of this town and off our beaches. Sicily is flooded with these Africans, but we have kept them out of Noto. You can go to Siracusa and see them selling openly in the street. You will never see that here, they know better than to try. If we let them in now, paid by the Romans, we will never get rid of them."

Paola smiled sweetly at him. "Yes," she replied carefully. "It is true that tourists note with pleasure that our streets are not full of illegal immigrants selling trash." They are full of your family and the poor kids from the villages selling the same trash, she said to herself. "But now we are in the winter, there are no tourists, and we have to move fast. The Romans will pay for these people to do the job. They do not want to pay our people. And perhaps our people prefer the warmth of their homes in this weather to being out on a freezing beach, don't you think?"

Across the table she caught the eye of the Mafia voice. There was just the suggestion of a wink. She held up her hand and cut off the hubbub of voices which was rising as the councillors turned to each other to vent their worries about the Africans coming to Noto.

"Perhaps our good member from inland can help us here," she said evenly.

"Gentlemen," the Mafia voice leant inwards. "And lady, of course," he acknowledged Paola. "You discuss a problem that will not be a problem. I can assure you of that. Let the Africans come to build the defences against the oil. They will be closely supervised. The beaches are ten kilometres from here, and not one of them will find his way inland to our city. Your women are safe, your children are safe, your businesses are safe. And when the defences are built every African will be taken back to Siracusa. Just say yes to the plans of the Romans. You have my word that Noto is safe from the blacks."

Paolo sat quietly and looked around the table. They all knew what his word meant, but the power of the Mafia was not as strong as it had been in the past. Would they accept it now? She waited. *They are getting older, like me. They need time to digest things.* She saw one councillor nod, then the others. It was done.

"Thank you," she said. "We pass the motion to demand immediate defences from the government oil spill contractors. I will call the Coastguard right away. That will keep the beaches clean. We rely on our friends from inland to keep our city clean."

****

"Noto?" asked Osman. "We cannot go to Noto, chief. You know those people they don't like us Africans, no Sir."

Osman Mohamoud shuffled his feet. He was trying not to show the Mafia enforcer that he was afraid. But he was. Afraid of what this mad Mafia man might do to him and afraid of what would happen to him if he went to Noto. Those illegal immigrants who had defied the Mafia enforcer in Siracusa had been left crippled, so he wanted badly to just say yes and go to work in Noto. But those from the camp who gone to the nearby city of Noto that summer to try selling in the streets had been pushed into a dark doorway and had been lucky to survive the kicking. They all knew better than to go anywhere near Noto.

"Listen, I talk to you because you understand Italian. You talk to the others. Tomorrow at seven o'clock a lorry will be here to pick you up." The enforcer pointed to the square behind him. "You will be taken to the Lido di Noto where you will work on building defences against the oil. No-one will bother you. You work for us, we protect you. Just do your work and a lorry will bring you back each night. Door to door. Rolls-Royce treatment. Guaranteed pay. *Capisce?*"

The enforcer was leaning towards Osman, looking out from under his hat brim. Osman could feel the menace. He doesn't like black people, he knew that. But I cannot say no to him, and he has paid us today for the work we have done here. I suppose the people of Noto who so like to kick us will also be afraid of this one.

He gave his best big comic African smile. He lives in a film, thought Osman, so he will expect me to behave like a film African.

"Yes, boss," he said. "I get the message. You tell me how many people you want here and I bring them at seven in the morning. We look for Noto, you look for us."

****

Simone was trying to ignore the self-satisfied looks which the bar owner was giving her. She knew she would have to deal with him one day soon, and she had to admit he had solved a problem for her. But not a big enough problem for me to let you into my bed, she thought.

The Bar Duomo was packed out. Journalists were sitting at all the tables and standing around the walls. All of them were clutching a glass of the prosecco which the owner, Antonio Cusumano, was handing out freely. Three camera crews were jostling for position. Simone had not seen a press turnout like this since the *Erika* spill. They are a bit bored, she recognised. They all rushed here for the catastrophe but so far there isn't so much to see.

She glanced at the two young activists who were beside her, holding large cardboard cartons with the lids shut. They grinned at her, this was a huge game for them. She took a deep breath and climbed up onto a chair, clapping her hands for silence.

"Thank you for coming," she said. She was pitching her voice to be heard over the rustle of pads and clothes. She was used to the classroom. Journalists are like children anyway, she said to herself. "I work for Marine Bleu. We fight to protect the seas and marine life. Siracusa, Ortigia, the coastline south of here, the Vendicari bird reserve, all are facing a major catastrophe. Eighty thousand tonnes of oil are descending on this area, a black tide of death. We need your help. Here in Siracusa we see that some of the local businesses and the authorities do not want to protect birds. We have tried to set up a bird rescue centre, but we cannot get any support. So I appeal to you, shame Sicily into saving the seabirds!"

She raised her voice as she came to the end, and then gestured to the activists. They opened the tops of the boxes. Inside each was an oiled seabird, feathers gummed black, in obvious distress. She heard the gasp of indrawn breath, and went on.

"This is what Sicily is ignoring. We can save these birds and many more to come. But we need places to work and money to buy cleaning materials and transport for the birds to clean areas. Please report this scandal, bring pressure on the authorities."

There was a flurry of questions. How many seabirds? Thousands. How long did it take to clean one? Two days. How much money was needed to save the birds? Nothing compared to the cost of keeping the oil away from those big white yachts moored behind us.

She stepped down from the chair and pushed her hair back behind her ears. She knew exactly how the cameras would see her. Clean, positive, young, caring, catching her looking down at the struggling bird.

There was another question, asked in a clipped Dutch-sounding voice. She looked up. A neat-looking guy in heavy glasses. Older than most of the press here. A corporate guy in a suit, she thought. Is he a spy for the oil company?

The question came again, mild but insistent.

"Can you tell me how many of the birds you will clean and save will die anyway within two days?"

"We save their lives because they are struggling in the oil," she replied passionately. "We release them into a clean area. They are wild creatures."

"Yes of course," the Dutch guy was looking up from his notepad. He spoke without passion, almost pedantically. "But are you aware of the studies done on the bird cleaning after other major oil spills? For instance after the *Sea Empress* spill in Wales, studies showed that seventy per cent of the birds cleaned died. They concluded it was less cruel to kill them after fouling, rather than stress them with cleaning only to die anyway. They also found that seabird colonies neighbouring the spill area increased in size. Can you comment on that please?"

Simone could feel the interest of the room turning away from her. This pompous middle-aged fascist was trying to derail her call for action.

She grabbed a box from one of the activists and jumped up onto the chair. She shouted back at the Dutchman. "Come on then, come here and kill this bird. That will not improve its survival rate, I think."

The room had gone silent. "Come on, you know so much, come and kill this bird."

Her passion had caught the room. The cameras were on her now. She could hear the murmur growing louder as journalists and cameramen pushed to get closer to her. From the corner of her eye she saw the Dutchman politely pushing a camera lens away from his face. I hate corporate pigs like that, she thought. Full of facts but no compassion. That has taught him a lesson.

****

"The way I see it, we can't miss out on this one," said Cesare Disario. He kicked his chair back and casually put his Docksider-clad feet up on his desk. "I can't let the board tie us down when we have a big chance."

He was convincing himself, talking to a small group of students who were clustered in his office. As a Professor of Oceanography he liked to encourage informality. Feedback, he called it. Especially when it came from the students who knew how to suck up to him. Not that he realised that they were. The group around his desk were nodding now.

"Oceanography might be white-man's magic to these fairy literary types, but this is a university on the Atlantic coast and we got a maritime heritage," he went on. "It's our duty to share our expertise with the world, especially when we have connections to the old country. I guess they got their noses in dusty books so deep they can't see the oceans."

Cesare laughed, and the students laughed with him. When they were alone they laughed at him. His short frame, his comic Italian gestures, his excitable nature and his affectation for nautical clothing made him a figure of fun. His attempts to pretend he was one of them were something to laugh about over a beer. If feedback meant making the professor feel important in return for good grades, then they were happy to lay on the flattery. If feedback meant supporting his crazy ideas of expansion, they were happy to support him. Even better if it meant he would go away on a trip.

One of the girls leant forward. She looked up at him with an expression of deep respect.

"You know, Professor," she said. "You have so much to offer. These guys in Italy will be shell shocked right now by this oil spill. You gotta help them."

She wasn't getting this all her own way. On the other side of the group a geeky boy in a yellow tank top raised his hand, catching Cesare's eye.

"It's only an idea, Professor," he said, "but what if you took a little from the operating budget and used that to fund a trip to Sicily? You could talk direct to the universities there, set up a direct connection. You speak such good Italian. We might have to cancel the next scientific cruise, but we would sacrifice that if it means the department will grow."

A less self-important man might have seen through this. A man more able to concentrate on what students meant rather than what they said would certainly have seen through it. But Cesare was not that man.

"These feedback sessions are so useful," he beamed. "You guys really help me, and I appreciate that. I'm going to do it. The University of Savannah is going to send its Professor of Oceanography to Sicily to advise on the oil spill."

The students glanced at each other. A result. The little puffed-up professor goes away, we get to miss a seasick trip in a squalid old research boat, and we get loads of kudos that will show up in our grades. They applauded wildly. It seemed the right thing to do.

CHAPTER TWENTY

Simone stepped down from the truck and smiled her thanks up at the driver. She looked around. She could see a rusty green-painted notice welcoming visitors to the *Oasi di Vendicari*. She was in a scruffy lay-by beside the road from Noto to Pachino. It had taken her three hours and two lifts to cover the thirty or so kilometres from Siracusa. Sicilians don't seem to like hitchhikers much, she thought. And they don't seem to know that they have a world-class bird reserve here. The truck driver had been hard to convince that this was where she wanted to go. She could see why. It looked as if there was nothing there.

She shouldered the ethnic bag which contained her camera and her bird books and set off down the rubble track heading away from the road. The track was bordered by high grass and she could see nothing, but after half an hour of walking she came to a small car park and a green fence with a gate and a thatched hut beside it. There was no-one in sight. She walked into the reserve and saw an old faded and dented metal notice with an outline map of the reserve and the walking paths. She could see now, there were two large shallow lakes slightly inland, separated from the sea by a narrow strip of sand. The map also showed an information centre and a tower and three hides overlooking the lakes. Boardwalks connected the hides and the paths and tower.

She wondered why she could not hear anyone. There was no noise. The air was still, she could not hear the distant road. She could hear nothing. Surely there would be noise if they are building sea defences against the oil, she thought. They must be being very careful not to disturb the birds.

Simone found the first boardwalk entrance and set off along the wooden pathway, following the signs pointing to the beach and information centre. She could see the first lake. It was alive with birds. She was excited, identifying them through her long camera lens. Herons, storks, flamingos, so many types of waders. She wanted to look them up but was in a hurry to see what was being done to protect the birds, so she carried on, walking quietly but purposefully towards the sea.

Suddenly the pathway opened out onto a strip of sand. In front of her was the sea, a sullen grey under the overcast sky. To her left she could see round a sand-lined bay to an old stone ruin and beyond that the grey tiled building that must be the information centre. From the extra metre height of the top of the sand strip she could see to her right, south down the coast. Inland was a second large shallow lake, also teeming with birds. She looked for the oil defences. Where were they? Where was everyone?

Simone began to run. Her heart was thudding. She could not believe this. In Siracusa she had heard the announcement on the television news that everything was being done to protect the coast. Here was the most precious part of the whole coastline, where Europe's birds came to overwinter. And there was no protection.

Her footsteps rang on the stone slabs as she ran across the yard in front of the information centre. As she got there the door opened. A kindly-looking man in a grey warden's uniform was looking at her.

"You will disturb the birds," he said mildly. "*Silencio?*"

Simone was struggling to find words in Italian, trying to ask why there were no precautions against the tide of oil coming down the coast.

"*Vous êtes française, mam'selle?*" asked the warden, smiling.

"I am French," answered Simone happily. She went on in French. "What is happening here? Where are the booms, the bales, the sand bars? The oil will be here any day!"

"You are French, and I am Sicilian," replied the warden, no longer smiling. "Look behind you. You see that building? There our people have been killing and processing tuna since the 16th century. People have made a lot of money from fish here. But they never made anything from birds. That is why we have rusty signposts, and bad paths, and no investment. But at least the birds are in peace, because no-one comes to see them much in winter."

He paused.

"Yes, *mam'selle*," he went on. "People here know how to make money. They like less having to spend it. There may be money being spent to protect these birds, but there is no protection. Birds have no votes, no value and no bank accounts, and no friends in Rome. There is just me to look out for them, and I cannot fight an oil spill alone, with no equipment. No money comes my way. So there is nothing."

****

The two men were huddled in the corner of the Bar Duomo. Apart from them the bar was empty. Antonio had served a few ristrettos to locals on their way to work and a few cappuccinos to journalists who found it too early to start on the wine and who wanted to begin the day in an Italian way. But now the bar was quiet.

Antonio could see his accountant was not happy. He explained again.

"Look," he said. "This is easy money for you. All I am asking is that you go back three years and make a new set of accounts for each year. You need to show a healthy profit for each year, especially around this wintertime. You are a man of figures, all I ask is you move the comma a little to the right."

The accountant was an old man. His fat neck bulged over the collar of his shirt, and Antonio was careful not to get too close. The heavy garlic-laden breath was too much, even for a Sicilian bar owner.

"Antonio," said the accountant, shrugging his shoulders. The fat under his jacket rippled. "Have you gone mad? I have worked for you for many years, and your father before that. I helped you keep hold of your money. To keep the profits hidden from those tax bastards in Rome. To keep our local family friends from draining you dry with *pizzo*. Now you ask me to undo all that good work. Have you been drinking, perhaps? Should I speak with your wife about this?"

The mention of his wife made Antonio sit up.

"My wife is my wife, she is not concerned with this," he said sharply. "I am not asking you to undo what you have done. For the tax people and for that Mafia clown we continue with the same books, the same accounts, the same pitiful profits. Do you think I am a fool? But there is a new game in town now. The oil that is coming onto Ortigia from the tanker is bringing money. There are people here from the insurance. They pay compensation for loss of earnings to local businesses. It's big money, a deep pit. To get my shovel in I have to show that I was earning a lot last year, and now I am not. So I need the books to show that I was making a lot of money every year, even in the winter, and that now I am not making money. With those books I can claim, and they will pay me for the money I am not making now. *Hai capito?*"

"I see it," replied the accountant, laughing out loud. Antonio recoiled from the gust of bad breath. "For years you make a misery in winter, and I make books which make that misery even more miserable. This winter you have every room full, your bar is full every night, you make more than you have ever made. But if I can show the good times were before and now is a misery these foreigners will pay you. I move the comma, they pay a cheque. Truly I am a magician and this oil is a tide of gold."

Antonio saw the door opening and he got up to serve the TV crew which was shouldering its way into the bar. They are not here to film, he thought. They are here to drink. I can help them with that.

"Two sets of books, my friend," he said quietly, tapping the accountant on the shoulder as he moved towards the bar. "And quietly done. One set as before, one set for the insurers. I need them this week. Do them well and there is a cut for you too."

****

David couldn't quite get his arm out of the rain coat. He felt ridiculous as he pulled at it, but the coat was too tight across his broad shoulders.

"I can help you," he heard behind him. The voice was laughing. He started to turn.

"Stay still one minute, Mr Chillingworth." She was holding his arm now, and pulled the sleeve gently away, releasing him.

He turned, embarrassed, then almost took a step back as he found himself too close to the smiling dark haired girl.

She laughed again.

"I don't think they make coats for men as big as you here in Sicily," she said. "Perhaps you came thinking it was hot, the summer?"

David had to smile back. His dignity was punctured and he was very conscious of the girl in front of him. He could read the name on her badge, Anna. She had helped him with setting up the Club's local accounts at the Banco di Sicilia.

"You have me there," he said. "I packed a blazer, rather expected some sunshine. Silly really. Had to buy this coat yesterday, biggest I could find."

For what seemed a long time Anna did not move, then she smiled and stepped backwards.

"Shall we go through to the office, Mr Chillingworth," she said, professionally now. "I have all the account documentation ready, and we can handle all your local payments, how you call them, disbursements?"

"David," he said, automatically. He was straightening himself taller as he spoke. "Please call me David. Yes, disbursements is what we call our payments. I think we will be handling a lot of those in the next few weeks. So we will work together a lot, perhaps."

"I shall be your account officer, David," replied Anna. "It will be a pleasure to help you here in Sicily."

****

Osman was cursing his father. Not out loud, he would not hear, his father had died before he left Somalia. But before he died he had taught Osman Italian, and that was what had put Osman in this position he did not want to be in. So he cursed him, because his Italian made him the spokesman and now he was trapped between a lot of very angry African immigrants and a Mafia gang boss who was about to get very angry.

"Chief," he said politely. He could feel the Mafia enforcer glaring at him, but he did not look up.

"Chief, these people have a problem. For two days we built defences at Noto. It was dirty work, but there was no oil. So no problem, and you paid us, thank you Sir. But today you make us work here in Siracusa. We have to clean up the oil which is on the beach. This is dirty work. We get oil on our clothes and on our hands and in our hair. Sir, these people say they will not work more at this. They see over there the Italian soldiers. They have clean overall suits, face masks and gloves. They see over there the young people, the volunteers. They have clean overalls and face masks and gloves. We have been given the dirtiest area of the beach, with the rocks and most of the oil. But we have nothing to protect us. They will not work more, Sir."

There was no reply. He looked up. The enforcer was slowly and theatrically lifting his hat, and leaning towards him. His eyes were locked onto Osman, who tried to step back. He could not, fear had frozen his feet to the ground.

"They have face masks and suits and gloves because they are Italian," hissed the enforcer. "You are not. You have no rights here. You should be glad of the work. Glad we do not throw you back into the sea. Tell your black friends one thing. Tell them that if any of them have the balls to stop working when I say work then they will wake up with their balls in their mouths. Tell them that, my friend."

He paused. Osman did not move. He knew his people were angry. How could he tell them?

"Tell them now," spat the enforcer. "Or you will be the first to taste your own balls."

He turned and walked off, carefully replacing his hat on his head. Osman felt his bowels churning. It is not good to be the only one who speaks Italian, he thought.

****

It was a mistake to comment. He had said it mildly, just as an observation, but now he was pinned up against the rough white limewash on the old stone walls. The tour guide could smell the breath of the Mafia don on his face.

"Don't talk to me of the world press." Guido Recagno was whispering, but the tour guide could hear every syllable clearly. "Here in this pit I do not see the world press. Here in this pit I do not care for the world press. And I do not care for your opinion."

The Mafia don released him slowly and allowed him to stand. He made no move to brush himself down. Guido remained standing very close to him.

"My cousin is stupid, and that is enough stupid in my life," he said. "He says the blacks will not work to clean up the oil because they do not have protective clothing. He says what should he do, he has money from the contractors for the protection clothes, but he has my order not to spend it. Should I change the order so he can spend my money to protect these black men? And then you mister smart arse tour guide you tell me that it looks bad to the world press to see black men cleaning up oil without protective clothing. You are as stupid as my cousin."

He turned and paced towards the other wall of the wine cellar. The tour guide released his breath, but slowly and carefully. He said nothing.

"Tell my cousin to spend a little of the money on new glasses for himself," the Mafia don went on. "Tell him that he does not see so well. The oil is black, isn't it? We did not ask for the oil to come, did we? These men come to our country without invitation to threaten our women and steal our work. We did not ask for them to come either. But they are black too. So black cleans up black. Tell my cousin that. They are black already so they have nothing to worry about from a little oil. And fuck the world press, and fuck you too."

The guide nodded and turned to go.

"One more thing," he heard, and stopped suddenly, turning to face the caged Mafia boss. "Just remember you are a guide. You earn your living talking. You need your tongue for that. You have only one tongue. Be careful what you say with it if you want to keep it."

CHAPTER TWENTY-ONE

Simone was getting angry. She had been waiting for an hour to speak to someone in the office of the Regional President. An hour sitting on the hard bench in the marble hallway of the old offices of the Provincia Regionale di Siracusa. An hour in which the receptionist had not looked at her once. An hour in which a succession of pretty young girls had tottered through the hallway on high heels, glancing at her with what she felt might be pity. Or contempt.

She knew she did not look her best. Hitch-hiking back from Vendicari had taken too long. She had had to fight off the last driver who thought it was OK to put his hand on her knee because she was hitch-hiking. She had gone straight to the offices of Castalia Mareazul to find out why there was no protection work being done at Vendicari. An hour wasted there in the Municipio, with crowds of fishermen eyeing her up. An hour waiting then five minutes with a fool in a suit who insisted that work was being done and who would not listen to what she told him. Then the shrug and the opened hands. It is all run by the Regional President, *Signorina*, we work through the regional authorities. If you have questions perhaps you can ask them of the President. Perhaps Signor Vinciullo will be able to help you. And a pitying smile for the mad Frenchwoman, she said to herself as she pushed her way out of the Municipio on Ortigia and set off at a run to the mainland and the regional offices.

She stood and tried again.

"Please, I need to speak to President Vinciullo," she said to the receptionist, stretching for her politest Italian. "How long before I can see him?"

The receptionist looked up at her slowly. She spoke with studied indifference.

"President Vinciullo has already left for the day, *Signorina*. Perhaps tomorrow?"

Simone did not know whether to shout or cry. She was tired, her bladder was bursting, this stupid rude woman had made her wait for an hour, and now she was blandly saying that the President was not there anymore.

She opened her mouth to speak, then stopped. She would not let them get to her. She was a founder of Marine Bleu. They were founded on direct action. Direct action is what these people will get, she thought. She turned on her heel and walked out. Tomorrow they would find out what direct action from Marine Bleu meant.

****

The noise inside the helicopter made conversation difficult. Ugo Vinciullo was distracted. He could feel Laura's left leg push against his right leg each time the helicopter banked to give them a better view of the coast. She still manages to show something red, he thought, even in a flying suit and helmet she wears a red scarf.

He pulled his attention back. She was speaking sharply now and he could hear her through the intercom. He could not pretend the helicopter noise was blocking out what she was saying.

"Ugo," he heard. "We are alone here, and I speak frankly. Only the pilot can hear us, and he is a good man, married to the daughter of a close friend. You have to act, and you have to act now. We are making a disgrace of ourselves, and of Sicily. And we are losing money."

Dino Cervetto had lent them the Coastguard helicopter to give them a bird's eye view of the coast. It had picked them up north of Siracusa and was now circling over the island of Ortigia. Below them the sea was streaked with heavy black oil. Thin slicks leached out south of the place where the aft part of the tanker had sunk, now marked by red buoys and surrounded by small boats ineffectually trying to recover the oil coming to the surface. Closer to the coast a heavier slick was strung out south and west of the sunken forepart.

As the helicopter banked again and turned Ugo could see the brown streaks on the sea reaching into the distance down the coast. Then the rocky foreshore of Ortigia came into view. They were almost over the military fort at the end of the island. The gangs cleaning the oil from the concrete breakwater blocks looked small from above. They looked hopeless to Ugo. How can they make any impact on this lot coming from the seabed?

Laura was talking to the pilot now, pointing him south over the Capo Murro di Porco and towards the beach resorts at Avola and Noto.

"You saw," she said to Ugo. "You saw them working there. We have hundreds of African illegal immigrants cleaning up the oil. They work without protective clothing. The Mafia is charging Castalia Mareazul full Italian wage rates for them, plus clothing allowance. I know it is paying them next to nothing. The world's media is here filming. They are not stupid. Or at least, they are not stupid when someone tells them what to look for and they have not been too long in the Bar Duomo. One day soon they will film and report the illegals cleaning oil without gloves and masks. They will ask where the waste oil and soiled sand and rocks are going to each night. They will ask why we have no bird cleaning stations. And look," she was tapping his knee and pointing down to the right. "They will ask why we have done nothing to protect our bird reserve at Vendicari."

He did not answer. She was right, the Mafia was making fools of them. The money that should be flowing through municipal and regional authorities was going into their pockets, and soon the authorities would be publicly exposed while having gained nothing. But he said nothing because he did not like a woman to correct him. Even such a woman as Laura Filippone.

She will not be so easily put off, he told himself. The Mafia may not be scared of her but I am.

"Ugo, you have to promise me you will sort this out," she said sharply. "Cervetto is an honest man, work with him, squeeze out the Mafia. I will back you." He saw her smile sweetly at him through her helmet visor. "It is always nice to work with you, Ugo," she said.

He did not know if she was laughing at him or not.

"OK, Laura," he replied. "The pilot can bring us back to Siracusa now. We can see how far the oil is. I will talk to Cervetto and we will try to get a grip on this. It's not what we planned."

He sounded confident, and he reached out to touch Laura's knee as he spoke. His hand stopped suddenly in mid-air as he caught her look.

God, he thought, this woman infuriates me. I am trapped between Laura and the Mafia. Life used to be so simple.

****

Across the Foro Siracusa Simone could see the small group of Carabinieri. They looked relaxed, in normal dress uniform, high peaked caps and polished leather shoulder belts. She looked behind her.

The police are going to have a shock, she told herself. I don't think they are used to street protests here. When we get going we'll shake up that *merde* Regional President. We'll take over his offices, turf that receptionist out, and we won't give up until they put proper protection in place for the bird reserve.

She had spent the evening before and that morning organising the demonstration. She felt full of life and purpose. It was like the *Erika* days, when they burned down the offices of the oil company, Total. It took her back to the north of Spain, when they demonstrated with the fishermen hit by the *Prestige* spill. She had stood on a table in the hostel the night before, urging them to join her. She had spoken of the unprotected birds. She had told them that soft politicians always give in to hard street action. She had taken them with her, they were here now. All the activists who had come to Siracusa. They were young, they wanted to save the birds. They jostled for position, to be in the front.

She could see the posters calling for action. They were written in Dutch and German and English and Spanish and French. Not so many in Italian, she saw. And a pity that the local fishermen had been so unenthusiastic about joining in the demonstration today. No local youths either, although she had sent groups of activists out to the bars and into the street to tell everyone about the demonstration and to call for support.

Simone was not worried. There were plenty of them, they were fired up, and the small group of relaxed policemen between them and the President's office would not stand a chance. She stood on a small wall around a flowerbed to look further. She could see the media in place, she had made sure to alert the TV crews. Almost unconsciously she swept her hair back. She knew that made her look younger. The cameras would be on her, leading the charge on the offices. She checked she had her Marine Bleu flag, and turned to the restless crowd behind her.

"*Mes amis*! My friends!" she shouted. "We are going to do this. We will occupy the office of that corrupt politician. We will show the world that these people are not acting. We are going to save the birds. Shall we do it?" She paused. "Can we do it?"

"Yes we can!" the crowd shouted, and as Simone jumped down and began to march across the square towards the police they surged forward behind her.

In front of her she could see the thin line of uniformed police squaring up. One produced a megaphone and stepped forward.

"Stop!" she could just hear the thin voice. "Stop now and leave the square."

Simone laughed out loud. Did they think that would scare Marine Bleu? She could feel the adrenalin flooding through her. I wish Yves was here, she thought. No I don't, she said to herself, suppressing the longing. Let the bastard stay at home. I am the leader now.

****

She is so naive, thought Michiel. She could use that energy to do some good. She has a way of attracting people and she's a quick thinker. But all she is doing is leading those poor youngsters into a trap.

He had tucked himself into a deep doorway upwind of the Regional President's office. He was three steps up from the pavement and hidden in the shadow of the lintel. Years of reporting street protests had taught him the safe places to be when the ruck started and the tear gas was thrown. He was looking across the square at Simone, standing on the wall and rallying the crowd. He saw her look at the small group of police.

She doesn't realise it's a trap, he said to himself. She put so much effort into trying to tell everyone about the demonstration yesterday evening and today. That gave the Carabinieri plenty of time to get organised. Around the corner from the square he could see the dark blue vans and armoured coaches that had delivered the riot squads via the side streets. They were out of sight of the demonstrators. He could see the groups of police in overalls and full body armour moving quickly down the streets parallel to the square. Each man had a small shield and a long heavy baton. As they marched purposefully away from him he realised they were going to cut the demonstration off from behind. They were swinging their batons, loosening up their arms.

To his right he could see the main body of the riot squad. Dark uniforms, no insignia, just bulky body armour and high strong boots. The men were restless, knocking their batons against their boots. Their helmet visors were down now. He could sense the anticipation. They are spoiling for a fight, he guessed. They are trained in crowd control, trained to be aggressive, but they don't often get a chance of a rumble with a group of young foreigners. For them this is a day out, a day when they can really hit out and be paid for it. He considered intervening. This is going to be horrible. Those idealistic kids are going to be crushed between two heavily armed groups of police who really want to teach them a lesson.

Michiel hesitated, but then it was too late anyway. He saw Simone leading the shouting crowd across the square. She was increasing the pace and broke into a run as she saw the thin line of uniformed police turn and disappear around the corner. He saw her look back and urge the crowd on. They think they have done it, that the police have run, Michiel saw.

Then the trap was sprung. Behind the crowd three large riot police units were marching forward, one blocking each road leading into the square. No-one was going home that way tonight. A whistle blew and the mass of riot police in the street beside the regional office began to move forward too. They were drumming their batons on their shields as they walked quickly. The front squad turned the corner as Simone was twenty metres away, turning to urge the crowd on. The police were beginning to run forward now. She swung back, shocked as the dark throbbing mob flooded towards her. The solid police line broke as it moved more quickly.

Michiel felt his stomach knotting up. They are running to be the first to hit a demonstrator, he realised. That stupid Frenchwoman is going to get hurt, and hurt badly. He could not move, the police were passing his doorway now. No-one looked at him, they were staring straight ahead, pushing forward for a chance to get at the crowd.

Michiel saw the batons rising and falling but could not see who was being hit. The police were past him now, pushing the crowd back across the square. Back towards the police units who had sealed all the exits on that side and who now stood ready, batons raised. The momentum of the police charge had hardly been checked as they smashed into the unarmed demonstrators. Then he saw her. Simone was lying in the gutter, blood streaming from the side of her head. She has to move before they come back for her, realised Michiel. She looks unconscious. They know she is the leader and they will finish what they started. When they broke up the G8 protests in Genoa all the protestors got a good kicking, and being a woman was no defence.

He knew he should not get involved. He was a reporter, he was there to document the event, not to be a part of it. But he ran forward anyway. He knew there were only minutes before the police turned and began to sweep up the demonstrators more purposefully. He reached Simone quickly and lifted her over his shoulder, then ran directly away from the square on the side which was now open, where the main police unit had come from.

CHAPTER TWENTY-TWO

Ugo Vinciullo was trying not to show his surprise. As a Sicilian politician he had heard every possible bare-faced demand for getting a piece of any cash. But this was special.

He smiled, and spoke carefully to the group of men across the table from him.

"Can I be sure I have understood correctly," he asked politely. He kept his voice very even. He was holding his temper in check, but only just. "You, Signor Spinelli, are the owner of the *Barbara S*, the tanker which is spilling eighty thousand tonnes of oil onto our beautiful coastline. Your tanker broke in two parts and is now the source of a black tide which will kill our seabirds, our fishing and our tourism. And you have come here today not to say you are sorry. Not to seek the pardon of the people of Siracusa. Not to offer your assistance and undoubted wealth to help to clean up the mess. My own villa is polluted with oily spray, and you come to me with a demand, not an offer."

Across the table from him he could see the muscles bunching in the shoulders of Enrico Spinelli's suit. Spinelli turned and glanced at one of the two men with him. Just as nasty looking, thought Ugo. Typical of Naples, the scum rises to the top there.

There was a long pause. Ugo knew better than to speak. He was not scared, but he was curious about these thugs.

"Presidente Vinciullo," replied Enrico Spinelli. He was staring intently at Ugo now. "I come with no demands. I can apologise if you wish. It would make no difference. And in any case, it is I who have lost a good ship and a good charter. You have gained the chance to line your pockets. My P&I insurance people are already here. They are making your people rich. Your people are queuing up to claim for their dreadful losses, and they are getting paid. They cry wonderfully as they put the cheques in their pockets. So please, don't ask me to cry for you."

He paused.

"No, no demand," went on Spinelli, leaning forward now. "A simple offer, one which it would not be good business to refuse. You are the regional authority. You have organised the waste disposal from this clean-up. All the fouled sand and rocks and recovered oil is taken away by contractors organised by you. But paid for by my insurers. Now, you see, my investors," he nodded to signify the two men who sat silently either side of him, "my investors are experts in waste disposal. The oil, in a way, is mine, the spill, in a way, is mine, the pay-outs you are getting from the insurers are paid for by my premiums. So it is only reasonable that a small part of the contracting is also mine. Or rather, given to my expert waste disposal people."

He spread his hairy, stubby hands out on the table in front of him and looked hard at Ugo.

"What could be fairer, Mr Regional President? I bring you the oil, you give my people the contract to take it away again."

Ugo almost laughed at the brazen request. But he knew better than to laugh at people like this. It has to be Camorra, he guessed. They have made a fortune by illegally dumping waste from Naples. Now they want to do that here. He was thinking fast, although his face remained impassive. I have Laura on to me to cut back the share of the local Mafia. That will be hard. Now I have the Naples Camorra muscling in. Can I fight two such groups at once? Can I get them to fight each other?

"Gentlemen," he said. "In the privacy of this office you are very frank. I for my part will be frank too. You know that the waste disposal and the people who are working are contracted here through powerful local interests. Very powerful local interests. Family interests. It would be very hard for me to change that."

The reply hit him hard.

"It will be very hard for you if you do not, Vinciullo."

The man to the left of Spinelli was speaking now, his Neapolitan dialect so thick Ugo could hardly pick the words out. "Stop the bullshit and the fancy talk. You have to face down your local families. They are finished. The family head lives in a hole in the ground, for God's sake. They won't fuck with us. The waste disposal contract for my company will be on your desk tomorrow when you get your fat arse into the office. You sign it, or your fat arse will be in a hole with your local families who are a bunch of has beens."

For a moment the office was silent, then the chairs were scraped back as the three men stood up to leave.

"Until tomorrow, Signor Presidente," said Spinelli, smiling.

****

Simone felt the strong hands lifting her up but she could not resist. Her head was swaying as she was carried away from the square. She forced herself to concentrate. She tried to punch the dark figure carrying her.

"Let me go, you fascist bastard," she tried to scream, but it was only a croak. Blood was dripping from her head onto the pavement. She felt a surge of vomit and gagged as it came out, wetting the trousers of the man who was carrying her. She was aware enough now to think that it served him right.

Suddenly the man stopped and she was lowered carefully to sit on a doorstep. She looked up, ready to lash out at the policeman who was arresting her. Her eyes widened in shock. It wasn't the police. It was that Dutchman, the self-righteous bastard reporter. What the hell was he doing?

"A nice way to pay back your rescuer," said Michiel. "But it is good you are awake. I could not have run any further and we need to get you to safety."

"Safety?" Simone was struggling to think. What the hell is he talking about? Then it came flooding back. The demonstration, the charge, then the shock of the dark wave of police washing over them, then the blow, then nothing. She tried to stand up.

"The demonstration," she said. "I have to be there. What the hell are you doing dragging me away?"

She had no strength and Michiel easily held her down with one hand on her shoulder. He spoke urgently but without passion.

"There is no demonstration. The police are right now taking all those activists away in their vans. The police are going to have fun and your friends are going to have a very nasty day. You are safe for this minute, but they will come looking. You have had a strong hit on your head. You need to see a doctor. But first you must get off the street. The police will be looking for you, and with that blood on your face they will find you easily."

Simone shook her head, trying to clear it. She felt sick with remorse for leading the activists into the trap. Sick with fear of being picked up herself. And viciously angry with this pompous middle-aged man for saving her. Why did it have to be him?

"I can go to the hospital," she said, trying to sound strong. "They can help me, then I will go to negotiate the release of my friends."

"Listen," Michiel was more urgent now, his hand gripping her shoulder firmly. "Listen to me. You cannot help your friends by being taken to a police cell and getting beaten up. The police will be at the hospitals, they know exactly how to do this. You will only be safe off the street. Let me help you."

He felt in his shoulder bag and produced a woolly beanie hat.

"Put this on," he said firmly. "Tuck your hair up and let me wipe the blood from your face. Then hold my arm and let's walk quickly to where you are staying."

Simone did as she was told. She was mute, embarrassed, but she knew he was right. She sat quietly while he wiped away the blood. She felt a little stronger now and she took care to tuck her hair away into the hat before standing up.

"OK," she said, "I can walk now." She did not want to hold on to him, but after a few paces her legs were like jelly and she was glad to feel his arm linking to hers and supporting her.

"I am staying in a room on Ortigia," she said quietly. Michiel nodded and led her south down the small road away from the square and closest to the sea. It seemed to take forever to cover the few hundred metres to the old bridge and then up the narrow lane to the *pensione*. They could hear police sirens along the main streets to the east of them but they passed no-one. They did not speak. Simone was using all her strength to walk, and she felt too angry and embarrassed to say anything. Michiel was silent, just firmly helping her along.

In the doorway of the *pensione* Simone pulled herself upright.

"Thank you," she said. "I will be OK now." As she turned to let herself in she sensed he was about to say something, but he remained silent. With a nod he turned and walked away, leaving Simone angry with herself, angry with him and angry with Sicily. What a bloody mess, she thought as she dragged herself into her room and pulled the beanie away to look at the damage. *Merde*!

And I don't even know his name.

****

Luca Consentini tried to hide his distaste. And control his temper. He was having trouble on both accounts. Across the table from him Giovanni Paci had slashed his grilled sea bream into bite size chunks as soon as the waiter had placed it in front of him. Then he had switched the fork to his right hand and was hoovering them up, talking as he ate.

"Luca, you godda take advantage of this, my friend," said Paci. "Opportunities like this don't come along every day. Just look out that way," he pointed seawards with his loaded fork. "The sea is covered in oil right?"

He waved the fork inland. "And here are people. You got people and you got oil, what you ain't got yet is any work for yourself. That's where I come in."

Luca was eating carefully. The small cuttlefish cooked in their own ink were delicate, but had to be treated with care if he was not to get a stain on his immaculate white shirt.

He took a small sip of wine and spoke quietly.

"Giovanni, you are very welcome here in Sicily. You are family and family is important. But I have to ask you to respect our way of working. Here we do not have a no win-no fee system, and we don't go out drumming up business. If any local business comes to me for help with compensation then of course I will take the case and do what I can. But if I go out in the Piazza Duomo with a sign up saying "Claims Handled Here" I will never be trusted again. Please respect that."

"You see, my friend," said Giovanni triumphantly. He had already finished his plate of fish. "You think we Americans are dumb. But I got the measure of this. We have had those Brits at BP over a barrel and shafted them and they don't like it but they pay up. We can do the same here to ENOL. You don't want to dirty your shirt, but you still eat squid, right? You don't want to dirty your hands with oil, but you can still make money from it. Trust me, Luca. I can get the business, you handle the local angles. I get down and dirty, you get rich."

Luca was pulling his thoughts together to reply when Giovanni pushed back his chair and stood up.

"I guess these guys don't do New Orleans portions," he said. "Quicker to eat this way, right? Not too much on a plate. So you finish up and I'll go get sorted. Paci & Delaney are in town and the action starts here."

Before Luca could protest he was gone. Luca took a deep breath, held it for a count of three then breathed out slowly. I don't know what he will do, he said to himself, but I do know it is going to be complicated for me. He picked up his knife and fork. At least I can now finish my lunch in a civilised way. The price of a good lunch in Ortigia had doubled since the spill. No fish, they claimed. The fish comes from the rest of Sicily, as it always does, thought Luca. These prices are midsummer tourist prices which match the full hotels and restaurants. Maybe he is right, I should profit a little instead of being profited from.

****

This isn't quite going to plan, thought Cesare Disario. What's wrong with these guys? There's going to be money going begging and they can't seem to understand.

The taxi had pulled up outside Palermo airport and the taxi driver was thumping the button on the meter. Each push of the button added five euros to the fare.

"I could have got a cab across the ocean for that price," he said to the driver, priding himself on his careful Italian.

The driver looked at him coolly.

"No special price for Americans, mister," he replied in English. "Extra for luggage, extra for airport, that's the price."

Cesare paid over the fistful of euros and looked ruefully at his fast emptying wallet. He had been in Sicily three days, had spent a fortune, and had got nowhere. Exactly nowhere. The local university in Siracusa had kept him waiting for three hours, then an old grey-haired professor with bad breath had told him, taking a long time over it, that his department was in touch with the Coastguard and the fisheries but that they got their grants from Rome and he could not see how that would change because of a tanker spill. The Regional President's office in Siracusa had received him politely but told him that the place to go was the university, which he had only just escaped from. The University of Palermo couldn't see the oil and couldn't see what their role in the spill might be, and in any case, Professor, as you know we are funded from Rome, Rome sends us money and we spend it, so if you want to help, you want money, then Rome is the place to go, Professor, and good luck in Rome.

He checked in for the Rome flight. He had booked a hotel ahead. Rome's hotels seemed to be the world's most expensive, even at this time of the year. I had better land some consultancy work for us there or I'm going to look stupid, he told himself. I spent the cash we were supposed to spend on the students' research trip coming here, so I have to bring something home. He saw a pretty girl in a rumpled linen suit going through security ahead of him. He cheered himself up. All roads lead to Rome. These Sicilians are small thinkers. The main Oceanographic Institute in Rome will surely see that we can add value, ENOL can pay, the shipowner can pay, and we can all benefit.

He smiled at the girl, but she didn't seem to notice him.

CHAPTER TWENTY-THREE

Simone pulled herself up from the bed. The tapping at the door was insistent.

"*Signorina*," she heard. "There is a man to speak with you. *Signorina, per favore, scusi!*"

She looked around. It was daylight, she must have slept through the night. She felt a surge of fear. Was it the police?

"Ask him to wait and I will come," she said. She heard the footsteps of the old woman who managed the *pensione* moving away and she went to the bathroom. I look awful, she thought, as she splashed water on her face. No sense in dressing up for the police though. She pulled a t-shirt over her head, slipped into her jeans and grabbed the heavy wool cardigan she had bought that autumn in the local charity auction.

Her legs felt wobbly as she went downstairs, holding tight to the bannister. She stopped dead when she saw Michiel standing in the hallway. Not him, a voice rang in her head. Not now. Instinctively she tried to stand more upright and with one hand pushed her hair back.

"I came to check you have not got concussion," he said formally.

"And you have my hat."

It was a flat statement. Simone remembered the day before and blushed. She was annoyed with herself and annoyed with this man. Had he really come just to get his bloody hat back?

"I'm alright," she said brusquely. "I will fetch your hat. I am sorry to have put you to any trouble."

She could feel him looking at her, sizing her up. He knows I am not alright and I know I look awful. I need to rest, not have this man getting in my space.

"Look," said Michiel. "Can we sit for a minute? I have a proposal to make." He pointed to the heavy old dark wooden chairs which were set in the large hallway. Simone sat down. She was glad to sit but did not want to show it. She did not trust herself to speak, so she just nodded.

Michiel looked right at her and spoke slowly and clearly. His clipped Dutch accent made the words seem more formal than they were.

"I think, if you are willing, we can help each other," he said. He saw her bristle. "You may not think so but we have the same interests at heart. You want to see the oil cleaned up and the birds protected. I want that too. You believe you can achieve that by direct action, by doing things yourself, by protesting. I believe that I can achieve that by showing the world what is happening here. I want to uncover the corruption, chase down where the money is going, force them to spend it properly."

He paused. Simone was paying attention now. She had been expecting some words of concern or of censure. Maybe even a come on, she thought, men are so predictable. She had not been expecting this calm, businesslike statement. He has not even asked how I am feeling.

She nodded and Michiel continued.

"Look," he said. "We can help each other. I can interview you and give you some publicity in major European papers. You can help me by telling me what you see on the ground, getting your friends and activists, those who are not now nursing bruises and on their way home, to keep an eye on what is being done and not done, so I can build up a picture which shames the authorities into action. It is a trade-off. Publicity in return for information. We both gain and we both get towards what we both want."

Simone was thinking fast. Can I trust him? Is it surrendering to the fascists if I work with him? Why did he save me? Why doesn't he ask how I am? What does he see when he looks at me? Her thoughts were jumbled.

Before she could reply she saw him standing up.

"You are tired," she heard. "I leave you now to rest. Please think about this co-operation. I will come back later today, in the early evening, to see if you are willing to do it. May I meet you here?"

I don't want him here. Not in my *pensione*, she thought.

"The Bar Duomo. After six o'clock," she heard herself saying. What the hell are you doing, said the warning voice in her head. Why did you just agree? "I am Simone."

"Michiel," she heard. "Six in the Bar Duomo."

Then he was gone and she did not know if she was angry with him or angry with herself.

****

"What the hell is going on?" Linus was almost screeching, his voice an octave higher than its normal prim level. There was a crashing noise at the door, making everyone in the claims office jump.

The smell of fish was overwhelming. David was on his feet now, gesturing his staff towards the back of the office while he strode towards the door, which was buckling inwards. The wood was splintering. Outside the office he could hear shouting and what sounded like a dump truck.

He reached for the door handle then hesitated. There was a massive weight pushing the door inwards, and he did not want to release that.

"Stand well back, everyone," he said. "Just let me look out of the window and see if I can see what's going on."

Out of the corner of his eye David could see Linus wringing his hands. Poor fellow, he thought, smiling to himself. Real life can be so untidy.

He moved a chair close to the bulging door and stood on it. There was a small tilting window in the glass panel over the door. He pushed the window open and looked down. A waft of rotting fish smell sent him reeling back, banging his head on the window frame.

"Shit," he swore, shaking his head, then looking out again more carefully. A huge pile of fish was filling the old stone porch and spilling out into the cobbled courtyard of the Municipio.

He looked up and saw Fortunato and a crowd of fishermen in shining oilskins staring at him across the yard.

"Good morning, Mister Insurance," said Fortunato. "I hope you are well? And Mister Procedures, your friend, is also well? We have brought you a small present."

David could not contain his temper.

"What do you think you are doing?" he shouted. "How is this supposed to help anyone? You could have hurt my staff!"

He saw Fortunato smiling. He knew he had scored a point, making

David lose his temper.

"You see, Mister Insurance, we have a problem," said Fortunato blandly. "Our problem is that you said forms, then people, then cash. We have done the forms, your people have been, but we don't have the cash. So we bring you these fish as a present. To make you remember that fishermen need money to live on when they cannot sell fish. Be happy, you are not alone. We are also bringing a good helping of fish to all the ENOL petrol stations, and to our good friends in the Provincial Administration. They too must pay. We have plenty of fish that we cannot sell. But if you give us the cash you promised then of course we can leave the fish in the sea in future."

David squeezed his hand on the window frame, pushing his temper into the pressure. He could feel his knuckles cracking but the pain calmed him down.

"We said we would compensate you for loss of earnings," he said, as evenly as he could. He was uncomfortable and knew he looked foolish with his head squeezed sideways out of the small window. "We explained that there are procedures. We are following those, and we will have interim payments ready for you in the coming days. This does not help. There is only one door to this office. If you block it, we cannot go to the bank, so we cannot pay you. I leave you to think about that. If there is fish in our door, there is no money in your pockets."

David did not wait for a reaction. He pulled his head back into the room, stepped down from the chair and looked at his staff.

"That should do it. Back to work," he said calmly. As they began to move to their desks he could not resist a dig at Linus. "I'm sure they'll clean up, Linus," he said. "You'll be able to wash your hands soon."

****

Paola di Bartolo looked around the Sala degli Specchi. Noto town council was in session. She could see each man twice or three times in the mirrors which lined the walls. We work in illusions in a room of illusions, she thought. I am one woman in a council of men, or in the mirror I am many women.

"Gentlemen," she began cautiously. "There is an issue of council revenue to discuss. As your Mayor I have met with my counterpart in Siracusa. She has told me that Siracusa council will be getting substantial compensation from the insurers of the tanker. Compensation for the fouled beaches and for loss of tourism."

She paused, giving time for her message to sink in.

"But here in Noto we are not getting any money. We cannot claim any because we have not apparently suffered any damages, nor lost any revenue. Thanks to our good friends from Rome, and the Africans, so well managed by our good friend from inland," she nodded to the Mafia council member, "our beaches are well protected. The oil which is reaching here on the sea is not getting past the defences."

The questions were coming now. The questions she had wanted to hear. How much was Siracusa claiming? How much could Noto claim? What good were defences if they kept the oil away but also kept the money away? If there is money we can rebuild the Lido di Noto, we need money to attract the tourists. Why are we so stupid, we only do a good job when it hurts us?

She let the discussion run, letting the natural greed in the councillors build up a good head of steam. Then she tapped the table, calling for quiet.

"Perhaps, gentlemen, we can find a way forward," she said. "We work in a room where everything is not as it seems. We look up at our beautiful trompe l'oeil ceiling, we know it is flat, but we see it as beautifully formed. We see what is not there. To get compensation for our city the insurers must see oil, but the oil is not there. I think, if I have your support, we can change that."

They were looking at each other. One or two of the councillors moved as if to speak, but then sat back. She saw them nodding. They did not want to put into words publicly what Paola was suggesting, but she knew they understood.

"I have your support then, gentlemen," she said. "Where there is oil, there is money, and I know where there is oil."

****

He winked at his secretary and went past her to the video conference room. She thinks I've gone mad, thought Giuseppe, smiling to himself. He had ruffled his hair and carefully smudged one cheek with boot polish. His tie was loose and his suit jacket hung awkwardly.

ENOL executives don't usually look like this, he laughed to himself, but then this is no normal call. This is a million euros in our pocket call, and Rome has to stay out of it.

He was connected through to the operations headquarters in Rome, and he smiled tiredly at the camera. Montalbano didn't act this good, he congratulated himself, as he saw the reaction of the General Manager to what he was seeing on his screen.

"Jesus, Mammino, you look terrible," he heard. "What the hell is going on?"

Giuseppe sat up and made what looked like a real effort.

"It's nothing," he said manfully. "Nothing. Just a little brush with some fishermen. They are mounting a boycott of our petrol stations and have dumped a lot of fish in all the gas stations around Siracusa. I had a little trouble to get through the crowd to get into the office.

People are angry because they need fuel, but the fishermen are stopping them."

They are buying the story, he said to himself. They have seen the news reports. Now I have to get the cash without getting them down here too.

"We can sort it out quickly, I think," he went on confidently. "It is all because the British insurers are being slow to pay out to the fishermen. If we can step in and pay them the issue will go away. But if we don't act the boycott will spread across Sicily. I've checked with our lawyers and they confirm that any payments we make to people affected by the oil spill can be reclaimed from the insurers and the IOPC Funds. So what I suggest is that you fly down here right away, bring a credit line and we can set you up with a claims office. You can make interim payments to the fishermen, deal with them direct. It will be quite safe, they mean no harm. That will stop the problem."

He slumped in his chair again and held his head in one hand. Don't overplay it, he thought, but they need to worry.

He could see the General Manager exchanging looks with his bag carriers. They don't want to come here and be pushed around by angry fishermen. He waited for their reaction. I think you have the message, now we will see what balls you have.

There was a long pause before the reply.

"Mammino, this is a busy time in Rome right now, better you handle this. You know all the local systems. Why don't you set up a claims office in Siracusa, handle things with the regional authorities? We can authorise an emergency fund, and you can make interim payments in return for lifting the boycott. It will help us with good publicity if we are seen to be helping all those affected by the oil."

Giuseppe did his best to look shocked.

"Well, of course you are right, we must make the payments. But these could add up quickly, some of the total oil spill payments have gone to over a billion euros in recent spills. You should be here to handle that, to feel the temper here. I am only the Regional Manager, it is a job for the General Manager."

"Man up, Mammino, where are your balls," he heard. He struggled to suppress a laugh. "This is no time for hiding. I will authorise the funds you need, you get on to this and start getting the pressure off our petrol stations. I will be in charge here in Rome."

"Very well," replied Giuseppe. "I will do it with your authority. Thank you for trusting me with this responsibility."

He cut the link. Arseholes, he thought. He talks about my balls, and gives me licence to spend a billion euros to protect his. He laughed and straightened his tie. This is going to be fun. Everyone likes people who give money away.

CHAPTER TWENTY-FOUR

"It has to be done with discretion, at night and quietly, is that clear?" Paola di Bartolo did not like what she was doing and it showed in her voice. She became more aristocratic when she was tense, she forgot to act the woman of the people.

She did not like the reply. These bastard Camorra play with us, she thought. I am asking only for a few trucks of oily waste to be spread on our beaches. They are well paid to take it away from the soiled beaches of Siracusa, and this way they have no disposal costs. But still they ask us for cash. They want to be paid twice for not doing their job.

"I understand you have expenses, Signor," she said calmly into the telephone. "I understand there are implications for everyone involved. And of course you will be recompensed for that. But the town of Noto is not so rich, and will not make so much money from this. If I arrange cash upfront then something goes wrong and we do not get the insurance payment, then we will be in trouble."

Paola tried to picture the man at the other end of the phone. He will be fat, very fat, she imagined. Dark greasy hair and horrible pudgy fingers. You can hear him down the phone, he likes to bully women. He's picked the wrong one this time.

"Signor," she broke in. There was steel in her voice. "It is not helpful for you to continue to list your demands in return for a small favour I ask of you. Let me help you see things more clearly. Let me put this plainly. You have got a contract for waste removal from Presidente Vinciullo, and he has asked my help to hold the Mafia in check so you can benefit from that contract. I have done that, and you are profiting each day from removing the oil and waste while I hold back the men in the mountains. But if I give the word then strange things will happen. Your tanker drivers will go missing. Your trucks will catch fire. You will have to bring in much more security from Naples, and they will be busy because this is our island. Do I make myself clear?"

She listened to the chastened reply. He is not used to women who stand up to him, she thought.

"So, we understand each other, Signor," she said. "Three trucks of waste spread on the beach at the Lido di Noto, enough damage to the defences to look realistic, and you will be paid when we receive our claim. Thank you for being so understanding."

She put the phone down and looked up. The ceiling in this room is just an illusion, she said to herself with satisfaction. And our friend in the Camorra has just fallen for a very old trick. Let's hope the insurers are as gullible.

****

David had felt ridiculous on the back of the scooter. His legs were too long and the scooter had struggled on the last few curves of the dusty road up the steep hill. But Anna had laughed at him when he said he knew all about Archimedes, and had laughed at him again when he looked surprised that she had suggested taking him up to the fort so he could show her what he knew. He did not know how to deal with a girl who laughed at him, so he had climbed on the scooter meekly and in ten minutes Anna had swept them through the traffic, out of Siracusa and up the hill to the Castello Eurialo.

"You see, David," said Anna. "Here is our ancient fort. A ruin, like everything in Sicily. You can tell me about Archimedes. But I would rather hear about London."

She was just touching his arm, leading him along the path through the heavy stone blocks. He liked the feel of her hand on him but could not quite believe he was here. They had met several times to sort out the bank business but had only discussed bank and payment matters. Anna was always open and smiling. She's pretty too, he thought. Why is she taking an interest in me?

"Look," she said, waving her arm in an arc. "From here you can see the whole of Siracusa, all of Ortigia. It is a historic view, but I think we learnt in school that this castle never won any battles."

It was late afternoon, they had left the bank at the end of the day, and now as evening was closing in David could see the bays north and south of Siracusa in the last of the daylight. From here there was no sign of oil, but he could see the skimmer boats at work.

"Well, clever Englishman," teased Anna. "Tell me what I do not know of our good citizen Archimedes."

David remembered his schooldays. Perhaps there were some benefits to a classics education after all.

"Well," he said. "Did you know that it was from here that Archimedes shone a huge mirror onto the sails of the approaching Roman fleet and set fire to them?"

"Our schoolbooks are written in Rome, David," said Anna. "They teach us only that Archimedes jumped out of his bath."

"He was killed by a Roman soldier who was about to tread on mathematics he was drawing in the dust," said David. "Did they teach you that?"

"There is so much they do not teach us, you have no idea," she replied. She held his gaze. "I have never been to Rome, and I have never been to London. There is so much I would like to see and learn."

David took her answer literally and began to explain more of the history of Archimedes and the Roman conquest of Sicily. He felt secure while he could talk about history. When women came close to him his words dried up, but he was able to talk to this lively young woman who was now leading him by the hand through the massive tumbled blocks which made up the ruined castle.

They walked carefully, looking at each other and at the path in front of them. That's why they did not see the two young men who had come up the hill behind them and who now watched them from behind a block near the entrance.

****

The wind was cold enough to make Simone hug her cardigan close around her. She should have been wearing a coat, but when Michiel had called for her she had grabbed the cardigan. That's what he has seen me in and I'm not going to change how I look for him, she thought. They were standing on top of the Talete parking building which disfigures the mainland end of Ortigia island. Michiel touched her arm and pointed.

"Look," he said. "From here it is very clear. The entrance to the marina is quite narrow, between those rocks below us and the breakwater over there. When Castalia Mareazul began work it was easy for them to string a boom across the entrance to the marina. That would keep the oil out, right?"

Simone nodded. If he talks down to me I'm walking away, she told herself. I'm not sure if I should be here anyway.

They had met in the Bar Duomo the evening before. Simone had been sore, confused and irritated. She did not want to spend time with this middle-aged stuffed shirt. But she felt a sense of obligation. He had saved her from the police. And she liked that he did not talk about that. She knew she had been naive and she did not want him rubbing salt in the wound.

She had been very conscious of the bar owner watching her sitting talking with Michiel. It might keep him away a bit, she had told herself. Or he might try to throw me out if he thinks he has no chance anymore. It would be so much easier if Yves was here. These *merde* men might leave me alone then.

Michiel was intense when he began explaining his point of view. It was simple. Whenever there is a big oil spill, there is major corruption and hypocrisy, and a nasty rush to get money from insurers and the oil company involved. Everyone was in on the racket, fishermen, port owners, local authorities, local businesses, academic institutes, lawyers. As he explained it, an oil spill was a golden tide washing prosperity into a coastal community.

Simone had banged the table at that point. She had spoken back sharply, pushing her fatigue and pain to the back of her head. She matched his intensity as she told him that he was unfeeling, he did not care about the sea and the fish and the birds and the natural ecology. The money was not enough to compensate for the terrifying impact of oil spills on birds and coastlines.

Michiel had quietly asked if she would eat something, and when the *tagliatelli carbonara* was in front of them he had replied. His measured words irritated her. He was so pedantic. Michiel had facts and figures at his fingertips. How much had been spent cleaning the beaches after the *Prestige* oil spill. How that part of Spain had more Blue Flag beaches after the spill than before because of the clean-up. How much had been spent on academic research after the *Exxon Valdez*. How much BP was paying out in the Gulf of Mexico for research into a clean sea. How art galleries in New Orleans were getting compensation from BP for the Gulf oil spill. How she should visit any of the places where she had fought oil spills and see them today, prosperous and with new houses, new roads, new fishing boats and plenty of wildlife.

She had needed the food or she might have walked out then. She did not want to be lectured by this boring man. She had seen him recognise that.

"Look," he had said. "I can see you do not believe me. But if I can show you one clear instance of corruption, will you agree to an interview, and get your activists to help me gather more information on what is going on?"

She had nodded and they parted awkwardly outside the café. Michiel had paid for the food and drinks without looking at her, and she felt ashamed that she had not offered to pay her part. Now in the morning the intense Michiel was back. He takes it so seriously, she noticed.

"Look into the marina now," he said, pointing to his left. "You can see that there is oil fouling on the pontoons and yachts. You can also see a big crew of Africans busy cleaning up. Now look here in front. Where is the boom? Swept away, the marina owners claim, swept away by the waves and current. Probably not installed correctly, they are telling the insurers right now. But I know the truth. I have photographs of the original installation. It was well done. I have recorded the weather. There were no storms since the boom was rigged. And I was able to come down in the night and photograph the men who came and cut the boom. They took a long time to fray the ropes through so it did not look like a cut. I have a video of them, I was hiding in the car park below us. I can show you that. Then will you believe me?"

"What will you do with the evidence?" asked Simone. She was indignant. "This is a crime, there are birds suffering because of this.

Why haven't you told the police?"

Even as she said it she felt foolish. The police are part of the problem, she realised, and instinctively reached up and touched her head where the baton had left an angry red lump.

Michiel took the question seriously.

"I have to build a picture," he explained. "There is no sense in going to any local authority about these things, because they are all part of it. They will be taking some kickback on the wages of the African immigrants, and getting cash from the insurers or oil company which they will use to line their pockets and build some new promenade next year. The only weapon against corruption is public exposure. But no newspaper will print this story without a lot of proof. I have to have evidence of systematic corruption. Then I can show how one incident links to another, and I can blow them wide open in the media across Europe."

When Simone did not reply he went on, urgently now.

"You can help, you have many people and you are in the thick of things, trying to help the clean-up. I want the same as you, clean beaches and healthy birds. It is just that I use different tools. Help me now, I cannot be everywhere. If you and your friends will be my eyes and ears we can make a real difference. Not just to this spill, where most of the damage is done, but to future spills. We can focus everyone on making sure future spills are tackled properly, not in a way which maximises the profits of the locals."

Simone looked away. It makes sense, she realised that. But when I start thinking pompous middle-aged men make sense then I must be missing something. I need to get rid of him, then I can rest and think.

"I will think about it," she said brusquely. Then without looking at him she walked across the square towards her *pensione*. She tried to walk upright and not show how tired she felt.

CHAPTER TWENTY-FIVE

Michiel held himself rigid. He would not react, he knew the prison warders wanted to get to him. The warder reached up between his legs and pushed his testicles one way and then the other, then reached round his waistband and with one rough gloved hand ran his finger down between the cheeks of his backside. In front of him another warder was watching him closely, enjoying the ritual humiliation.

"Our Captain does not get so many visitors," said the warder. "He has hurt our country. Why does a foreign journalist want to speak with him?"

Michiel was deadpan.

"I have here the signed permission from the governor of Catania prison to meet the prisoner Captain Anand," he replied.

There was silence as the warder doing the body search indicated that Michiel should remove his shoes. These were examined in minute detail, and his briefcase emptied out onto the desk. The warders picked over the contents with disappointment. Nothing here to stop the interview.

The senior of the two warders spoke briefly.

"Take your things. He is waiting for you. And we are watching you."

He was led to a harsh grey room containing only a table and two chairs. In one he saw Captain Anand. God, he looks ill, thought Michiel. He could not imagine that this small, old grey-haired man was a ship's Captain. He looks broken.

The Captain spoke first.

"Are you from my owners, or are you asking me again to confess what I did not do?"

"Captain Anand, I am neither. My name is Michiel van Roosmalen, and I am a journalist. I am concerned that you are being held here in jail and that no-one is telling your story. I want to do that," said Michiel, holding out his hand in greeting.

He saw that Captain Anand did not move to respond to his handshake, and then he saw that he was handcuffed. He saw the Captain look at him, and look at the warder who was close behind Michiel. He does not want any trouble, he thought. The warder looked as if he would move to restrain Michiel if he moved any closer.

Michiel sat down and began again.

"Captain," he said politely. "I am a campaigning journalist who believes that you are being wrongfully treated. I followed and reported the Captain Mangouras and *Prestige* case and the publicity helped to get him freed. I believe if we can tell your story we can do the same for you. Will you talk to me?"

He waited, he could see the Captain thinking. Was this a trap? Then the answer came, with a firm dignity which he did not expect from the grey, beaten-down figure opposite him.

"Well, Mr van Roosmalen," he heard. "I am glad of a chance to tell my story. Since I have been here the authorities have been making up a story for me to sign. It cannot do any harm for me to tell you the truth. Where shall I begin?"

Michiel led the Captain through his background and experience to why he was on the *Barbara S*, and finally to the fateful decisions of that dreadful night. He guessed the conversation was being recorded by the prison, but the Captain spoke without exaggeration. He ended with a simple, direct plea.

"I saved my crew. That is the final duty of a Captain," he said. "But now the owner is ignoring me, the state wants to blame me, who will help me to go home? Will you, Mr van Roosmalen?"

Michiel closed his notebook and stood up. He began to reach out his hand again to say goodbye, but pulled it back just before the warder behind him had the chance to reach and restrain him.

"Captain," he said. "I have your story and I will make sure it gets aired. People will listen. They should not be holding you here, it is unjust. But powerful forces always like to blame the Captain. Be strong, be patient, and you will get home. I will do my best."

****

David left the claims office at the Municipio and turned left down the broad Piazza Archimede towards his hotel. He stretched himself tall. It had been another tough day. Lines of fishermen and restaurant owners and tourist boat owners and yacht owners and every other person in Siracusa and fifty miles south, it seemed to David. No-one leaving happy. They all came in wanting money, but few left with any. Either they had not completed the claims forms, or they did not have the evidence, or they were simply trying it on, he thought.

He shook his head to clear it. All day he had been thinking about Anna. Nothing had happened at the castle. They had walked about, looked at the view, and he had explained the history of Siracusa's most important historic citizen, Archimedes, to Siracusa's best looking bank manager. Why was he thinking like that? Nothing had happened, but some boundary had been crossed. Should he have kissed her? Perhaps she would have kissed him if he had tried. Why didn't you try, you fool, he thought. She had dropped him off at Ortigia with a cheery wave, and was gone. There must be more, but what? What does she want? What do I want? He felt his stomach tighten, half with fear, half with anticipation. There is a bank meeting set for tomorrow, he thought.

He was restless. He could not face the hotel, the heavy carpets, the dusty curtains, the stuffy room, the nuns singing quietly in the distance. I need to look at the sea. See the oil. See what this is all about. He turned and walked south down the narrowing streets towards the seaward point. It was evening but there was still light as he emerged on the lookout place. Below him groups of workers were swabbing at the thick oil lapping onto the rocks. He felt a surge of anger. Dispersant out at sea would have stopped this, he thought. No-one should have to do that filthy job. He looked left and right. Wherever he looked black oil smeared the rocks. Clean-up debris was everywhere. It's a mess, and we are paying for this. He swore under his breath.

David turned to walk back. He did not see the two figures stepping back into the shadows. He was thinking about how to call Dino and get dispersant into use. And what would he say to Anna tomorrow?

He stepped away from the lookout and into the narrow cobbled alleyway. A few yards in he turned right into another narrow slit between the tall old buildings. He heard running footsteps behind him but before he could turn something smashed into the back of his head. He stumbled forward onto his knees. A foot pushed him hard in the back and he crashed face down onto the cobbles. He felt his nose crack and hot blood flowing onto his face. He pushed with both hands to lift himself up but was too late to avoid a swinging kick which caught him on the left side of his head. He tried to shout and choked on the blood. He fell back and was bracing himself for another kick but there was silence.

David rolled over painfully and sat up. He was shocked, the attack had come out of nowhere. They didn't try to steal anything. What the hell was that about? With his handkerchief he staunched the blood flow from his nose and then slowly stood up. For a second he rocked on his feet, then held his balance with his left hand against the wall. It must be a warning, he realised. They don't like not being paid immediately. I'll warn Linus and we'll get more security for the office and our hotel tomorrow. We need some more muscle. What a bloody place.

****

Simone stepped to one side so the stall hid her. She was browsing the market in the Via Trento, looking for some cheap fruit. She still felt sore from the baton strike and was not yet ready to throw herself back into the clean-up effort. One more day of rest and I will be ready, she had told herself. One day, but I need to eat, so she had come down to the street market to buy what she could. I can't face another meal in the Bar Duomo, she thought. It will either be the landlord or that Dutchman, and I don't want to see either of them.

But now she had. Three stalls down Michiel was trying to buy some ham. She watched him trying to catch the attention of the stall holders. It looked as if they would not serve him. He turned away from the stall, and she saw he was being hassled by a small crowd. She realised that they must know who he is. The TV that morning had carried a report on the ill-treatment of the ship's master, building on Michiel's piece in the Herald Tribune. They don't like him, they don't like the truth, she thought.

She stayed hidden as she saw Michiel trying to walk away with dignity, but being jostled and mocked by a tight knot of bulky men in oilskins. More were coming up the road, and stall holders were pointing them towards where Michiel was. This is looking bad, she thought. She saw his glasses knocked from his head as the pushing became more violent.

Right in front of her two Carabinieri were standing beside the road. Their uniforms were immaculate, high hats exactly in place, black leather gloves folded neatly over their gleaming shoulder belts. They can see what is happening, she said to herself. But they will do nothing. She began to move towards them. I'll make them save him, she thought. But then she felt the mark on her head. If they see me they'll arrest me, she realised, and shrank back into the shadow.

She felt relieved when she saw Michiel break free of the group and walk away quickly. They were jeering at him, and a tomato flew through the air and burst on his head. The police did not move. He won't be so neat and precise now, she thought. She was surprised to feel almost pleased. Then angry with herself for thinking that. At least he is safe, her conscience told her.

She slipped away from the police back towards her *pensione*. Her mind was working fast. I still haven't answered him. Perhaps he is right though. He must be doing something powerful if people react so strongly. He might be useful to us.

****

I never felt this bad even after the Varsity match, thought David. He was nursing a splitting headache and the bandage across his nose was irritating him. He had been to the bank meeting that morning looking forward to seeing Anna, but she had been off for the day. Her colleague had been polite but distant. He felt relief and annoyance. He wanted to see her, but not like this.

It's good it is quiet, he thought. But there must be something going on. Yesterday we were worked off our feet. Then I got a beating because we are not paying out fast enough, and suddenly the claimants dry up today.

He looked up. That's what I need now. This dried up Swede with a huge sense of importance and all puffed up.

Before he could speak Linus began spitting out words. His lips were drawn tightly, his body was quivering with anger and his elbows stuck out. Like chicken wings, imagined David. He is such a fool.

"David," said Linus. "David, we must act. I know why there is no-one here today. The oil company ENOL has set up a claims office. They are making payments to everyone who comes in the door. We must take control of the situation."

He almost stamped his foot, thought David. How the hell does he think I can stop an Italian oil company chucking money at people? He was slow to reply, and Linus could not wait to speak again.

"You understand that it is the duty of the IOPC Funds to manage the claims process with respect to the cargo owner. That is my responsibility. ENOL is usurping that. They are not using the correct forms, and they are not validating the claims. I have seen it, David. With my own eyes. The office is in the regional presidency, in Siracusa. There is a queue down the street as news is spreading. This is a disaster. All control of expenditure is gone."

His outburst gave David time to think.

"Linus," he replied slowly. "I am so, so sorry to hear your system is being bypassed. Of course I understand that it is a trifle annoying for you. But perhaps there is a benefit for us in this? First of all, it takes the immediate heat off us. People with money are not so likely to attack us."

David pointed to his bandaged nose and bruised head.

"And it is their money they are giving out, not ours. Of course ENOL will try to claim it back from you and from the Club. But they will have to prove in court the claims they have paid on and the awards made. That will not be easy. So I think we should not be so unhappy about this. I for one am happy not to see an angry fisherman today."

David could see that Linus was bubbling over and about to explode. An untidy and uncontrolled claims process not under his direct control was something he could not live with. David thought rapidly.

"We can benefit from this in another way," he said, reaching out a hand to place on Linus' arm. "We make a rule that every claimant here has to declare any cash received from ENOL and we deduct that from anything we were intending to pay. We can ask ENOL to give us a list of payments made each day, and perhaps ask anyone who comes here to produce any documents ENOL has given them. That will stop double counting."

And it will give your nit-picking little mind something to focus on, said David under his breath. He could see Linus thinking it through.

"Of course, David," replied Linus primly. "We must avoid double payments. I will immediately draft a formal note to ENOL to ask for a list of payments each day, and I will revise our procedures here to ensure we do not pay out to anyone in receipt of ENOL cash. It is most irregular, but it is what we can do."

He turned and bustled off across the office. David put his head into his hands. What a mess. And where was Anna today? When will I see her again?

CHAPTER TWENTY-SIX

Capitano Dino Cervetto was angry and he was embarrassed. He did not want to show either emotion, but his formal stiffness gave him away. He was sitting very upright in full uniform.

"Mrs Jones," he said, the words almost ground out through his teeth. "Your question is quite correct, and you already know the answer. The Ministry of the Environment has in fact given permission to use dispersant to break up the slick out to sea. We have the spraying aircraft tasked and the weather is set fair. That is good news. Unfortunately there is a small delay, as the stocks of dispersant are held up at Catania airport. We hope to move them soon and begin tasking the aircraft."

Don't ask me to say any more, he pleaded mentally, or I might just tell the truth. He was seething with anger. Three days of intense lobbying had finally got permission from Rome to use dispersant. Then the contractors had reported that the local stocks of dispersant were somehow not to be found. Which thieving bastard had sold them off he did not yet know, but he would find out when this was over. He had twisted more arms and called in favours in Rome, and a planeload of dispersant had arrived at Catania civil airport that morning. And there it sat, because the airport cargo workers wanted a bonus to handle what they had suddenly decided were hazardous chemicals.

He realised he was staring at Kate Jones, and he turned his head away. She must think I have gone mad. It is enough to send anyone mad. We have the biggest oil spill in the Mediterranean for years right on our doorstep and the only people who don't see it as a way to make money are sitting around this table. Everyone else has their hand out.

They were in the briefing room at his Coastguard office. Across the table from him were David Chillingworth from the P&I insurers and Kate Jones, the oil spill specialist from ITOPF. Ranged either side were the oil spill contractors from Castalia Mareazul, the salvors and his duty officers. He did not turn his head, but he knew what they could all see behind him. The large plot showed red reaching down the coastline as a swathe of black oil was carried by the current towards the main beach resorts and the bird reserve at Vendicari. They did not need to discuss the plot, they all knew when the oil would reach the next part of the coast. And they all knew the damage it would do.

"I am sure," continued Dino carefully but with biting force, looking at the Mareazul manager, "that the hold-up is temporary. The dispersant will be moved from Catania and the spraying aircraft will begin work while we have daylight. If not we may begin considering deploying military aircraft." He paused and he realised the room was completely silent, "and applying military discipline to those who are holding up our work."

Dino could see the contractor manager squirming in his seat. He is caught between a nasty rock and a very hard place, realised Dino. Powerful forces here want him to spend locally to clean up the oil which hits the coast, and I want him to spend on aircraft and dispersant to stop the oil hitting the coast. We shall see who is harder, he thought grimly.

"There is some good news," Dino continued. "With this settled weather the offshore skimmers are having some success at recovering oil as it surfaces close to the wrecks, and specialist teams with ROVs will be on site in three days' time and will begin assessing the wreck sites and what we can do to stop any more oil outflow. There is also some bad news. A deep depression is building in the North Atlantic, and we may expect in a week or so to see storms here again. In the time before it comes we must do our best to restrict the oil outflow, stop what is out at sea coming ashore by breaking it up, and strengthen the defences to the south of here."

Dino was looking around the meeting, waiting for questions. He wondered what had happened to the English insurer. His nose broken by the look of it, and a bad bruise on the side of his head. Dino did not want to ask, and in truth I don't want to know, he thought. I have enough battles to fight to get this mess cleaned up. Probably he got too close to a Sicilian girl, or was too slow to pay a fisherman. He is learning a little while he is here.

He signalled to his duty officer to run through the routine reports and the plans for the next two days then called the meeting to a close.

"Thank you all for your input," he said formally. "We meet again tomorrow afternoon to assess the dispersant spraying programme and adjust our plans accordingly."

He was looking at the Mareazul manager as he spoke. He saw him wriggle. "Spraying starts today, or someone goes to the military jail."

****

This is not a call I want to deal with, thought Ugo. I'm Regional President, I am a man of power, and yet I am sweating. I am pushed one way by Laura and I know she is right. I am pushed another way by Cervetto and his sainted Coastguard, so pure they want to do everything right every time. But I have to deal with this man.

He was waiting for his mobile phone to ring. Word had been sent that he needed to talk with Guido Recagno. But you cannot call a Mafia boss who lives in a bunker, Ugo mused. He lives in a hole, no-one sees him, yet we still fear him. I am the President but I have to wait for his call.

While he waited he was flipping through the press cuttings his staff had collated for him. He was in his study, darkness already wrapping the villa. He did not want to go outside for his cigar. The smell of the oil on the coast invaded his garden. His wife did not like him to smoke in the house. He fumbled with the cigar, then pushed it away, suddenly angry. That Dutchman is causing us trouble, he thought. There had been his reports in the press about the treatment of the ship's Captain. Now today there was a story alleging deliberate fouling of the marina. There was a photo of an African cleaning the marina. The caption pointed out that he had no protective clothing and that the boom protecting the marina had given way in mysterious circumstances.

Van Roosmalen, Ugo had read in the byline. We should have the right to expel these parasites. They report nothing good. With Berlusconi's channels you get good reporting presented by pretty girls. With this Dutchman you get only accusations.

He grabbed the phone as soon as it rang.

"My dear Guido," he said. "Thank you so much for calling."

"Recagno to you, Vinciullo," replied the flat, hard voice of the Mafia don. "What do you want?"

It must be the isolation, Ugo told himself. If he had any manners he is forgetting them. Even Mafia bosses should not speak to a President in this way. He was angry. Angry with the Dutchman who was making them look bad. Angry with Laura for forcing him to make this call. Angry with himself because of the fear he felt in his stomach.

"Recagno, we are in trouble," he said. "Your people are taking too much and giving too little. The immigrants need to be paid more and to have protective clothing. We have the world press looking at us. One Dutchman is already reporting it and soon we will have to answer the accusations."

He paused. The phone was silent.

"*Allo*," he said. "Are you there?"

"Go on," he heard. "You want some more of our money and you are afraid of a Dutch journalist. What else?"

Ugo realised he was not putting things correctly. He had not meant to talk about the press, just to push for a better share of the clean-up cash.

"The issue is that we need to reorganise…" he began but was cut off.

"We need to do nothing," said Recagno. "The arrangements stand. Dutchmen can be dealt with."

The phone went dead. Ugo realised his bladder was about to give way. He ran towards the toilet. Now what will I tell Laura?

****

Cesare opened his mouth to correct the old professor, then stopped and closed it. He looked up and realised the ENOL manager had seen him. He felt embarrassed, and it did not help when the ENOL manager winked.

They were seated in the back room of the Ristorante Antico Porto. Across the room from them the television was tuned to CNN at what seemed maximum volume. When they had been shown to the table Cesare had hung back, trying to take a seat out of range of the professor's bad breath. But somehow the smooth-looking ENOL manager had taken that seat. Now every time the professor turned to speak to him a gust of decaying garlic breath made him wince.

It wasn't just the breath. The TV was showing clips of the *Barbara S* oil spill, then it switched to a studio discussion with experts. One of them was the professor who was head of Woods Hole Institute. He was talking about all the studies his institute had done after big oil spills and how they had recently discovered worse than expected long term damage previously unnoticed around the *Deepwater Horizon* spill site.

"You must be very proud of your track record, Professor," he had heard as he flinched from the breath. That was when he had opened his mouth to point out that he was not from Woods Hole but from the University of Savannah. And then he had stopped himself speaking, because if this old fool thinks I am from Woods Hole, so much the better. As long as we get to sign a decent contract for co-research into this spill.

Cesare realised that the ENOL manager knew what he had been going to say, and also knew why he had not said it. But he wasn't going to kill the deal. What the hell is going on, he wondered?

The old professor from the University of Siracusa introduced them courteously,

"Professor Disario, this is Giuseppe Mammino, he is the head of ENOL here in Sicily. And my son-in-law. Giuseppe, this is Professor Disario, from the American university. He has come to help us study the oil spill."

He paused, signalling to the hovering waiter.

"Allow me to order? Yes, we will all take the *fritto misto* and a little sparkling water, thank you."

In the US of A we think guys drink wine in Sicily, Cesare said to himself. But what the hell, if I pull this off I can buy any wine I want.

"Giuseppe, it's great to meet you," he said, reaching over to shake his hand. "I've been to your office in Rome, with the team from the National Oceanographic Institute. They have told me how keen you will be to work with us to ensure that all the consequences of this spill are rigorously studied."

I didn't mention how keen they are to get a little science on their side just in case things turn nasty, he thought. He saw that Giuseppe was thinking, but before he could speak again Giuseppe was leaning in to the table and answering effusively.

"My dear professors, we are indeed lucky to have such a concentration of scientific knowledge at our fingertips," said Giuseppe. Cesare half thought there was a note of sarcasm, but his Italian was not quite good enough to be certain. "We at ENOL are of course very anxious to do what we can to mitigate this spill, and also to be seen to be doing everything possible. Only the most rigorous scientific investigations can ensure we achieve that. So I am delighted to appoint the University of Siracusa as our scientific advisors in this issue, and I am very pleased they can draw on your undoubted expertise, Professor Disario. Let us agree quickly. You prepare a proposed list of studies and associated costs and let me have those tomorrow. Tell me what we need to know and how we will find out. I will set up a budget for that. Is that OK? If so, we can enjoy our fish. It is a very good lunch here. And perhaps a glass of our excellent Purato Catarratto Pinot Grigio? It is a good Sicilian wine, not the pinot grigio we export."

Cesare could only nod and smile. He put his doubts about ENOL's motives away. He had suffered days of despair, traipsing round universities in Sicily and Rome, now within seconds he had landed a contract with the oil company and local university. The students will like this and the board will have to swallow it when I come home with the dough.

He did not notice the slight grin which Giuseppe Mammino permitted himself as he turned away to signal to the waiter. He did not know that they were celebrating another way for Giuseppe to get money from Rome, money which would look clean and some of which would stick to Giuseppe's hands on its way to fund this research. Let them look for what they like, Giuseppe was thinking. As long as they spend and Rome funds it, I win.

CHAPTER TWENTY-SEVEN

"I got the angle now, Luca. We godda get moving. The goddam streetcar is rolling and it's time to step aboard."

Giovanni Paci was stabbing the air insistently as he spoke and bouncing in his chair.

I hope he doesn't break my furniture, worried Luca Consentini. They were in his office. Giovanni had marched in and pushed the curtains wide. Luca had tried to close them a little. He preferred the more intimate light of shuttered windows and a desk lamp. Giovanni took no notice. His red hair contrasted with the orange tweed of his jacket. It would not look so bad with the curtains shut, thought Luca.

He was going to ask which streetcar Giovanni was intending them to travel on, but he was too slow.

"Look, Luca, it's like this. We got them on toast two ways, now we need the jelly," explained Giovanni. "ENOL is the oil company, right? They've already set up an office paying out to every bum who comes in. There's the IOPC and P&I office, who ain't so ready to pay but who are gonna pay in the end. So we got two places who want to pay, we just godda find the people who need our help to get their hands on the money. And that's where I come in. Because I've got a contact and I've got an idea. We're gonna get rich, my friend. By the way, you keep any cookies in this office, any coffee? Making money is thirsty work."

Luca rang for his secretary and explained carefully that his American colleague would like a coffee. But not a proper coffee, he wanted a large mug filled with water with a coffee poured into it. The secretary looked at Giovanni with horror.

Giovanni was pacing up and down the office now, his energy making Luca nervous.

"I met this guy, Disario, he's a professor in oceanography from Savannah. He's here on the money trail, got himself a sweet deal with the local university, and they are getting cash from ENOL. So here we go first off. This scientific stuff is long tail, they can keep pulling on the oil company tit for years. But to make that work they need to back it up with legal action against the insurers. ENOL has to do that to get paid, got it? They give out the cash now, get it back from the insurers."

He did not wait for a reply, just spun on his heel and paced back across the office, grabbing the coffee mug from the startled secretary who was carrying it on a small tray towards the desk.

"So here's our first in. We are gonna work with this Disario guy to make sure his claims for scientific study stack up legally, and we're gonna handle those claims against the Brits on behalf of ENOL."

He could see Luca was looking surprised.

"You got anything against working for an oil company, Luca? They got deep money."

Luca had a chance to reply as Giovanni took a swig of his americano.

"I have nothing against working for oil companies, Giovanni. But they will appoint their firm in Rome, who will then appoint a local lawyer. That's the way it works."

"That's the way it used to work before I got into town, Luca my friend," replied Giovanni. "I already got the signature of this guy Mammino here. He's the regional ENOL boss. He wants to keep this all in Sicily. Maybe he's got a motive, but that's not our issue."

****

Antonio Cusumano was rubbing his hands together. He could not help looking pleased with himself. Every night his Bar Duomo was full with free-spending journalists and contractors. All his hotels and *pensiones* were full and every room was let at double or triple the usual rate. Except to the thin French girl, he thought, rubbing his hands a little more. She is paying less for her room but I think she will know how to make up the balance, she knows the bargain. Better still, his wife was worked off her feet keeping the hotels going, which meant she had less time to shout at him. And less time to keep an eye on him, he said to himself as he wriggled slightly, picturing the French girl. Thin, but good breasts under that jumper, I think.

And in front of him was the cream on the cake. His accountant had wobbled his fat old body into the bar, wheezed as he squeezed into the corner table, and slobbered as he drank a small vermouth. Antonio did not mind any of that because he had brought with him the new accounts for the last three years. They had looked at them together. Last winter's official accounts had shown a small loss throughout the winter months. Not enough to arouse suspicion but enough to keep the Roman taxman's hand out of his pockets. And low enough turnover to keep the *pizzo* manageable and the Mafia happy.

Now in a splendid feat of creation the same period showed healthy earnings and full bookings at high prices, with low costs and a steady profit. Antonio had slapped the old accountant on his ample shoulder, sending the fat in his jacket into a shiver.

"You are a magician, a money wizard," he said. "Tomorrow I will go to the offices of the English insurers and get a claim form. You can help me to complete that. With this work of art as evidence we will get a good pay-out."

Antonio had taken the accounts with him behind the bar and was looking at them between serving customers. It seemed too easy. Were the English so stupid they would fall for this? He had heard they were paying, and so were ENOL. He rubbed his hands again, then looked up with a start.

Right in front of him the light was blocked by the square body of the Mafia enforcer. He could not help looking down at his accounts again, then up again to meet the cold, still eyes which did not blink.

"Good evening, Signor Cusumano," said the enforcer. "I came to give you a message from my cousin. He knows that your bar and hotels are full, so when I return tomorrow on my regular visit to your lovely bar he expects a significantly larger contribution. He asked me also to pick up your accounts. It is kind of you to anticipate my requirements."

Antonio could not move, and he could not speak. He stood frozen to the spot as the enforcer reached over the bar and picked up the open account book.

"Until tomorrow then, Signor," he heard as the enforcer turned theatrically to leave. "We will look at these tonight and discuss them with you tomorrow."

****

"My cousin is disappointed, Signor Cusumano." The voice was not much above a whisper. But in the damp silence of the cellar Antonio Cusumano could hear every word. "My family is disappointed. They have asked me to express their disappointment to you."

Antonio could not take his eyes off the open razor which the Mafia enforcer was stropping slowly, stopping every three swipes to feel the edge. He could not turn his head away because he could not move.

"In this way with you *incaprettato* you perhaps can concentrate on what they want me to tell you, Signor Cusumano," the enforcer went on. He did not seem to want a reply.

Antonio was lying face down on a table, his head pulled backwards by the wire around his neck so he had to look up. His knees were bent up behind him and the wire around his neck was tied to his ankles, which were firmly bound together. If he moved to stretch his legs the noose on his neck tightened. He was shivering with fear and he could smell his own shit. His bowels had let go when the enforcer had appeared suddenly as he had opened the bar that morning and hustled him down into the old cellars under the bar.

"In our village we tie up goats like this when we are taking them to slaughter," went on the enforcer. "It is an effective way to keep them quiet, don't you agree."

There was no question mark, just a flat voice and a steady sharpening and testing of the razor.

"It seems, Signor Cusumano," the voice went on, quiet and relentless. "That you have not been honest with us. You have enjoyed our protection for many years but you have not paid us for that."

Antonio whipped his head back, then it fell forward and he choked as the enforcer suddenly stepped closer to him.

"Worse than that, you have laughed at me, my shitty friend." The whisper was more intense now, full of hate. "You think I am stupid and cannot read accounts. You think I am a stupid peasant from the stupid mountain villages. But I am not as stupid as you, because you did not think that your accountant would be happy to explain your new accounts to me. He was quite happy to explain them last night. Quite happy once I had explained what would happen to his old wife if he did not. His wife would not look right with one breast removed. Don't you agree."

Still no question mark. Through his fear Antonio could sense that the enforcer was holding himself in. He wants to hurt me, he thought. What will he do with that razor? His bladder gave way and he felt hot urine flooding onto the table, soaking up into his shirt and trousers. He moved his legs slightly and felt the wire cut into his throat.

"It was for the insurers, just for the insurance," he screamed. "I have not lied to you. The books are false, for the English. I was going to give you a cut."

"Yes, a cut," was the menacing reply. "It is now you who will get a little cut. Just a small one, where only you will see it. Each time you piss you will see it. It will remind you to be honest with the people who protect you."

He felt the big hand pushing him onto his side. His arms were bound, he could not move and the razor was passing his face and going down towards his trousers. He opened his mouth to scream and a cloth was stuffed between his teeth.

He felt the hand tearing open his trousers but he did not feel the razor. He fainted when the first cut was made.

CHAPTER TWENTY-EIGHT

He couldn't have got the timing more wrong. But then he did not know that the Mafia boss had been told by the Regional President that he was causing trouble for everyone in the region. And he did not know that the Mafia enforcer had his name and knew what he looked like. Even if he had, he could not have foreseen that just when he decided he would go for a morning cappuccino in the Bar Duomo he would meet the Mafia enforcer coming out of the bar. An unhappy Mafia enforcer who had just punished the bar owner, but who was frustrated because he was working under very strict instructions not to go too far. The enforcer liked to really hurt people, but he had not dared to hurt Antonio more than he had.

"I want that fat bar owner so scared he will never try anything on again," his cousin had told the enforcer, his voice hard to hear down the mobile as the wind whipped across the dark mountainside he was calling from. "But I want him able to work, able to walk, able to earn money for us. And no marks that anyone can see. Got it?"

So the enforcer had a head of steam up and wanted very badly to hurt someone. He wanted to feel some bones crunch and see blood running.

Michiel did not know any of that. He had had a late night filing copy from his hotel room for three different websites in the US, and was getting more and more traction for his stories. He just needed some more proof of corruption for the story to catch fire. He was hoping the activists could help with some evidence, and that Simone would ease up and agree to help him today. She annoyed him, so naive, so married to her idea of marine purity she could not see their mutual advantage.

Now he was on his way for a coffee and croissant and he half hoped to see her there in the bar. He wondered idly if there was anything between her and bar owner. He had seen how the owner had looked at her. Surely she is not that silly?

He was conscious of someone inside the bar about to leave so he stood aside to let them pass. The door opened and he took another step back to make room for the squat muscular man who was pushing through it, head down under a fedora hat. He saw the man's head lift, and he saw a look of recognition on the man's face. Then he saw the cathedral dome wheeling across the sky as he was pushed violently backwards, striking his head on the stone cobbles. He did not see the enforcer take a small deliberate step sideways out of the bar door, to give himself room, and he did not see the enforcer swing his leg back before kicking him as hard as he could in the ribs.

The waiters in the bar could have seen the next kick, which Michiel felt as a crunching blow in his side. But they knew better than to watch, so they saw nothing. The shopkeeper opening his newspaper shop across the street could have seen, but he saw nothing. The Africans on their way to the contractor's office at the Municipio saw nothing either. Seeing nothing when a Mafia enforcer is administering a warning is a good way to stay healthy in Sicily.

****

There would have been a third kick, and a fourth, doing real damage to Michiel. But the kicks did not come. Michiel was bracing himself for the next impact when he heard a shrill scream and sensed that his attacker had looked up. He used the moment to try and stand but his legs would not obey him.

The local populace of Ortigia knew that it was healthy not to see a Mafia beating, but Simone did not. Even if she had she would not have cared. She had come into the square on her way to the bar for breakfast and seen the enforcer kicking a man on the ground. She screamed and ran towards them. No-one should be kicked like that.

The enforcer heard the mad foreign woman and looked up. Better to avoid a fuss with the police, he remembered. My cousin does not like having to pay the police to get me out when I go too far. Each time the price goes up. He looked down again.

"Just a little warning to watch what you write, buster," he said in English, straining for his best Godfather accent. Then he straightened his hat and walked away slowly. Fast enough to get out of the square and round the corner before the mad woman had every Carabiniere in town there, but slow enough to impress on anyone watching that this was his decision and he was in charge.

Simone was breathing heavily when she reached Michiel. He saw the surprise in her eyes when she realised it was him. Then he saw her smile.

"*Voilà*," she said, "it seems I am not the only one who needs help. This is a rough town."

Michiel could not see anything to smile about. His head hurt, his ribs hurt, and as Simone helped him to sit up he was suddenly and violently sick down his jacket. The attack had come out of nowhere, he felt disorientated. He hated not being in control.

"I know," went on Simone. "You don't want a doctor. But you do need help, so don't be the big tough man who will not be helped by a woman."

She was helping him slowly to his feet. His legs wobbled but her hand held him. Her thin arms were surprisingly strong and he was glad of the support. But he was angry and embarrassed at the attack, at being helped by Simone and by the vomit and blood mingling on his clothes.

Simone was brisk now. She looked around. The square was deserted. No faces showed at any window.

"We have to look after ourselves," she said. "You helped me, now I will help you. Where is your room? I will take you there. Come on."

The last words were a command and Michiel obeyed meekly. He pointed the way and leant against her as they set off across the silent square towards his hotel.

****

David felt washed out. His nose hurt, his head hurt, and he could not get Anna out of his mind. And each time he looked up from his desk his headache intensified. The queue was getting longer and longer, people were getting noisy, and he could see that his claims handlers were struggling. The four ex-Ghurkha soldiers the P&I Club had employed through a London agency to provide security were stretched as they tried to stop the crowd surging into the office.

It's all or nothing, he thought. We had huge queues, then they all went to hold out their hands to ENOL, now suddenly they are all back here again. I wish I knew what was going on. I wish I could understand these people. I wish I could see Anna. Why had she avoided him since they went up to the fort? What had he done?

Linus was moving officiously from one desk to another, picking up claims forms and files and making notes on a clipboard. His rimless glasses glittered as he marched around, ramrod straight and radiating disapproval.

I'll find out what is upsetting him soon enough, David told himself wearily, turning back to the report he was putting together to email to his head office that night.

Before he could rally his thoughts he sensed Linus approaching his desk. That was quick, said David to himself, and certainly sooner than I wanted.

"It's an American lawyer," Linus burst out. "Annoying chap, red hair, never stops talking."

"American, lawyer and annoying go together," replied David with a slight smile. "Sit down for a second Linus, and tell me what this particular chap has done to upset you."

Linus shifted busily from one foot to the other and remained standing.

"He has teamed up with the university and some American professor to dig up reasons for damages, and he is going round telling people he can get money for them from us and from the oil company," said Linus, outraged. "Today you have seen the queues. They are all submitting the same forms, very well completed and reasoned, and with a mass of supporting evidence. We have shopkeepers from the main road, we have window cleaners, we have pasta makers, we have a piano tuner, we have even had a lady of dubious virtue, I should say a whore, who claims to be out of pocket. This is organised fraud."

"Well, Linus," said David mildly, "there's your answer old boy. If it is a fraud we don't have to pay. And if it isn't a fraud we have processes to decide what to pay. Do you think I could finish this report? Perhaps we can agree to meet tomorrow with the senior claims handlers. We can look at the pattern of claims and take a view. Tomorrow, old boy, what do you say?"

He ended breezily, looking at Linus with a forced smile. He smiled a genuine smile to himself when he saw Linus tutting and turning away.

It must take him hours to get up in the morning, thought David. If everything isn't just so he can't function.

He turned back to the report. I must finish this. Perhaps I will see Anna when I go to the bank tomorrow?

****

Michiel's room was small and the only chair was hard and upright. Simone made him sit down and carefully pulled his jacket and shirt off. She crumpled them inside out and tossed them into his shower. He was quiet, letting her take charge. They had both noticed that the desk clerk was nowhere to be seen when they had entered the hotel. They were on their own. No-one would help them.

Simone looked around the small bathroom for something to use to clean up Michiel. She smiled to herself when she found a large packet of tissues and a pack of antiseptic nappy wipes. And as she expected, he had a small personal first aid kit. He is so fastidious, she thought. Ready for anything. Everything in the bathroom was neat and tidy. But he is not so neat and tidy himself now. Not so high and mighty mister know-all.

Michiel flinched slightly as she used a wet wipe to clean away the blood on the back of his head and then applied a plaster to the small cut.

"Lucky your hair is thinning," said Simone. "It is only a small cut from the pavement and this will stop the bleeding. Now let me check out your ribs."

The enforcer's heavy boots had broken the skin on one side of Michiel's chest and an ugly bruise was beginning to form. Simone made him flinch again, strongly this time as she probed his ribs with her long fingers.

"I cannot feel any broken rib here," she said. "You were lucky. Let me clean this up now and with some rest you will be OK. But you had better choose where you go for breakfast more carefully in the future."

He said nothing as she slowly and carefully cleaned up the cuts and dressed them. Simone was touching his muscles, cleaning the blood from across his chest. He has a good chest, said the voice inside her. Not too hairy, and he keeps himself in shape. What are you thinking, she could hear another voice, this is not the man and not the time to think that.

Michiel was very still, and Simone was suddenly conscious that the air in the room had become very thick. Her hand was moving more slowly, changing from an efficient wipe to a softer caress.

In her head the second voice was urgent. What are you doing? But she seemed to have lost control of her hands. Both of them were touching his chest, stroking it, and running up to his shoulders. She did not want to look up at him. She felt her face blushing. She was looking down and could see a bulge forming in his trousers.

Not so hurt after all, said the first voice. Stop this nonsense now, said the other. Her body was not taking any notice of either voice. She felt warm and liquid and her breath was shortening.

If Michiel had moved then she would have stood up and moved away. She would have been embarrassed and annoyed with herself. But he was still, rock still, and silent.

Her rebellious hands moved down his chest and over his stomach. Good and flat, said the approving voice. Don't be an idiot, came the reply. Her hands began to unbuckle his belt and her voice joined the rebellion.

"I think we need to check you out a little more," she heard herself say.

CHAPTER TWENTY-NINE

Fortunato had never been to the university before. He thought, as he walked through the courtyard, that perhaps this was a mistake on his part. The courtyard and corridor were full of groups of students. Most of them seemed to Fortunato to be very attractive young women. They were all wearing that winter's fashion of long thick tights and very short tops, leaving very little work for his imagination.

"There would be good fishing here," he said out of the side of his mouth, and the two fishermen with him laughed.

Fortunato saw the slow old porter who had met them at the entrance smile.

"You would have to climb over some of the professors," he said. "They are the ones who can give out the good marks."

The porter led them to a meeting room.

"Here are the Americans," he said. "Good luck trying to understand them."

In the meeting room Fortunato courteously greeted the old oceanography professor. All the fishermen knew him, he was often down in the port discussing catches, and they kept an eye on his research vessel when it was out at sea. It was he who had asked Fortunato to come to the meeting today. With him were two Americans. One was dressed in expensive yachting clothes and was introduced as Professore Disario, from America, and the other was an impatient looking bulldog of a man, who the professor introduced as "our lawyer Giovanni Paci, who will explain how we can help you."

Fortunato shook hands with both men and sat down. His two heavy companions sat each side of him.

"It is not how you can help us that I worry about," he said forcefully. "It is what you are doing to ruin us."

He turned to the local professor. "*Professore*, these Americans are bringing fishermen from outside Siracusa to claim for the oil. I have seen boats from Marzamemi, and yesterday from Portopalo. Tomorrow we will see them from Catania, I am sure. They told me these Americans are encouraging them to ask for money. It is our money, they have not suffered. But they will suffer if my friends get angry. They will wish they had not come here to steal from us. I hope it will not come to that. For the sake of your friends here."

He saw that the American professor flinched backwards as he understood the threat. But the lawyer did not flinch. He was bouncing in his chair, leaning in to speak almost before Fortunato had finished.

"You godda understand, Fortoonato, my friend, that there's no limit here. These guys get money, it ain't money you mighta got. The oil company has got a lot of money it wants to give away. They don't like having their filling stations attacked. Those British insurers and the old Swedish frog that keeps the books got no real limits either." Paci spoke urgently, jabbing his finger towards Fortunato. "We are using science, Fortoonato, to show how all the fisheries are being affected by the spill and by the use of dispersants. And the more fishermen we get who can't fish because the science says no, the bigger the claims get and the more we all make. You fish and you are happy if you catch a net full. This science is going to get you a boatful, every day."

Fortunato was not intimidated by lawyers or professors, and he did not like the way this excitable little man mangled his name and his language. But he liked money.

"Let me get this clear," he said. "You can show that the oil is affecting a much wider area than we can see. So you are helping these new people to make claims. That makes for a bigger cake. And with a bigger cake, you will help us to cut a bigger slice?"

"You got it, Fortoonato," said Paci. "We are bringing American expertise to the situation. Where I come from we think big. You gonna get more pasta. So be happy that these guys from Portopalo are here. Treat 'em as fellow sufferers."

And you will get richer the more people who claim and the more they claim, Fortunato said to himself. But if we get more, then fine. He looked at his companions, who nodded, and turned back to Paci. No-one was paying any attention to the two professors.

"Let's begin with us," said Fortunato. "We have our claim papers here with us. All the details of our boats. All the details of what the English and ENOL have paid us. Show me some more money. If you can do that then these foreign boats coming to our port may in fact not suffer any strange and unexpected accidents. But if there is no more money for us I fear that boats will burn tonight. My men are angry." He paused, just long enough for Paci to open his mouth to reply, then cut him off strongly. "Very angry."

****

Simone did not want to move. If I move he will wake up, she thought. What will I do then? How did this happen? I've woken up in the bed of this middle-aged corporate journalist. He will think I am a tramp. How could I be so stupid?

She wanted to hate herself, but she couldn't find the bad feelings she needed. Her body felt warm and relaxed. Though the curtains she could see it was bright daylight. We must have fallen asleep and now it is lunchtime. She almost giggled. Well, it wasn't all sleeping.

She remembered the sex now. The tension between them had been like a controlled explosion. He may be a patronising ice cold middle-aged suit wearer, she thought. But he knows how to please. Michiel had been courteous, controlled, urgent. She wriggled slightly as she remembered how she had undressed him. Those boys I date in Dunkerque are always ready to promise anything if they can get into my knickers. Then it's wham, bang but not even a thank you ma'am. Michiel didn't ask, but he gave and he wanted me to be there with him.

She had not realised that she had moved again, and she opened her eyes to see Michiel smiling at her. If he laughs I will hit him, she thought.

"It is a nice memory, I hope," he said. "For my part, certainly worth getting kicked for."

Simone could not stop herself. She laughed out loud.

"It must have been a surprise for you. It was certainly a surprise for me," she said.

They were both laughing now and there was no tension in the air. Then Simone saw him suddenly look serious. She stopped laughing. Here it comes, she felt the fear suddenly. The put down.

He was very formal, speaking in his Dutch-accented English.

"Would you mind very much helping me to get up? I really need to go to the toilet and my ribs are very sore," asked Michiel. "Then perhaps we can manage another surprise? You can kick me first if that is necessary."

For a second she was confused by the formality and the foreign language. She saw the worry appear in his eyes, and liked him for that when she realised what he was saying, and felt a surge of warmth.

She found the right words.

"You appear to be a gentleman so I would have been disappointed if you had not got another surprise in you," she replied equally formally. "If only as a way to say thank you for the help I provided this morning."

She could feel him hardening against her leg.

"I don't believe a kick will be necessary," she said.

****

In Brussels it was already dusk at four o'clock. But the lights shone brightly in the debating chamber and offices of the European Parliament. This dark January afternoon, five hundred and twenty-six of the seven hundred and twenty-three Members of the European Parliament were in the chamber. Of the rest, a sizeable number had not yet left the abundant lunch tables of Brussels' finest restaurants, eight were in hospital, five were suspended because of irregularities and no-one could track the rest because they were signed in as present but were in fact not.

Among the five hundred and twenty-six present, emotions were running high. The European Parliament was in a lather about safe shipping. There was not one single MEP with any experience of the global shipping industry, but that did not hold them back. Shipping is always a good target for European regulators because it is transnational and has no votes. A motion calling for strict new standards to apply to all ships sailing near European coasts had been tabled by one of the MEPs for eastern Sicily. She was putting all her personal assets into backing the motion.

Those assets wobbled dangerously in the very low cut top she was wearing. They had found her this job when Berlusconi had seen her presenting the weather on Sicilian TV and invited her to his Sardinian villa. She did not hesitate to deploy them to attract the attention and backing of the mostly male MEPs. Her party wanted to see the European Parliament acting on ship safety. It would take away the scrutiny of what the local authorities had done to create the mess of the *Barbara S*. The Sicilian MEP did not know the motive, and she did not know anything about the *Barbara S* incident except that it was on the TV every day and her constituents were upset about it. What she did know was that she liked this soft job with good expenses and she liked manipulating the men around her in the Parliament. So when the party asked, she gave her best.

She was in full flow, turning from side to side so that her assets could be appreciated from all sides of the chamber. Her anger seemed almost genuine, and her excitement sharpened the interest in ship safety of the men watching her. In her account, all these flag of convenience ships were dangerous wrecks that threatened the livelihoods and coasts of Europe. They had to be banned.

Across the aisle from her sat the MEPs elected as members for the UKOE party. UK Out of Europe had a lot of support in Britain, and was the natural home of red-faced men who liked their women busty. The UKOE MEPs were very much enjoying the show.

"I don't know about you, old boy, and I don't know about flags of convenience," said one in a stage whisper to his neighbour. "But if she is looking for support I'm more than up for it. Up already, in fact."

The smutty laughter that rippled across the UKOE group did not deter her. That was several votes she could count on for her motion.

And sure enough, later that evening, four hundred and twelve MEPs voted for stricter control of non-European flag ships. A year later the Council of Europe would quietly let the measure die, but the MEPs felt they had done their job.

****

Michiel tried to sound positive, but he guessed that he wasn't hitting the right note. He could tell that the foreign editor did not like what he was hearing.

"Look, Michiel," said the editor. "I'm in the newsroom here in Rotterdam and I can see on three different TV channels that they are reporting a catastrophe for Europe's birds as this oil spill hits the bird sanctuary at Vendicari. They've got pictures, they've got people filmed on oily beaches, they've got struggling birds. We've got our experts here lined up to tell us about the birds we will miss next spring here in the Netherlands. What we haven't got is an on the spot report from our on the spot man, because he keeps telling us about corruption stories. I don't want corruption. The readers don't think corruption in Sicily is news. My readers want to know if they are going to see a robin redbreast next spring or not. And that's what I want from you."

Michiel had not got the strength to argue. He wanted to say that the film of oily beaches was not at Vendicari. He wanted to say that the birds the editor could see on the television were not at Vendicari. He wanted to say that the oil had not yet reached Vendicari. But he was tired, his ribs and head hurt, and he wanted to be paid.

"OK," he replied. "You've got it. I'll hold on the corruption until I have a story and photos to blow your socks off. Tomorrow I'll get to Vendicari and file an eyewitness report. And I've got another angle that your readers will like. We have a lot of activists here from Northern Europe, some of them from the Netherlands, and they are right at the heart of the clean-up. I've got the leader, an attractive

Frenchwoman, to agree to an interview. It will be good human interest for the Saturday paper. What do you think?"

"I think you have begun to talk sense again, Michiel," said the editor. "Give me the oil, give me the birds and give me the sexy activist. Get a Dutchman into the picture, or better still a Dutchwoman if you can. Copy tomorrow by five?"

"I can do that," said Michiel, and cut the call. Now how am I going to tell this attractive Frenchwoman that she will be a feature in Saturday's paper? Did I really say that, he asked himself? She is not a woman anyone can take for granted.

CHAPTER THIRTY

Dino had taken an instant dislike to the American professor but he was doing his best to hide it. The Greek salvage master and the SCOPIC representative from the P&I Club were not being quite so diplomatic.

"Gentlemen," said Dino calmly, "and lady of course, I apologise, Mrs Jones, you are most welcome, can we focus on the issue please? We should not talk of interference. Our focus must be on getting the best outcome, and that may mean changing our plans if the science changes."

There will be no change as long as I am in charge, he thought to himself. But I can't afford to brush these professors off. They seem to have ENOL and the Ministry in Rome sewn up.

"Our very experienced salvage team from Kalargyrou has come forward with a detailed plan to seal the wreck of the forepart and to tap off the remaining oil. I think you have all seen the plan?"

Around the table in the Coastguard office were the salvage master, the P&I Club expert, the stuffy Roman manager from the oil spill contractors, some Coastguard officers, and Ugo Vinciullo and his staff. Kate Jones from ITOPF had joined the meeting at the last minute. The old oceanography professor from Siracusa University was sitting opposite Dino, and with him was Cesare Disario. His bright nautical clothes looked out of place. Everyone else was sombre in a suit or crisp in a uniform.

He probably thinks all Italians go to work in a designer shirt, Dino realised. We don't need this idiot, but I have to handle this carefully.

He saw them nodding, and went on.

"Now we are most fortunate to have with us a distinguished professor from the University of Savannah who is proposing further collection of data and more studies before we proceed with the plan. He has submitted an outline of a monitoring programme, and he has been funded by ENOL, the owners of the oil, to prepare this. He has a close liaison with the Ministry of the Environment. I think that it is important to listen to what the professor is suggesting, but it is also important that we do not lose this current window of good weather for setting up the operation. For that reason I have asked you to join me today, to ensure that we decide on a course of action which we can all support."

He gestured to Cesare. "Professor, the floor is yours, please outline your ideas and explain to us how you see the benefits of holding off before we act."

Dino sat back and let Cesare speak. He kept his face impassive. He is doing my job for me, thought Dino. Cesare was waffling about sub-sea plumes of oil and about the dangers of the oil getting released during the tapping process. Twice the P&I representative tried to break in, and twice Dino silenced him with an upraised hand. He wanted to let Cesare have enough rope to hang himself.

When Cesare tapered off and looked around the room with a smile Dino could see that no-one had been taken in. You will have to do better than that to convince a room full of professionals, thought

Dino. But I don't want to be the one to shut him out. My career is already broken, but Maria warned me only today that this professor has a lot of friends. I need friends of my own now, not enemies with friends who will be my enemies.

Help came from an unexpected quarter. Ugo Vinciullo spoke.

"Professor Disario," he said, "As Regional President I am delighted that we have your expertise here to supplement the local knowledge and to help our brave salvors. I of course, I say so modestly, am not an expert like yourselves here today. But as a politician I can help you. On the one hand we have our local experts who want to get to work. On the other we have an international expert who wants to collect more data. And for my part I have a coastline to protect."

He paused. Dino had to cover his mouth with his hand. He was afraid he might laugh. I have heard it all now, he said to himself. The man who stopped the ship going to shelter, the man who stopped the use of dispersant until it was too late, and now he talks of saving his coastline.

"If I may make a humble suggestion, we should listen to all our experts. So Capitano Cervetto, of course this is your decision, but my suggestion is that you give the go-ahead to the salvor's plan to seal off the wreck, and at the same time Professor Disario gets the permission he needs to set up increased monitoring. We cannot lose from taking action now but also watching what we are doing while the action proceeds. And if we learn something from the monitoring which makes us think we should change our actions, then we can take a different view."

Dino sensed everyone except Disario sitting back. They know they have what they want, he thought, and now so do I.

"Thank you, Presidente," said Dino politely. "As always you see to the heart of the issue. We shall proceed like that."

The meeting broke up and Dino was surprised to hear Ugo's voice very quietly just beside him as people were leaving. "Let him spend ENOL's money, Cervetto," he heard. "But if he tries to tell us here in Sicily how to do things then we will send him back to Uncle Sam."

Then Ugo was past him and shaking hands heartily with the two professors, loudly wishing them good luck with their endeavours.

One liar lying to another who knows they are both lying, Dino said to himself. Oil is easy to handle, politics is a lot dirtier.

****

The narrow street was noisy with children. The brightly lit stalls backed up against the stone walls each side were laden with toys of all sorts and the kids did not know where to look next. They were dragging their parents from stall to stall, skipping and sliding over the wet cobbles. For a second Bianca came into Michiel's mind. This should have been them, playing with an excited chid on Epiphany.

"Are you dreaming, Michiel?" asked Simone. She squeezed his hand and he came sharply back to Ortigia.

"I must be," he said, smiling. "I came here to report an oil spill and the waste and corruption that follows it and I have been seduced by a committed French environmentalist who is almost convincing me that saving birds is a good thing. Almost, but not quite yet."

Simone was suddenly serious.

"You joke," she said. "Because I took you to bed you don't take me seriously. But you do want my help now, if only to get a story into your newspaper. I should be more careful."

"To be accurate, you did not take me to bed. You jumped into mine," replied Michiel in a formal, deadpan voice.

Simone looked at him sharply. I am going to hit him and walk off, she thought. I have made a fool of myself. Then she saw he could not contain his smile and they both laughed.

"So, Madame Marine Bleu," said Michiel. "I am very happy that you did, and I am very happy to be walking with you now. But I have a suggestion."

He was conscious of Simone looking at him steadily. If I suggest going back to bed she will leave, he sensed. She doesn't trust me yet, and she is annoyed with herself.

"It is this. Let us leave the happy families to their toys and go to a quiet restaurant. There I will buy a bottle of good wine as a present to ourselves for Epiphany. While we drink it we will make a plan. A plan which will respect your point of view, respect my point of view, and which will allow us both to go back to work with a purpose tomorrow. You want to save birds at Vendicari, I want to continue reporting."

He paused. "And I want to go on seeing you," he said simply.

Simone was still looking at him, not showing any emotion. I hope I didn't get that wrong, he worried. Suddenly he felt like an awkward teenager.

"It is a little too early to talk of going on seeing each other," said Simone briskly. "We had sex, it was not an offer of marriage. But I agree with your suggestion. With good wine and good food we can make a good plan."

He sensed there was more coming. She was looking at him slyly now. She spoke quietly.

"And as your plan does not include going back to work until tomorrow, perhaps after we finish planning I may have another little suggestion."

****

Fortunato would never normally drink in the Bar Duomo. It was not a place for fishermen. It was a fancy place for tourists and politicians and bankers with too much money. But this evening he had come from the Municipio with a cheque in his hand. Finally an advance from the English insurers. The first bar he had seen was the Duomo. He felt good, he had money in his pocket, so he went in. I am as good as these fat cats, he thought. Now he was at home here. He had two warm *aperos* and two *grappas* in his stomach, and he might be warm in bed later as well. This Frenchwoman was happy for him to buy her drinks. And why not? He was rich tonight.

Simone had been in Vendicari all day. The oil was already lapping against the beach there. It was broken into tar balls and slicks by the dispersant spraying, but with no booms or other protection the oil that the waves brought was already fouling some birds. She had come back to Ortigia tired and angry. She wanted to tell Michiel about the oil, and the birds, but he had said he would be busy filing copy. I will not push him, she thought. I don't want to look needy. But I do need a drink and a meal.

Her group had dropped her at the entrance to Ortigia and gone on towards their hostel. She could have gone with them but was too tired. And their youth was getting on her nerves. When did I start to get old? she asked herself.

She pushed into the bar and smiled at the waiter as she took a small table at one side. He nodded and brought her a glass of wine. She asked for the menu of the day and was happy to feel the wine warming her.

"This is not such a good wine, Signorina," she heard Fortunato and looked up at him. He's big, she saw with a start, and a bit drunk. I don't need this corny chat up.

"I am a fisherman, a boat owner, and we like our good wine with our good fish," went on Fortunato. "Let me show you."

Before she could protest he had pulled out a chair and was shouting to the waiter to bring the best Nero d'Avola and plates of calamari and prawns. Simone was thinking quickly.

A fisherman with too much money and half drunk. Perhaps he will help with Michiel's story. She looked at him again. I don't think there's anything here I can't handle, she calculated.

"Well," she said smiling. "I am hungry and thirsty so that is kind. Tell me about your fishing boat. Surely you are not working now with this oil spill? Should you be spending money on women you do not know?"

CHAPTER THIRTY-ONE

"You are a strange man, Michiel," said Simone. She was not sure if she was going to laugh or get angry. "You want to report about corruption, we agree I will help you and I tell you I have met a fisherman who is benefitting from corruption. I know I can get a story from him. But you are not pleased. In fact, I think you are jealous."

"It's not jealousy," replied Michiel. She could see he was blustering now. "But this is a nasty place if you upset people and I don't want you to get hurt."

"Are you going to start telling me what I can do now?" Simone was suddenly and visibly angry. "One fuck and you think you have to protect me? How did I manage before you came along to look after me?"

They were sitting side by side on Michiel's bed. Simone had shaken off a very drunk Fortunato with a promise to see him again the day after. Then she had come straight to Michiel's hotel. She had lit up inside when she saw that he was pleased to see her. She had told him how Fortunato was boasting of all the money he was getting from the oil company and from the insurers, and how an American professor and an American lawyer were helping everyone to get more money.

His reply had annoyed her. Instead of getting excited and pleased at a new source, he was worried about her. Deep inside a voice was telling her that it is nice to have someone who cares about you. But Simone was used to fighting for her place in a male environment. Perhaps he really is as old-fashioned as he looks, she thought.

She pulled away from him and stood up.

"Perhaps you have a fluffy little wife at home," she said bitingly. "I will leave you to protect her."

He reached out his arm but Simone pushed it away and grabbed her coat.

"We have a plan, and we can follow it," she said. "In some ways we want the same thing. But I am not looking for a father. I will call you when I have more about the crooked fishermen."

She turned to the door, expecting Michiel to reply. But he said nothing, and she found herself walking quickly down the stairs and out into the street. *Merde,* she thought. I am not a drama queen. Why am I making a mess of this?

The fish and wine were churning in her stomach, and it seemed a long, cold walk alone back to her room.

****

The restaurant was tucked away in one of the tiny narrow alleyways that divide the tall yellow stone buildings on Ortigia. There was no menu outside and the discreet sign on the door said simply Casa Luigi. It was not a place for tourists, and Luigi's prices were not set for people who needed to ask how much things cost.

Tonight the five tables in the front room were all full. On a typical January day Luigi's wife would cook for five or six of his regulars, businessmen and politicians who came for her sea anemones, her tender young kid stew, her roast suckling pig, her delicate pasta and

Luigi's extensive wine list and gentle encouragement towards the best parts of it. But this oil spill was bringing money into town, and tonight his regulars were entertaining their friends. Luigi moved between the well-spaced tables, suggesting, guiding, joking, always making the diners feel a little special. In the kitchen his wife was working at full stretch, her two daughters called away from their families to help. Since they had moved here from Bologna they had prospered, but never like this.

He checked the front room was under control then slipped down the corridor to the private room at the back. Here there was only one table, round and crafted a very long time ago from deep-lustred rosewood. Luigi had found it at an auction. He guessed that this table knew a lot about how things worked in Sicily. And he knew it would learn a little more this evening.

He did not always know the people who ate in this room. Sometimes the phone call to reserve it would say only that there was a special guest. Sometimes the people looked rough and ate with real hunger. Sometimes they were politicians, sometimes men from the mountains, but pale looking, as if they spent too much time indoors. And always they ate the best food and were served the best wine and they did not get a bill. Luigi knew it was a small price to pay for a quiet life, good prices and products from his suppliers and a steady stream of well-paying custom for the front room.

Tonight he knew two of the four men in the room. Everyone in Siracusa knew Ugo Vinciullo, the Regional President. His florid face spoke of how often he ate and drank here. With him was Giuseppe Mammino, the ENOL man. Another regular. And two Americans who spoke bad Italian.

He tried not to listen as he laid out the small plates of delicate seafood *antipasti*.

"We are bringing the fish from the west of Sicily," he laughed. "I hear from my colleagues in Rome that they are complaining now in the Vatican that their delicacies are going up in price. That's because we are taking the best fish for Ortigia."

He was about to explain what was on each plate, but the red-headed American was already reaching in with a fork, spearing up the delicate balls of stuffed lobster and pushing them into his mouth. Luigi caught the eye of the President and held himself back.

He poured wine for the four men. He heard part of the conversation, Vinciullo was telling an elaborate story about power. He will have to be a little more direct, Luigi said to himself. I don't think these two visitors are getting the message.

Ugo had invited Giuseppe to the meal and asked him to bring Giovanni Paci and Cesare Disario along. He wanted them to understand who ran things in this area. He thought a good meal in a place of power and a subtle warning would be enough. Giuseppe knows how power works here, but foreigners perhaps don't. Let's just get these two Americans clear about what they can do and what they cannot, he had said.

Before Luigi brought the delicate multicoloured bow tie pasta shapes bathed in sage butter, Ugo had told a story about a shepherd who was confused about who was in charge of his flock. Was it him, or his dog, or was it the wolf on the hillside? He could see that either they did not understand the language or they were not open to the message. The lawyer, Paci, seemed more interested in getting some pepper sauce to put on his pasta. What the hell is pepper sauce? he asked himself.

I will have to be more direct, Ugo decided. They treat our best food with crudeness, so I will be a little crude as well. He waited until Luigi had cleared the pasta plates and signed him to give them a few minutes alone.

"Gentlemen," he said in English, not meaning the word at all. "I am pleased you can join us here tonight as our guests. Guests are always most welcome in Sicily. We have a tradition of fighting between ourselves but of being very hospitable to foreigners."

He paused. He had their attention now, even Paci had stopped cleaning out his teeth with a fingernail.

"That tradition works as long as the guests are guests. Not when they begin to try to change things here. We are a long way from America. A long way from Rome too. But we are very close to our powerful families. The families like only guests who respect their position. This can be an uncomfortable country for those who do not show proper respect, am I right Giuseppe?"

Giuseppe nodded, but Paci and Disario did not move. I've never had to be this direct before, thought Ugo. But they seem to be listening now.

"So tonight you will leave this room with a good dinner inside you. And good wine from Sicily to relax you. Paid for by our good families and protectors. Take also with you this message. Everything you do here is watched. Everything you do here must be to our approval. We run Sicily, not Rome, not the law, and certainly not Americans."

Better they don't answer. It was clear enough, even for them. He could see the shock on their faces.

He broke the tension. "Luigi," he called. "What has your lovely wife cooked for us tonight?"

CHAPTER THIRTY-TWO

Simone could feel Fortunato's leg brushing against hers. She was trying to look uninterested and sexy at the same time. I'm trying to channel Carla Bruni, she laughed to herself, but she was listening hard.

She could just about follow the rough *Sicilianu* that the fishermen were speaking. They clearly thought that this French bird that Fortunato was showing off was too dumb to understand, but Simone was used to being in noisy groups with activists from all over Europe. With a good grasp of Spanish and Italian she could get the sense of the *Sicilianu*. I won't take any chances, though, she thought.

"What are they saying?" she asked Fortunato naively.

"We are speaking *Sicilianu*, Simone," he said. "It is our first language, but no-one can understand it outside Sicily, so it is dying out. These guys are just bitching that they are not getting as much compensation as us, that's all."

She smiled but spoke only to herself.

And they are talking about your chances with me. Which are zero, but you don't know that yet.

They were crammed around a table in a small trattoria on the quayside at Portopalo. Fortunato had invited her to see the coast with him. As leader of the fishermen in Siracusa he was going to talk with his colleagues in the fishing ports down the coast. She had accepted, and been shocked to see how broken down the ports were. Portopalo was dirty and grey, dominated by an old warehouse and processing plant. From where she was sitting she could see wrecked boats rotting in the mud and the whole port looked tired and neglected.

"Do they make a good living normally?" she asked.

"Not so bad," said Fortunato. "But it is a few bigger boats that get all the catch here, so the small, old boats are pushed out. The fish farms are killing them too. They get EU money. These boys get subsidies from Rome, but now they want to find a way to show they were earning big time, so they can claim loss of the fishery from the insurers. I'm telling them about the Americans. I can get that red hair down here and he can help them."

You are telling them that, she thought, but you are not translating what they are saying. Which is that the fish farms have all been protected by Castalia Mareazul, but the owners are going to wreck the protection so they can get cash too. There was a rumble of anger as one of the old men explained this. They don't like the fish farms, realised Simone, they take their jobs.

The anger ebbed as Fortunato explained to the locals that the money was a bottomless pit. "Let the fish farms have a share," he said magnanimously. "You will not go hungry if you listen to the American. Tomorrow I will bring him here to meet you. Now I have other business."

Simone knew exactly what the envious glances meant but she did not react. I have to tell Michiel about these fish farms, she thought. He can photograph them before they have a chance to damage them, and watch for sabotage. So I need to get back to Ortigia.

Then I'll have to tell Fortunato he will have to wait a day. He'll be alright if he thinks he is on a promise.

She squirmed slightly. If I can make things right with Michiel then he won't have to wait. And tomorrow I'm going to be out of town, cleaning birds at Vendicari with the others. Tough luck on this idiot fisherman. She gently moved away and stood up.

"Shall we go back to Ortigia?" she said with a smile.

****

Michiel parked the car below the crest of the hill, out of sight of the coast. He had driven forty kilometres south of Siracusa, past Vendicari and the fishing port of Marzamemi, to the small gulf which sheltered the fish farms just north of Capo Passero. The badly kept narrow road snaked between uncultivated fields, moving in and out from the coast. There were no villages here, just wasteland. When he had seen the road turning towards the coast he had pulled over and tucked the hire car into a gateway. There were no buildings around, and he had not seen another vehicle for ten minutes.

Hitching his camera bag onto his shoulder Michiel walked quickly along beside the stone wall. He did not feel threatened but he did not want to be seen. These photos would be dynamite if the fish farms were fouled.

Where the road slipped over the edge of the hill the bay opened up in front of him. On the still grey sea Michiel could see the fish farms. Nets, walkways, piles in a dense black pattern of dots above the water reached out from the shore into the middle of the sheltered bay. There was no oil on the sea, but Michiel knew it would reach down this far south any day now. Below him, at the water's edge, he could see the ugly breeze block warehouse which he supposed was the fish processing plant.

He stood by the wall, hidden from view by a large blue sign sporting the EU stars symbol. Pacino Principiale Mariniere, it said. Fish farms financed by the EU Regional Development Fund. He grunted and put his camera bag down. He could not see any sign of life at the fish farm, but he did not want to take any chances. He needed the longest lens for this, he did not want to go closer.

The EU funding notice made a good support for his camera and long lens. The Nikon SLR was old, first generation digital, but it produced terrific shots. The only drawback is how heavy it is, and how fiddly to change the memory card, he thought, as he zoomed in for his first shots.

Michiel was in automatic now, systematically zooming in on the booms which were secured in a double row across the bay, protecting the fish farms. Simone was filling his thoughts. She had come to see him the night before. She had been excited, animated. The news of the plan to foul the fish farms had tumbled out. He could see she was pleased with herself. She could have called my mobile, he had thought. But she chose to come and see me. He was trying to listen to what she said, trying to work out what that meant, and trying to suppress jealousy and fear. She shouldn't be putting herself at risk with these fishermen. Not for me. But he could not say it. He was afraid she would get angry again.

The tension in the small hotel room had been unbearable. They spoke to each other formally and kept a distance between themselves. Michiel wanted to take Simone in his arms. He wanted to thank her, he wanted to say she should not take risks. He wanted to take her to bed. Badly. But he was afraid to make the wrong move and he did not know what the right move was.

Finally Simone had left. It was an awkward parting and they did not kiss. Michiel had not slept well, thinking of what he should have done. I should have told her I want her. I am sure she wants me. I have to find out how to get close to her. He decided to call her that night and ask if they could start again.

He relaxed back from his crouched stance and ran back through the pictures. It took a few minutes as to swap the memory card for a second one, then he reshot the key points of the oil defences onto the new card, just to be sure. The pictures were clear, and positive proof that this fish farm could not be hurt by any oil coming in from seaward, unless there was a major storm. It's good stuff, he thought, and Simone will be pleased when I tell her I have the evidence. She is a tough woman, she took risks, but I can show her they were worth it. I have to show her how I am grateful.

Thinking of risks made him glance around. No-one to be seen, he thought, and packed the camera and lens carefully before walking efficiently back to the car.

No-one to be seen when he looked, but if he had glanced up earlier he would not have missed the boy who was watching him from the curve of the road, and who turned his bicycle swiftly and rode away back down the hill. No-one to be seen, but if he had not been absorbed thinking of Simone and how he could call her that evening he might have been more careful. He might have noticed the motorcycle that joined the traffic behind him as he approached Ortigia, and he might have noticed that it stayed with him until he parked his car and shadowed him until he reached his hotel. But he noticed nothing, because all he could see was Simone, and all he could think of was how he could make things right with her.

****

"It is the starfish story," Simone explained. She saw the baffled look on the face of the old warden.

"It is the story that first made me want to help birds in trouble," she explained. "Yves told me it, when we were setting up Marine Bleu, and it is everything I need to do what I do. The story is that there was a stranger walking on the beach in Madagascar. It was low tide, and as the tide went out it had left thousands and thousands and thousands of starfish stranded in the baking sun. The stranger began to bend down and throw the starfish back into the cool sea, one by one. A local villager saw him and said, 'Why do you do that? There are so many, you cannot make a difference.' The stranger bent down and threw another one into the water. 'I made a difference to that one,' he said."

The warden smiled slowly as he took the story in. Simone was speaking half Italian and half French, but they had built a good understanding.

"We are making a difference here too," he said. There were twenty young activists there today, each busy helping to clean oiled birds. Simone had shown them how to set up a cleaning station and the warden had helped them set up tables and safe holding areas for the oiled birds in the old tuna factory.

Simone wanted to smile back, but she could not. She was pleased to be working with the warden and the youngsters. Pleased to be helping the birds which were increasingly getting oiled as more streaks and tar balls invaded the narrow beach separating the bird lagoons and the sea. But she was angry with Michiel, and the anger filled her head.

He could have called me last night. I gave him the opportunity, I let that filthy fisherman think he was going to shag me, and he doesn't even tell me how it went. All day the day before her mobile had been off, they did not want to scare the birds, and in any case there was very little reception at the bird reserve. But in the evening she had walked up to the road where the signal was strong. All the activists were camping at the reserve now, and Simone camped with them, but she did not want to miss Michiel. So while they made a fire on the beach and sat quietly passing a bottle of wine, she trudged up the dark lane to the main road.

There was a signal, but there was no text message from Michiel and no missed call. Simone waited in the dark, cold and afraid. I am a fool, she thought. A fool to take him to bed and a fool to be here in the dark and cold. "He is a fucking bastard *merde* pig," she had said out loud. But still she wanted her mobile to come to life and to hear his voice. It stayed silent.

Today she worked mechanically. Her mobile was off, she had no way of knowing what Michiel was doing. She told herself not to think about him. It did not work.

CHAPTER THIRTY-THREE

"You are a man of many questions, Mr van Roosmalen," said the neatly-suited public relations consultant. He spoke perfect English with a mid-Atlantic accent. "But finally there is only one more question. Shall we put you in feet first or head first? My good friend here prefers feet first, it takes longer for you to die. But the rest of us prefer head first, it is quicker and we do not have to listen to your screams for so long."

He was speaking loudly, forced to raise his voice over the noise of the log chipping machine which was idling behind them.

"Of course," he went on relentlessly. "The fish do not mind. Either way they get a good protein supplement."

Michiel heard the Mafia enforcer behind him snigger. His arms were bound tightly to his sides and his ankles were also taped together. He was lying on the concrete floor of what he had taken to be the fish processing shed when he took the photographs. Now inside he could see that there was no processing machinery, just some sacks of fish food and this industrial diesel-driven mincer which fed into the fish food holding tanks.

"You cannot do this," he said. "The police will trace me, and I have sent my pictures to a safe place where they will be found. You cannot get away with this."

He tried to struggle but could only wriggle on the hard floor. It was cold and he felt the roughness of the concrete along his body.

"Ah, Mr van Roosmalen, you are a great believer in doing things right." The man was laughing now. "And so are we. So are we. We very publicly came to your hotel to invite you officially to visit our fish farms. I am very definitely and publicly well known as a public relations consultant for many businesses here in Sicily. The police know exactly what sort of businesses. But you did not know the sort of business I work for, and it was most kind of you to come here today. Of course, you could not refuse, because you did not know that we already knew that you were here yesterday. That you were here yesterday spying on us. Taking photographs without our permission. But we have answered your questions, have we not? Even the ones you did not actually ask me. Yes we are run by the Mafia, yes we lose money on the fish but we make a lot more from EU and regional grants. And yes we plan to damage the defences and spill oil onto our fish. They are not making much for us, so with oil on them they will make more. I feel we can claim a lot. So you have the answers. And later today a man who looks very like you will drive back to Siracusa wearing your jacket and carrying your bag. He will leave the car where you normally do and will walk back to your hotel and leave the bag in your room. So the trail will end there, not here. You will end here, but only the fish will know that."

Michiel did not reply. He was cursing himself. I am facing death, he thought. But I don't feel fear. I feel anger. I'm only angry with myself. Angry that I was so absorbed researching these fish farms on the internet that I did not call Simone until too late last night. Her phone was off when I called and I did not know what to say in the message. Bianca always got angry because I forgot time when I got stuck into a story. Now I have let her down, and I have let Simone down. I have walked into a trap like a naive fool, and she will never know that I wanted to get closer to her.

"Can I make a call?" said Michiel. "It is to a woman. Just a message. It will be important to her."

"No, Mr van Roosmalen, you may not," replied the consultant patiently. He might have been discussing a contract he did not care much about winning. "You have already caused us trouble with your articles. You have ignored a friendly warning from our friend here. I am afraid you are out of options."

He signalled to the two oilskin-clad workers who had first pinioned Michiel's arms when he had walked into the shed, and who had stood there looking into space while he was bound by the Mafia enforcer. Michiel had recognised him as the man who had knocked him out and kicked him, but he had not said a word until now. Now he stood aside as the workers picked Michiel up horizontally. They waited. The enforcer pushed forward the throttle on the wood chipper and the noise of the motor and grinding teeth filled the shed as it accelerated.

"Feet first," he said.

****

His words were going round and round in her head. What did he mean? Was he going to push her away? If he is going to do that I won't give him the chance, Simone ordered herself. I will not give that dried up workaholic the satisfaction of using me then dumping me.

He doesn't mean that though. He wants to see me. He was busy, I was out of contact, he is busy again tonight, I have to give him a chance. She remembered what she had done when she had washed his chest and taken him to bed, and she blushed. There was no-one to see her and it was pitch dark, but she looked around guiltily, afraid someone would notice.

"Where the fuck is he now?" she said viciously. I'm going mad, talking to myself, she thought. She stabbed his contact on the phone again, but again it went straight to voicemail. *Merde!*

All day she had worked with the birds. The warden and the other activists had sensed she did not want to talk so they had left her alone. She worked efficiently, her long fingers cradling the oiled birds and carefully swabbing the oil from their feathers. Every water bird that summered in North Europe was here in Sicily for the winter. Too many will not be back next summer, thought Simone. This is a mess. How can we change things so that birds are not made to suffer like this? But her mind was not on the birds, it was on Michiel.

In the evening she had waited and eaten with the others and even joined in while they laughed around the fire. But finally she could not bear it any longer and she had walked up the road in the dark until she was out of earshot of the reserve and had a phone signal. Her heart leaped when she saw a missed call and a message from Michiel. Both were timed at midnight the night before.

"Er, hi Simone, this is Michiel," she heard. "I, er, wanted to talk to you. I'll call you tomorrow. Er, call me if you get a chance."

Very helpful, typical man message, she told herself. He is so stereotypical. Has to say it is him, when every idiot knows who it is because the phone says so. But no useful information. Is he well? Did he go to the fish farms? Did he wake up this morning and wish I was in his bed? And now when I call him his phone is off.

She felt frustrated. I can't wait here in the dark until his lordship decides to answer me.

She dialled again and left a message. "Michiel, you need to think up a good reason why you are not there to take my call. Tomorrow I will come back to Ortigia to arrange more supplies for the team here in Vendicari, we are busy here. I will try to see you and I will try to listen to your excuse."

She set off back to the reserve. Let him figure that out, she said to herself with satisfaction. And I hope there is some of that red wine left.

****

David was baffled. How had this happened?

The neatly suited man had come quietly into the claims office and from an expensive looking briefcase produced a thick dossier. It was a fully detailed claim supported by photographs and accounts. And it was so big that David's claims handler had asked the man to wait and taken the file straight to David.

David glanced through the file and asked the claims handler to show the man to his desk. He had introduced himself in perfect English with a mid-Atlantic accent as a consultant working for Pacino Principiale Mariniere.

"That is the fish farms complex just above Capo Passero," he said. "I am so sorry to bring this claim to you but it is a disaster for us. Our fish stocks are dying in the oil, and many local people will lose their livelihoods because of this dreadful oil spill affecting our farms."

"I know where the farms are," said David. "At a recent planning meeting with the Coastguard the state oil spill contractor Castalia Mareazul assured us both that it had deployed extra precautions to protect your nets. The whole bay was to be protected. We know how important the farms are economically. So I am at a loss to understand how they can have been fouled."

The consultant looked mournful.

"Indeed you are correct, Mr Chillingworth," he said sadly. "We have both been let down by the state contractor. We relied on their expertise and equipment, and indeed they spent a lot of time and I presume a lot of your money installing equipment. Tragically it has failed, and with the first of the oil and a few small waves we have seen the labour of years written off."

He looks as if he will cry, thought David. This is just too fishy to be true. We need to take a really tough look at this one.

"Well," David was scratching his head. He was embarrassed because he did not want to say to the man's face that this was an obvious fraud. He could see the consultant was enjoying his discomfort. He became very British. "We shall pass the file to our experts and they will be in touch for an onsite inspection. It does seem jolly unreasonable, I must say."

"Mr Chillingworth, if you have invested millions of euros in a fish farm venture to bring a little prosperity to a poor island and then a sinking tanker writes off your investment, it is indeed jolly unreasonable, as you say," said the consultant, with a perfectly straight face.

He is laughing at me, David realised. I'll do my best to see through what is going on here.

He stood up to indicate the meeting was over and politely shook the man's hand. It felt cold, almost clammy, and David wanted to go and wash.

"We will be in touch," he said.

"We will, Mr Chillingworth, we will," came the reply as the consultant strolled out of the room.

Bloody man got the last word now, thought David. But I'm going to do my best to make sure we get the last word in the end.

****

"Gentlemen," said David Chillingworth. "I've asked you to come here today for this meeting because I believe we have to act together. We are facing a claims tsunami which is getting worse every day. I'm afraid that only by working together can we contain this."

He had hardly stopped speaking when Giovanni Paci leant forward and answered sharply.

"We don't need to contain nothing, Mr C," he said aggressively. "You guys need to contain the oil. You get a handle on the oil that's hitting all these poor folk and you got a chance to get a handle on the claims. Co-operation ain't part of this. The old lady who can't sell her postcards no more, she don't want to co-operate. She wants compensation. The fishermen gotta put shoes on the feet of their kids, they don't want no co-operation because co-operation don't pay no bills."

David was taken aback. He had called the meeting because this American lawyer, Paci, was behind many of the new claims, and because he could see that confusion was building up with what ENOL was paying out and what they at the P&I claims office were paying. It seemed only sensible to him that the parties most involved should talk the issues through.

Across the table from him were Paci and Giuseppe Mammino, the ENOL manager, and beside him was Linus Eerlandsson, the IOPC director. David glanced at him. He was seated very square to the table, his hands in view and fingers steepled together. He was careful to avoid David's eye.

I don't know why I look to him for help, said David to himself. All he does is moan about the legalities and the paperwork. I want to tackle the issues.

David looked at Giuseppe Mammino.

"It is a matter of fair play, I think," he said mildly. "Don't you think?

It's not fair to encourage all sorts of people to claim who may never get anything, or who may ensure that the legitimate claims of some of the badly affected people have to be reduced pro-rata. This is not a bottomless pit of money, after all."

David was still looking at Giuseppe and expected him to answer. He had not seen the increasing look of disbelief on Paci's face. He was taken aback again by the sudden vehemence of his attack.

"You godda hand it to the limeys," said Paci. He waved his arm around to take in the others. "I guess it's that full English you have for breakfast, what the hell is that? Where's the fair play in you guys running an old tanker into the ground and then spilling oil all over this island? And where's the limit on payments, who the hell are you to tell us there is a limit? When the courts get done with you there ain't gonna be no limit, let me tell you. British Petroleum ain't seen the limit yet in Louisiana, we got the Brits over a barrel there, and I guess these guys in the Sicilian courts don't do no fair play fancy shit neither."

There was a sudden silence in the room. It was broken by a dry cough from Linus.

"Strictly speaking, you may in fact have a case that there will be no limit, but it is most unlikely," he said very formally. "Personally I think we should rely on due process and correct administration. Emotional involvement will not help us or the claimants."

"No shit," said Paci. "So why are we here then?"

He was getting up to leave when Giuseppe spoke. His voice was reasonable and inclusive.

"Let's not be too hasty, Signor Paci," he said. "We all have different priorities, but that is no reason for us to fall out."

David thought he saw a sharp look pass between Mammino and Paci, who sat back down. Surely they should be on different sides, he queried. Paci wants to rape ENOL as much as he wants to rape us. It doesn't make sense for them to be in this together.

"Look," went on Giuseppe, smiling, "We have a particular problem, which is that we are an Italian oil company spilling Italian oil from an Italian ship onto Sicilian beaches. So we are dealing with an emotional subject, and one with political and regional pressures. We at ENOL cannot afford to sit back and leave this to you to handle. We have to be seen to act, and to help people. Reputational damage will cost us much more if we do not pay a little over the top here. I think you can understand that, David. May I call you David? Thank you. For me it is always a pleasure to work with the British. So I am open to your proposals."

David began to lay out his ideas for co-operation on claims handling. He could see Paci fidgeting.

I'm wasting my time, he realised. But I'm blowed if I'll let the nasty little fellow out of here until he has at least heard me out.

CHAPTER THIRTY-FOUR

There had not been any girls at David's school. I wish there had been, he thought. I need someone to ask what I say now. If I had some girls as friends I could call them. For a second he considered going back and asking one of the claims handlers who had come over from his London office. They were bright, confident women who scared David a little. Better not, he thought.

He ran his fingers through his hair and went into the bank. He had dressed carefully this morning. His red shirt with a white collar, pinkish tie and neat blazer looked rather good, all things considered, he had told himself. He had polished his brogues, and once they were laced up he had felt more prepared. But now he was afraid again.

The clerk looked up and smiled at him.

"Hello, Mr Chillingworth. Take a seat and I will fetch the manager," she said.

He felt a surge of relief. That means Anna. I won't have the embarrassment of having to ask to speak to her personally. He smiled his thanks and moved over to the waiting area, then sucked his stomach in as he saw the door to the back office opening.

He was stepping forward with a big smile on his face when he realised it was not Anna. It was a woman he did not know. Smart, professional, good looking, he noted. But not Anna.

"Good morning, Mr Chillingworth," she smiled. "May I introduce myself? My name is Marlena Dozio. I will be handling all the club moneys from now on."

David was frozen to the spot. He saw the look of confusion on her face and glanced down. She was holding out her hand, waiting to shake his. Embarrassed, he flushed and took her hand, shaking it with too much force.

"Oh, er, I'm er, glad to meet you, Marlena," he said. "But what about Anna, she was handling our accounts?"

He knew he sounded too eager and felt foolish.

"Anna took a transfer," she replied coldly. She was shaking her hand ruefully. "Perhaps to avoid your handshake, Mr Chillingworth. Now, please come into the meeting room, and we can make a start."

****

The old lady in the reception of Michiel's hotel had not looked at her when she asked for him. She had simply handed over the room key and looked away.

She thinks I'm a whore, thought Simone, suddenly angry. Why did I get tangled up with this man?

She knocked on the door and waited, then let herself in. The bed was made and it had not been slept in. She looked around. Michiel's canvas shoulder bag was on the desk and his camera bag was on the bed. His car keys were beside the bag. Something made her pause. Her heart felt suddenly small as fear ran through her. Michiel did not put his things in here, she realised with a start. The bags and keys had been tossed down casually. Michiel would have unpacked the bag and arranged his things neatly.

She felt the hair on her neck stand up and she looked around. Was there someone here? She took two paces and picked up the shoulder bag. Inside was his phone, but not his notebook. The phone was off. What the hell was going on? She reached for the camera bag. The camera was there, and she turned it on, pushing at the buttons to find the picture files. There were no pictures on the card.

She was scrambling now, panicking. Something has happened. He must have gone to film the fish farm. But where is he now? She held his phone button down. Typical of Michiel to have an old-fashioned Nokia phone, she thought. And not to lock it with a pin. So careful, so meticulous, and just a little less worldly than he thought he was.

There were missed calls and messages on the phone. One from her, and one from someone called Bianca. Simone listened guiltily. She must be his wife, she thought, although she does not sound as if she loves him. She could not understand the Dutch but she guessed from the harsh tone that his wife was asking where the hell he was.

Simone looked in the shoulder bag again. There was his wallet, with cash in it, and credit cards. I should not look more, she told herself, but she did. In the wallet was a photo of a woman. Dark-skinned. Young. She is beautiful, said Simone inside herself, feeling a stab of jealousy. That must be Bianca. She stuffed the photo back into the wallet, and her fingers touched something hard. She pulled it out. It was a photo card.

She was fumbling as she slipped the card into the camera and scanned its contents. She felt her breath catch. There were clear shots of the fish farm and all its protection.

Simone almost dropped the camera. They must have seen him, and somehow they have taken him away. This is my fault. If I hadn't been so pushy and clever to get the fishermen to talk, if I had just left him alone, he would be here. Now they must be hurting him. They warned him once, what will they do now?

****

The Carabinieri Sergeant was not trying to hide his mirth.

"There is no need to get angry, Signora. Calm down. I am writing down your problem, Look, here I am writing it."

He looked up at Simone, who was tense and almost hysterical on the other side of the police station reception counter.

"Let me go through it again. You have lost a man. He is not your husband, not your brother and if I understand correctly, not quite your boyfriend. He is a Dutchman, who is very neat, and his name is Michiel, but you cannot remember his surname. You think he has been taken by the Mafia because he did not sleep in his bed last night. You know this because you have been in his hotel bedroom and because he has not answered your phone messages. You want us to find him."

He is making me sound stupid, thought Simone. How can I make him understand?

"Do you not think, Signora, that there is another possibility? Siracusa is full of men from Europe these days, all with money to spend. So it is also full of women who can help them with that. And if I am not mistaken we know you as well. You were leading the demonstration. There are many women in your group. Some are quite young and pretty. Younger even, and perhaps more beautiful than you, Signora, if such a thing is possible. Is it not also possible that this Dutchman, who is not your husband and not perhaps your boyfriend, has found another lady to accommodate him?"

"You don't understand, he was researching an important story of corruption."

Simone heard herself and realised she was screeching. It sounded ugly.

"You may have been watching too much of the handsome detective Montalbano TV shows, Signora," said the Sergeant, dismissive now. "Because we are in Sicily you think everything is corrupt. We have work to do. If you are short of a man my colleague will no doubt be willing to help you. Otherwise come back if you find a body."

Simone was struggling to follow the Italian. She heard the words help and colleague and for a second thought she had got through. Then she realised what he had said. One of the two Carabinieri standing close to her had reached out a hand and was running it down her bottom. He was laughing.

"It will be a pleasure to help you, Signora," he said.

Simone leapt back and slapped his hand away. She turned and ran out of the police station. Behind her she could hear the laughter. She was glad she could not understand what they were saying. She felt dirty and anger was making her stomach contract.

Michiel was right, she realised. The authorities will never help. But the press can. She began to run back towards his hotel.

****

The anger was hardening now, turning into a steel resolve. Simone sat on Michiel's bed and took deep breaths, consciously slowing her breathing. I am not going to let Michiel down, she told herself. And I am not going to let these men make me look stupid. I'm going to prove what he was doing and expose this corruption. She felt a tiny spark of hope. And get him out of wherever he is, she thought.

She looked up at the crucifix on the hotel wall. I would pray too if I believed it would help, she said aloud. But you were a man, she said. I don't suppose I would get much help.

When she had arrived panting and red-faced back at the hotel from the police station the receptionist had again handed her the key without a word. She knows something, thought Simone. She knows, but it is useless to ask.

In the room she had gone carefully through Michiel's phone contacts. She found the editor of the Herald Tribune and of the Dutch paper he had mentioned. Two calls later she had heard the same message twice.

"Michiel is not on our staff. Yes we know him, and yes we know he was trying to build an oil spill corruption story. But we cannot help you find him and with no evidence there is no story. A journalist out of touch for two days in Sicily is not a story either. Please give him our regards when you find him." Different words but the same indifferent message each time. She was on her own.

"Useless bastards," she said out loud. Sitting in your warm newsrooms in lovely safe and quiet Holland. Going home to your little wives tonight. You don't believe me. You don't know that Michiel is caught somewhere. They will be hurting him. Oh Jesus, she said as the thought hit her, I hope they have not killed him.

Simone banged her heels against the bed and went through her options. Then she stood up and packed Michiel's camera. She pocketed his car key. She knew what she would do.

****

Linus tapped the file twice before passing it to his left. The young claims handler waiting beside him added it to a growing pile.

"Our tenth fishing boat this morning, David," said Linus. "It is not yet ten o'clock and we have okayed twenty-eight claims to make a provisional payment on. We are in fact a money factory with a well organised production line."

His voice was flat and his face expressionless.

Why does he always do that double tap, thought David? And why can't I tell if he is complaining or giving himself a compliment for setting up a good system? Prissy sod. I think he is winding me up.

He decided to ignore Linus. They were holding the daily claims meeting. Today he, Linus and the senior claims handlers were joined by Kate Jones from ITOPF and two of the P&I Club expert surveyors.

"We turn to this fish farm claim," he said formally. "It is the largest single claim to date from a private company. It is well documented. But it feels wrong to me. I am sure these farms were well protected and there seems to be just too much pollution there too quickly."

He turned to Kate.

"Kate, I know you have no official role in this but you are the most experienced of us here." He was conscious of Linus snorting but he went on. "Have you had a chance to look at this?"

"David," she said. He could hear that she was angry. "I'm with you. I think they are having you over. But I'm buggered if I can see how they've done it. We know the contractors protected the farms, but my people didn't get down there to photograph the defences in time. We thought we had a day or two more before any real oil got down there. So we can't prove the defences were in place and properly done. And to be honest, we can't discount a tongue of oil on a rogue current reaching there when they say it did. It's not very bloody likely, but it isn't impossible."

David nodded and looked at the Club surveyors.

"We have checked the site thoroughly, Mr Chillingworth," said the senior man. "There is wreckage of booms there, but no sign of deliberate tampering. There is substantial oil in the fish farm nets and traces of it on the coastline to the north. There is nothing to the south of the farms yet, so it looks as if the hand of God sent an arrow of oil straight to these farms. If you are a man of faith you can believe that, but I'm a marine surveyor so I did a lot more digging. We checked their accounts carefully, and the records of fish in and out and production. We even checked their fish food bills. It all tallies up. It is a smooth operation run by smooth people. It is very odd that there is hardly any machinery in the shed, just a big log chipper they use to grind fish feed, but they can show they sell the fish for processing elsewhere. I have to report what we found, and it all adds up. But I do think it is a bit fishy. Pardon the pun."

"Well," said David reluctantly. "We have checked it thoroughly our side. I've never seen such a professional and detailed claim. So against my better judgement I suppose we have to pay it."

"Better than getting another black eye, David," said Linus, with just a hint of a supercilious smile.

He tapped the folder twice and passed it on.

Bastard, thought David.

CHAPTER THIRTY-FIVE

"Capitano Cervetto, it is most decent of you to come for lunch," David welcomed Dino to the secluded table in the corner of the quiet hotel dining room. "A small *aperitivo*, perhaps?"

"I will take a glass of wine with lunch, thank you David, and please call me Dino," came the brisk reply.

David noted that Dino was out of uniform today. *He knows I did not want to draw attention to our meeting.*

David was worrying about the fish farm claim, and he felt he was not getting to the heart of what was going on behind all the claims. His instinct was that lunch with someone in the know might help him. That was the way he was used to doing business.

"I hope you will agree that today is off the record, old chap?" asked David. "I just need to get a steer on a few things. I can't seem to pin down what's going on. Perhaps you might be able to help me with a bit of background on how things are done here in Sicily."

Dino smiled.

"You chose a good place for this lunch, David," he said. "You know this hotel is run by nuns, so we are eating in a confessional. And there is an old saying in Italy that the thick walls of a church hide many secrets. May I suggest we order, then we can talk without interruption?"

David was happy to let Dino suggest that they trust the nuns to bring a selection of *antipasti*, and to follow they would take *cosciotto di agnello* with some *caponata*.

"We will eat well, David," smiled Dino. "The Church in Italy looks after its servants. And it is not unknown for them to take a glass of good wine, so I have taken the liberty of asking for two glasses of Etna Rosso. It is grown on the slopes of our famous volcano, but it will not blow you up too much at lunchtime."

"Now," Dino went on when the nun had left the room with their order. They were alone in the slightly tired old dining room. "You ask a question which would never be asked of me in Italy. You ask me about Sicily. But I am from Genova. We are very different people."

He paused.

"But perhaps you are right to ask me, because if you ask a Sicilian you will not get an answer. I am fortunate enough to work here and to have married here. I do not say that I understand Sicily now. That would be impossible. But I can at least explain a little of what I know and help you to understand. I think the Genovese have something in common with the British, certainly more than we do with the Sicilians."

"I have the feeling that I am missing something," confessed David. "I like it here, some people have been very hospitable, but I feel there is something going on, another world I am not getting to. And I have some huge claims, such as for the fish farms, that really cannot be explained rationally, but which look perfect."

"It is a feeling common to those who come from outside to work in Sicily," said Dino ruefully. "What you see in Sicily is not always what you get. But look, here is our antipasti. Try this warm salad of octopus, and these clams. These gamberi. These are simple, and true, and in this case what we see is what we get. They would never bring frozen seafood from China into the restaurant of the nuns and pass it off as fresh seafood from Lampedusa."

Dino watched David helping himself and tucking into the octopus. He tasted it himself.

"It is not as good as Maria makes," said Dino. "But it is good. I see you like the food."

David nodded as Dino went on.

"There is the first thing, David," he said, suddenly serious. "You are very open. That is not always a good thing here. Everybody can see you like Sicilian food. And everybody knows that you like Sicilian women. One of them, at least."

He could see the look of shock on David's face, his loaded fork frozen halfway to his mouth.

"When you got on the back of the scooter with the lovely girl from the bank half of Ortigia saw you ride out to the castle. And the half that did not see you heard an even better story before the day was out. So now she has had to move to Rome, and you have a black eye. Sicilian girls are very impulsive, but a little more caution from both of you would have been sensible perhaps."

David put his fork down slowly.

"Do you mean I was attacked because of an hour with Anna?" he asked. "I thought it was because I was delaying claims pay-outs."

Before Dino could reply he suddenly flushed red.

"My God," he said. "Is Anna alright? They didn't hurt her did they?"

Dino touched his arm.

"Anna is OK, David. But she did something unforgivable here, she made her boyfriend look stupid. So she has gone to Rome. It is better for her. The bank has many jobs she can do there. And as for you, Anna's boyfriend and his brother saved the Mafia enforcer from a little job. Since the attack you have been paying out very fast, I am told. So they are happy and you are safe."

Dino ate a little more of the seafood and let David absorb the news. He was clearly shocked.

The old nun came in quietly and cleared away the antipasti. Dino did not speak while she served the roast lamb and caponata.

"Now, David," Dino was speaking in his clear naval voice. "Eat some of this. It is delicious. Tender lamb cooked with prunes and anchovies, and served with the national dish of Sicily. I fear you will need a little strength for what I will tell you next."

David took a gulp from his wine glass.

"Go on," he said. "I've made a fool of myself with a woman. What else?"

"Well," Dino swallowed a mouthful of caponata appreciatively. "In Sicily things are not always as you expect. You drive down the road, and you see a sign warning you that there is a traffic light ahead. But when you get to the junction, there is no traffic light. How can that be? Because the money for the sign was paid to one man, who put the sign up, and the money for the traffic light, which is a much bigger contract, was paid to another man, perhaps to a certain family, and so the light was not put up. You do not ask, where is the light? You just look, and if all is clear you drive on."

Dino pointed to the food.

"It will get cold, David, eat up."

He waited while David began to eat.

"Now I can use the food as an analogy," said Dino. "You taste this caponata. It is rich, it is sublime, it has multiple layers of flavour. It is full of history and no two Sicilians will agree on exactly how it should be made, but they will all agree that it is good to eat. So you can do just that. Eat it, enjoy the richness, the flavour, the history, the culture on your plate. Don't ask what is in it. If you do, you discover that what looks like a vegetable dish has also sweet fruit in it. It has sharp vinegar. It has many components that alone would not taste so good to you, and do not make sense together. So you don't ask, you just enjoy. That is Sicily."

"I can see that, and if your wife can cook like this then I can see why you wanted to marry her," said David. "But how does caponata help me with the fish farm?"

"David, we are off the record. So I will trust the word of an Englishman. But I could not say this outside of these holy walls. There are three things with the fish farm. First you do not believe that it made such profits as they claim. Second you do not believe the protection could have failed. And third you do not believe that the oil could have got there in such a quantity. Am I right?"

He cut himself a mouthful of the lamb and chewed with relish, noting that David had nodded and was waiting for more.

"You are right three times, David," Dino went on quietly. His naval officer voice had dropped from quarterdeck volume to gale whisper. "As I said, everything is not what you expect. We all know, and you can never prove, that the fish farm has never made a single euro of profit. It was set up by the Mafia using funds from the EU Regional Development people, and it is a big enough business to be very useful for laundering money from other less public activities. Tuna do not farm well, but farming whores and drugs is very profitable. That profit appears in the fish farms.

"As for the protection. Imagine you are an engineer from Rome, sent by the oil spill contractor to be in charge of a gang of local labour and you have to protect this fish farm. You order the work to be done, you see the equipment supplied and you see, from a distance, that it looks perfectly deployed. But you do not do one vital thing. You do not inspect how well it is secured. Why not, you will ask? Because before you go to make the inspection a very well-dressed and well-spoken man from the fish farm will tell you that only that morning your youngest daughter went to school happily with your wife. He will remark on what your youngest daughter was wearing, only that morning. And you will understand and your stomach will fill with acid and you will not go to check the work of the local labour. Instead you will sign the sheet to say the work is well done and you will get in the car and you will drive back to Siracusa and you will call your wife and you will feel relief when she answers and all is normal."

Dino was watching the play of emotions across David's face.

"This is not a good story for making appetite, David," he said. "Do you want me to go on?"

David nodded. He was shocked, but it was what he had suspected.

"Now, the oil. How did it get there in such a quantity? I will tell you, David. You paid for it to be delivered."

Dino saw David sit back in amazement.

"You remember that the contract to move the waste oil cleaned from the beaches and rocks of Ortigia and Siracusa was let to a big national waste contractor? Perhaps you do not know that they are a Neapolitan company. They are famous for being a front for the Camorra, which Naples is cursed with as Sicily is cursed with the Mafia. They have made billions by illegal waste dumping. They elbowed their way into this because your principal, the shipowner

Spinelli, is in debt to the Camorra. And it is good business for them.

"First of all, every day you pay for them to take several lorries of waste oil away from the coast and to a legal disposal site. Off it goes, and its route and its unloading is checked from time to time by your people. But at night it goes back into the trucks and is delivered further down the coast, to foul the next place, first the beaches of Noto, and then in this case the fish farm. Your people do not see that, because they are eating and drinking in the bars in Ortigia. The next day the place which now has the oil files a compensation claim. Your people validate it, there is the oil, they can see it, and again you pay. Part of that money goes to the waste firm for their helpful delivery. So they have been paid twice. Then you send a clean-up team, who load the oil into the trucks again, and you pay a third time for the oil to be taken to the disposal site. Again."

David was shocked into silence.

"It is a productive economy," said Dino. "Don't you think, David? They are doing efficient recycling. I laugh now, and I laugh because I do not want to be sad. That this can happen is a national shame, but it is happening and nothing you can do will prove it or stop it. It is like the caponata, eat it and enjoy the taste, don't ask any more."

David was shaking his head.

"It is hard to believe, but it all makes sense," he said. "My experts have been saying that you insist only twenty thousand tonnes of oil have so far leaked out of the sunken hull, but they find they are handling fifty thousand tonnes of waste. I knew it was crooked. Dino, I thank you. I will not let anyone know you told me. But I am going to find a way to stop this."

Dino inclined his head.

"I suspected you would think like that," he said. "But let me suggest one thing. Do nothing today. Sleep on it. Enjoy the wine now and do not waste this fine food. There is a big change coming. I have been watching a storm building over the western Mediterranean. I can feel it coming here. It is in my bones. Tomorrow and the day after we will be hit by terrible weather, worse than the storm which broke the ship the first time. That will change everything. Wait only until the storm has passed."

CHAPTER THIRTY-SIX

Simone left Vendicari as the afternoon was turning into a winter dusk. She drove south towards the fish farms. She had used Michiel's car to deliver supplies to the campsite and had spoken with the warden and the activists. They were busy, they had cleaned over three hundred wild fowl and wading birds and there were more waiting. She had started to help but the warden had come quietly to her and asked if they could talk.

He had drawn her aside, away from the others.

"You are nervous, Signorina," he said sympathetically. "The birds notice that and it upsets them. Let the others work, you have done your share. Go and do what it is you need to do. We will be OK, the birds will be OK, you must make yourself OK."

Simone had to turn away. His kindness almost made her cry. But she was angry with herself. I should not care so much that everyone can see what I am doing, she told herself. She touched his arm and went to the car.

"I will see you tomorrow, I hope," she said.

Now she waited a little while longer, parked beside the EU sign which told everyone that passed that way that their taxes had paid for the fish farm. She could see the nets of the farm stretching out seawards below, and here on the hill she was conscious of the wind strengthening. I hope the wind doesn't bring more oil to Vendicari, she thought. Those birds need help. So do I. I need it to be dark enough so they don't see me. But just enough light for this camera to get an image on maximum low light settings. She did not know the camera, but she had always photographed birds and it did not take her long to work out the aperture and shutter speed settings.

When it was almost dark she pulled her scarf up over her face and set off down the path to the fish farm. Her eyes were accustomed to the gloom and she sought out the thicker shadows. She did not want to be spotted. No-one had moved in the half hour she had waited up the hill, so she guessed the fish farm was unmanned. They've oiled it, they've killed the fish, there is no reason to stay, she reasoned. The bosses will be in town filing their compensation claim right now.

Simone climbed carefully over the rusty chain link fence surrounding the fish farm and walked quietly towards the walkways which led out over the water. They were wide, almost a metre, wooden slats built on bearers which floated on pontoons. They must go out to every fish-keeping net, she calculated. They have to get food out there and the fish back. She stepped cautiously onto the first slat. It was silent, so she began to walk forwards, moving gingerly. She did not want to slip into the sea or make any noise.

There were small waves coming into the bay. They made the walkway move, and even at sea level the wind was picking up. She could smell oil now, and could not sense any movement in the nets she was passing. They are real pigs, she thought. Somehow they have not only destroyed the protection put up by the state contractors, they must have found a way to put extra oil in to kill these fish so quickly. She knew that the oil coming ashore at Vendicari was increasing, but that was still a relatively small amount and it was ten kilometres north and not in such a protected bay.

Five minutes took her to the end of the first walkway. She was at the seaward end of the fish farm now. She felt exposed and the movement of the walkway was more pronounced. She had to brace herself with each step so that she did not slip as spray wet the wooden slats. She turned and looked at the way she had come. There was nothing moving. Her heart was hammering so loudly she was sure it could be heard. Calm down, she told herself. You are Marine Bleu. You are doing the right thing. You are exposing deliberate pollution of the beautiful sea.

You are trying to help Michiel, said the voice at the back of her head. She shut it up. I need to concentrate on doing this properly, she told herself. She knelt down and looked carefully at the edges of the pontoon ends. That's where the protection booms were secured in Michiel's photos, she thought. There was nothing there now, no rope, no cut end. It is evidence, but not enough, she told herself. But I must capture that and look for something more. She bent forward and framed the securing point in the lens. As she touched the shutter release she almost fell backwards in shock. The flash had gone off, blinding her.

Merde, she said inwardly. There must be an auto flash on this low light setting that I did not see. She stayed crouched down, peering towards the shore. There was no sound. No movement. She counted to thirty, keeping very still, then worried that it was not enough and counted to thirty again. Still nothing moved, so she stood up slowly and peered at the camera. As her eyes re-adapted to the dusk she could just make out the settings menu. Three clicks through menus and she found the flash setting and disabled it. Then she walked swiftly but silently towards the next walkway junction.

I'll get to the other side, see if there is any evidence of cut ropes, she thought, then I'm out of here. She was afraid but adrenalin was pumping through her. I can do this, she told herself. No-one saw me, and with this evidence and Michiel's photos of what the defences looked like the newspapers and the English insurers will have to pay attention.

She reached the junction of the walkways and turned towards the seaward end again. She felt her stomach fall as she suddenly saw a dark shape ahead of her. It was a man. He looked big, heavy set. He was dressed in a thick oilskin jacket and trousers that reflected what little light there was. He was silent, standing in the middle of the walkway, blocking her way.

Simone turned to run back the way she had come. Another man was there, only ten paces away, silently blocking the way. He is dressed like the other man, she registered. They must be the workers here.

"I just came to have a look," she said, trying to sound calm. "Just a look. I'll leave now."

She turned again. There was still another walkway at the three way junction, she would run that way. But it was too late, it was blocked. Another dark figure was there, silent, menacing.

Simone heard a footstep behind her and turned to shout, but no sound came. The heavy cosh struck her just below the right ear and she dropped like a stone.

****

Antonio Cusumano did not much like this big fisherman coming to his bar. His brooding presence made the journalists edgy. He knew why he was there. He is trying to find the Frenchwoman. That makes two of us, thought Antonio.

He had not seen Simone since the evening that Fortunato had been chatting her up and buying her dinner. That must have been a couple of days ago. She hasn't cleared her kit out of her room. So where is she? I was worried that maybe this ugly great lump had muscled in on my little prize. But he was here last night looking for her, and he is here again. So I guess we both lucked out.

He felt a stab of annoyance and jealousy. She must be tucked up with that Dutchman. I help her, give her a room, hold a press conference here and this is how she repays me. Chats up dirty fishermen in my bar and then disappears.

He moved to where Fortunato was leaning on the bar, his big hands cupping a large glass of red wine.

"Not a day for fishing, my friend," he said. "The weather is losing its temper again."

Fortunato looked up.

"I thought I had caught a little mermaid, and so did you," he said. "But she has slipped both our nets. As for the weather, it is good for me and good for you. This is a big storm now, and before it is over it will be one of the biggest we have seen. It is good timing, a gift from the Three Kings."

Antonio was looking confused. For him bad weather usually meant fewer customers.

Fortunato was not drunk, but close to it. He spoke more than he normally would.

"Look, the longer this fishing ban and oil spill last the more time I will have for mermaid hunting. My boat is on hire to the clean-up people, but it will not go to sea in this, so I get paid for doing nothing. Then I get paid because I cannot fish. Double pay for doing nothing is not so bad. And for the Cusumano family, the weather blows in more money. These winds and waves will tumble the wreck and release more oil. More oil means more journalists, more contractors, more money, and all of it coming through your bars and hotels. Maybe even more thin Frenchwomen. One for each of us. Now, why don't you share your good fortune with your local compatriots, and give me another glass of this Nero d'Avola?"

Antonio smiled thinly. He looked around to check that his wife was not in earshot. He did not want any talk of mermaid fishing or Frenchwomen to reach her. This guy is right though, he thought. We will have a rough day or two now, but it will give a new edge to the emergency. Maybe these fishermen will have even more to spend, so they will be more welcome here.

He rummaged down below the bar and produced another bottle of wine. He wiped it carefully and held it up to the light before stripping off the wax and pulling the cork.

"You are right," he said. "Good wine for good news. Here is a fresh glass to try this one. It is with my compliments. I too will take a glass with you. What shall we toast? To the weather, that blows us good fortune and thin women?"

****

Ugo Vinciullo sniffed the air. There was something he could not put his finger on. Something different.

He stepped out into the garden of his villa and looked up at the sky. It was a washed out blue and the sun was shining brightly.

Maybe there is something in this global warming nonsense, he thought. That was a hell of a storm, and it is the second one this winter. He remembered the first storm. That brought us the tanker and we did not see that as a benefit at first. Now my problem is how to manage all the fingers in the pot.

He wondered idly what damage this second storm had done. Two days of gales must have hit the salvors and work on the tanker wreck. There will surely be more work on the beaches for the oil spill contractors after this. No-one had called him during the last two days which he had spent at the villa, so he assumed there was no big infrastructure damage in his region. So the storm meant money to spend but nothing needing money spent on it. He took a deep, contented breath. Sometimes it is good to be a Regional President, he thought.

Then it hit him. That was what was different. There was no smell of oil. Since the spill the air at his villa had smelled of oil. You could not breathe deeply in the garden. He had to take his evening cigar in the house and listen to his wife complaining about the smell. Of the cigar or of the oil he did not know, and did not ask. But suddenly this morning there was no smell.

He crossed the garden and unchained the gate that led through the high concrete wall to the seafront. Out on the beach he looked left and right. There was nothing to see. Nothing. No oil. No people. The beach was piled with stones. They looked freshly scrubbed, glistening slightly as the morning sun dried them.

He took out his mobile phone and stabbed at the contacts until he found the Coastguard office.

"Cervetto," he said without preliminaries, once he had been connected to the regional commander. "I'm outside my little seaside place and the beach is clean. There is no oil and there are no people working here. What's going on? Has the storm caused some sort of catastrophe?"

"Good morning, Signor Presidente," Dino replied courteously. "Not a catastrophe, I think. But certainly a major change. It is a little early to say exactly how major. We will know more soon, my officers are out collecting information and the helicopter is airborne now on a reconnaissance. But so far all the indications are that the storm has cleaned up the oil."

To Vinciullo Dino sounded just a bit smug. What the hell was he talking about, the storm cleaning up the oil?

"How the hell can a storm clean up oil, Capitano?" he demanded. "Talk sense will you?"

"I can assure you that it is a recognised phenomenon, Signor Presidente," said Dino carefully. "It is quite possible that the very high energy waves have completely dispersed all the oil and cleaned the beaches. It is a natural process. It has happened before on many occasions. I will report fully to you later through the formal channels...You might say, Signor Presidente, if you are religious, that the Lord giveth, and the Lord taketh away."

He is laughing at me, thought Vinciullo as he cut the call.

No oil, no clean-up? That means no more money.

He redialled and got his personal assistant.

"Get me that American professor," he demanded. "We are really going to need him now."

CHAPTER THIRTY-SEVEN

There was an expectant air in the room. Everybody was restless and the duty Coastguard officer struggled to hold their attention. He was running down a long list of beaches and coves and reporting the status of each. Clean, this one. Slight residual fouling, that one. No oil in sight, the next one.

Dino raised his finger and stopped him.

"I think we have the picture, thank you, Lieutenant," he said. He looked around the room. He was flanked by the salvage master and his duty team, and on the other side of the table were Kate Jones, David Chillingworth and the P&I Club experts. Two of the Castalia Mareazul team had come in late and were hunched at one corner of the table. No-one had turned up from the local administration.

"I see it is a picture you like," he went on. "Frankly, I have not seen you all smiling before. It makes a pleasant change."

The meeting erupted into laughter.

"Not been a lot to smile about until now has there?" said Kate. "But this is the real deal. Nature is stronger than all of us."

"So, we go on," said Dino. "We have heard from Miss Kalargyrou and her salvage master. They have scoured the seabed with side scan sonar this morning and they confirm both parts of the wreck are completely broken up now. The waves have smashed them, so we know there is no more oil to come. We have heard from our friends in the Air Force that there is no sign of any oil on the surface. With the good visibility they can be certain of that. And we have heard from Lieutenant Fraille, at some length, that there is no more oil on the coastline, or at the most some small localised fouling. The waves have scrubbed the coast clean. We can assume the oil is fully dispersed into the water column and will be carried away on the current. Which leads us to a decision time. We have salvage tugs and oil spill clean-up vessels and aircraft on hire, we have thousands of clean-up crews, we have tank trucks for waste on standby, we have a full system in place to control the spill from the wrecks. But the spill has gone and the oil has gone. What shall we do? I propose, subject to any other suggestion you may have, to stand the whole operation down. Do you agree?"

He looked around the table at each of them in turn. No-one spoke, but they all nodded in turn as he caught their eye.

"Excellent," said Dino. "I then order the clean-up response to the *Barbara S* to be stood down and all contracts to be brought to an end. Let me say one last thing. I thank you all for your professionalism during a very difficult time. It has been a pleasure to work with you."

Applause rippled round the table then chairs were pushed back and papers gathered.

Dino leant to his left and spoke quietly.

"Fraille, pass the orders to all the onsite units and log this decision, then inform the HQ in Rome, please. Oh, and do all of that before you call your uncle. He will know soon enough anyway."

****

The sunshine that lit up the Foro Siracusana hardly penetrated the thick curtains of the meeting room in the offices of the Provincia Regionale di Siracusa. Just one finger of sunlight reached through a gap in the curtains. It reflected off the red Chanel jacket which Laura Filippone was wearing.

Across the table Paola di Bartolo was dressed more conservatively. Trust Laura to choose that seat, she said to herself. She looks great in that jacket. But we both know there is more than one way to get these men to do what we want them to.

Paola looked around the table. At the top of it she could see Ugo Vinciullo, slightly elevated in his presidential chair. She noticed that he could not stop glancing at Laura, although he was trying to hide it. She keeps him wondering what he missed at school all those years ago, thought Paola. She is clever.

Either side of Ugo were two men she had not seen before. Both were obviously American. One was dressed too young for his age and was also looking at Laura. The other was an energetic-looking redhead who was too busy talking to Ugo to look at anyone. He did not look as if he cared how he dressed.

Around the table were regional deputies, but there was no sign of Capitano Cervetto or anyone from the oil spill contractors, Castalia Mareazul. A lot of mini-meetings seemed to be going on simultaneously, everyone talking but no clear direction. Now it is my turn, she thought. Laura is getting their looks, I just need their ears.

Paola rapped her knuckles on the table. The sudden noise cut through the chatter and everyone turned to look at her. She was aware of Ugo turning red. He hates to be interrupted or made to look irrelevant, she thought.

"Colleagues," she said forcefully. "We are talking, but I did not come here from Noto today for talk. I came because I was invited to a meeting at which we would decide how to tackle the premature cessation of oil spill protection and clean-up activities. Can we do that? Or do I need to go and see Capitano Cervetto myself?"

There was silence when she finished speaking, then Ugo began to bluster.

"I was about to tell the meeting that I have been in touch with the Coastguard, both locally and in Rome. They insist that the local decision is in the hands of our dear Capitano from Genova, who is a very upright man. And he will not change his mind. He insists the clean-up is at an end. He will not authorise another euro of expenditure."

Paola looked surprised.

"Signor Presidente, perhaps you are a little premature to know what he will do or not do? He may be from Genova and he may be a brave or stubborn man. I have heard he is both. But he has a young Sicilian wife and if he felt that our mutual family friends were going to make life, shall we say, uncomfortable, for her, then perhaps he would reconsider his decision?"

She spoke carefully, as if for dictation, but the threat was clear. Put the screws on Cervetto's wife and he would do as he was told.

No-one wanted to answer. They knew that Paola was close to the Mafia, they knew she meant what she said, and they would have been happy if she had done it. But they did not want their fingers on the crime.

The red-headed American broke the silence.

"Look," he said, stabbing his finger towards Paola. "You dames maybe got some tough friends, but you're off the point here. You don't need no strong arm tactics and you don't need no Coastguard. You godda look at what the rest of the world has done and wise up.

Just because you can't see no oil don't mean you don't get no money. No sir. Not at all."

Ugo sat up straight and tapped the table with the small gavel beside him. Paolo stifled a laugh. He wants us to know who he thinks is in charge.

"Ladies and gentlemen," he said pompously. "Shall we begin again with a little order? First allow me to present Professore Cesare Disario, from the University of Savannah, and Counsellor Giovanni Paci, from the New Orleans law firm Paci & Delaney."

He looked around and there was a slight emphasis on the I when he spoke again. He wanted them all to remember who had brought these men along.

"I have invited them here today because they bring renowned experience with big international oil spills. They can explain to us how we can ensure that our beautiful Sicily is protected and compensated, even if our local Coastguard does not see any oil or any problem."

He looked from left to right and back.

"Counsellor Paci, you have begun. So can I ask you please to continue? Can you outline the legal mechanisms for managing this situation? Then we will listen to the scientific picture from Professore Disario. I feel confident then that we will be able to agree a way forward."

Paci needed no encouragement.

"It ain't difficult, in outline," he said. "You godda get a good scientist to show that although there is no oil to see, the oil damage is still there. Then you godda get a good university to work out that the damage is costing you a bucket. Then you need a good lawyer who knows how it works to make that claim stick on the shipowner's insurance, the IOPC Funds and the oil company. It's all about persistence. Look at Spain. These guys in La Coroona had the *Urquiola* spill. The got peanuts. They had the *Aegean Sea* blow up and make a big spill. They got peanuts. So when the *Prestige* bust up because they sent it out to sea, they were ready. They didn't settle for no peanuts. They cleaned the place up in months and went on claiming for ten years. They got four billion US out of it. Now we Americans think big. So when BP got caught with its pecker in the mangle in the Mexican Gulf, we were ready. We're on twenty billion US and climbing. You can come over and see. There ain't no oil, nothing ain't working, but BP is still paying. Transocean owned the rig and they godda pay out a billion greenbacks just to support research. It's down to good science and good lawyers. I'm the good lawyer, this here is the good scientist."

Cesare Disario looked up. He preened himself for a second and looked around to see who was looking at him. Paola saw that Laura was not, and almost laughed again. Laura is wasted here, she thought. She could have made a great career on the stage.

She waited until Cesare had opened his mouth to speak then cut in. He was left gaping.

"I am sure we have as much experience in trompe l'oeil as you do, Counsellor," she said. "We know how to make things appear which are not as they really are. We were doing that before New Orleans existed. Long before. From what I know American lawyers and American scientists don't come cheap. Are you perhaps suggesting we pay for your services, just when our revenue is cut? If so, I prefer my way. It is crude, I agree, but it costs nothing. And it works. Always."

She could see that Cesare had not understood what she was saying. Probably they don't have trompe l'oeil in Savannah, she thought.

"You cannot see the oil," explained Cesare pedantically. "But the oil is there. It is broken into droplets in the water column. We have already shown in the Gulf of Mexico that plumes of oil can exist under water. We can show that dolphin colonies are not healthy. There are all sorts of damage mechanisms. The beauty is that we don't know what all the ways we can be damaged are yet, so we have to be funded to find out. The courts have made BP and Transocean pay billions of dollars for scientific research. The research finds more damage, so then BP and Transocean have to pay out more compensation for the damage and then they have to pay for more studies to ensure that there is no further damage. The scientists provide the fuel, the lawyers are the lubricant, and the wheels of justice turn and drive the press that prints the money. Some of the money pays the lawyers and the scientists, and the rest is spent by the local authorities."

He paused. Paola was looking around the room. She could see the minds of the deputies churning. It seemed so clever and so simple. Why had they not seen it themselves?

"I buy it," said Laura.

All eyes swivelled to the red jacket. That's it then, thought Paola. Trust her to get the last word.

****

Giuseppe Mammino was on the phone to Fortunato Redivo. He wasn't happy.

"Fortunato, my old friend," he said angrily. "Something odd is happening. It must be a misunderstanding. I have heard that groups of fishermen are blockading some of our petrol stations again. We are making payments to your people and the agreement we had was that you would call them off unless I told you we needed a little more pressure. We don't need that now, so can you get them to lay off? I need to sell petrol."

"It is no misunderstanding at all," came the growled reply. "And I am not your old friend. My people are angry. They were chartering their boats to the oil spill contractors, but now all charters have stopped. But we still cannot fish. The English insurer is packing up and running away. You have money, it is your oil that stops the fishing, so now you have to pay more."

"We are paying," replied Giuseppe. "You know that. And you will still be paid by the insurers for loss of the fishing until you can fish again. I cannot get more money from Rome."

"Come to the streets and explain that to my boat skippers," said Fortunato, and cut the line.

"Shit," swore Giuseppe. What have I started now? There is no oil to see, no newspapers here to keep them excited in Rome and Rome won't pay more. How the hell can I put these guys back in their box?

****

Simone was shaking with fear and shock. She felt filthy and she wanted to see herself in the mirror but she could not lift her hands. They were tied together and a loop passed around her legs to keep her arms down.

She held her head down, trying to keep the bright sunshine out of her eyes. She did not know how long she had been in the dark shed. When she had come to she had been lying on a concrete floor in a dark building. She had screamed, but no-one came. Her hands and feet were tied. Her head throbbed and she could feel a lump under her right ear, but she could not reach up and touch it.

Hours went by and at some point she wet herself. She cried with tears of frustration. She had been caught. Michiel was probably dead and now she could not help him. She drifted in and out of consciousness.

Suddenly a door opened and a man came into the shed. In the shaft of light she recognized the squat muscular man who had been kicking Michiel in the Piazza Duomo in Ortigia. That seemed a very long time ago. He was wearing the same ridiculous fedora hat. Her stomach was knotted with fear. He will kick me now, she thought.

He had not kicked her. He had picked her up and carried her like a parcel and sat her in the front seat of the car. Michiel's hire car, she realised. Something else was odd. The sky was bright blue, it felt cold but the sun was shining. It felt unreal, after weeks of gloomy weather. Fear had hold of her. He will take me and kill me. He's going to take me to where Michiel was killed.

The man said nothing. He drove fast, pushing the car as hard as he could, cutting corners, overtaking on blind bends and pumping the horn at anyone who delayed him. Simone did not care. She had given up. She knew she smelt of her own urine. She could not bear this.

The drive seemed to last a long time and Simone realised she must have slept or fallen unconscious. She looked up and saw they were slowing to turn off a motorway. The sign pointed to Catania Airport.

They came down the slip road and after a mile turned up a track. Here is where he will do it, she thought. And there is nothing I can do. She felt the fear knotting her insides. I hope he is not going to rape me before he kills me.

Just beside a small concrete barn, out of sight of the main road, the Mafia enforcer pulled the car to a halt and spoke for the first time.

"You got lucky," he said. "You got a chance. Your bag is in the back of the car. Your passport is there, your money is there. The airport is one kilometre that way. You can get on the plane and get out of Sicily. This is your one chance. Your friend didn't take his chance. Turn the right way out of this lane and you are on the road to your old life. Turn the other way, talk about this, and your chance is

296

gone."

Simone's tongue was stuck to her mouth and she could not answer, but he did not seem to want an answer anyway. He took out a handkerchief and wiped the steering wheel and gear lever. He did it methodically. Then he got out and walked round the car, moving slowly and theatrically, opened her door and lifted her out on to the grass verge. From his pocket he produced a knife that opened with a sharp click. He cut away the ropes and tape on her ankles and arms and bundled them into an old plastic shopping bag.

Simone sat still while he looked into the car and checked it carefully.

A dusty red car was reversing up the track towards them. Simone sat silently, watching him and slowly moving her hands and feet.

The enforcer removed his hat and opened the passenger door of the red car.

"Remember, turn the right way," he said, then the car was off, leaving only a cloud of dust as it went back to the main road. She was alone, and now the tears came.

CHAPTER THIRTY-EIGHT

David watched the claims handlers bundling up the files. They were packing them carefully into numbered cases for shipment back to London. Out of the corner of his eye he could see Linus pacing across the back of the office. He is sniffing around, looking to check we have not left a piece of paper behind, thought David. He didn't want to come here, he hated being here, but now he is making shutting the office up and moving the whole claims process back to London as difficult as possible.

For a moment David wondered about Linus. Does he have a wife? Perhaps he is gay. Probably he doesn't do sex, just looks at himself in the mirror and tidies up his flat when he needs a thrill.

He could not quite believe that they were leaving. The whole experience had been surreal. He thought his life would never be the same again. The excitement of the spill itself, setting up the office, the huge claims, dealing with the fishermen and the aggressive American lawyer. Dealing with Linus. Learning to like the strange food, nothing like the Italian food he knew from restaurants in London. They don't even have those big pepper grinders here, he mused idly.

His thoughts were buzzing without a pattern, but he knew what he was trying not to think about. He did not want to think about Anna.

Her bright smile, the unexpected scooter ride, the walk around the castle. He could feel her back against him as he sat on the scooter. Had he upset her how he had held on? I tried not to touch her, he thought. Perhaps I should have done.

His mind was racing now. Her boyfriend must have been watching us. I hope he didn't hurt her. Perhaps she can come to London.

"Just got to check something at the bank," he heard himself say. Then he was out of the door and down the narrow street to the bank.

When he got there he did not know what to do. Can I send her a note? Will I look stupid if I ask Marlena to give her a message?

Don't be such a weakling, he told himself, and marched into the bank. Marlena was standing behind the counter, talking to the cashier. She looked up and waved as she saw him, then walked round and opened the meeting room door.

"Mr Chillingworth, it is a pleasure to see you again so soon," she said, although she did not hold out her hand to be shaken. "Did we forget something? I thought we had resolved all the outstanding issues for now, pending the transfer of claims handling to London?"

David shifted his weight and stood there tongue-tied.

"I, er, I was wondering if you could, perhaps, if it was possible…" he could not finish.

"If it is possible to give a message to Anna?" Marlena finished the sentence for him.

He nodded, feeling foolish. He felt even more foolish as Marlena eyed him up and down frankly. He felt she was sizing him up.

"Well," she said with a smile, after what seemed too long to David. "Perhaps I can guess why Anna will be glad to hear from you in Rome. Write your personal phone number down here and I will make sure she gets it."

David left the bank walking on air. He did not look back. So he did not see Marlena exchanging glances with the receptionist then throwing his phone number into the bin.

****

"You are going to give how much to the Mafia? Even a donkey such as you who has his brains in what passes for balls cannot think it is right to pay such a *pizzo*," shouted Antonio Cusumano's wife. "Perhaps your Donkeyness has not noticed that the bonanza has gone? The hotels are emptying, the bar is empty, I am sending the girls back to their husbands, may the Lord protect them, the sacks of money we were making last week are not going to be full this week, and you want to give such an amount to that Mafia clown?"

Cusumano held his head in his hands. To be trapped between this wife and the Mafia. What did I do to deserve this, he thought?

"I have to pay," he shouted back. "Woman, stick to your kitchen and your sheets. I have to pay because he has seen the pumped up accounts we did for the claim, and because if I do not pay he will finish what he started, and cut off my manhood."

He had not heard his wife laugh for years, but she laughed now. And it hurt.

"You are worried that he will cut off that little thing," she said scornfully. "It would be doing us all a favour. It has done me no good for years, and the girls who come to clean the rooms which you make so much money from come to me to complain when you try to use it on them. You wanted to show it to that skinny Frenchwoman, and look, my fine cockerel, she has left without paying the bill. She did not pay her bill, and the Dutchman who had a cock more to her fancy also did not pay his bill. Perhaps without that thing you would think more carefully. Let the Mafia have it. I prefer to keep the money we have made thanks to this tanker, may the Lord bless the man who broke it here."

****

He was trying to help, but he should not have spoken.

"I don't care to hear about your sister," said Guido Recagno. His voice was low and full of pent up menace. "Your sister in Ortigia has seen with her own eyes that the oil has gone from the coast and it is all clean. It is a miracle, she says. Well, I cannot see anything from in here, but I can tell you that it will be a miracle if you go home with your balls still hanging there if you mention your sister again."

The tour guide could see the fury and frustration in the Mafia don's pallid face. Why did he not learn to keep quiet? He thought his bladder would let go.

Recagno turned away and paced across the room.

"This is not a miracle, it is a setback. When you have money flooding onto your beaches and it dries up that is a miracle only to stupid women like your stupid sister, who is more used to seeing the ceiling while she fucks the fishermen than she is to seeing miracles. You bring me bad news, and no-one likes bad news."

The guide felt his left leg begin to tremble. He tried to hold it, tried not to move.

Recagno was thinking.

"God has sent one miracle, he cleaned up the oil. But America has sent another miracle, a scientist and a lawyer who can bring it back. Tell my cousin to do two things. First to visit all the bars and hotels and to take the *pizzo* now, before they forget that they have been full for two weeks and earned a lot of extra money. Then to make a little call to our good friend Presidente Vinciullo. Just to give him a gentle reminder that he took away part of our legitimate business, the waste disposal, and gave it to those robbers from the Camorra. He owes us for that, so he must be sure to use these Americans well to keep the compensation money flowing. There may be no oil to see, but that should not stop the money."

He paused and smiled.

"And change your trousers before you bring his reply," he said.

****

Osman Mohamoud looked at the handful of euros. He could see that it was only half of what he should have been paid. His mind was racing. Did he dare to complain?

He knew the Mafia enforcer was waiting for him to say something. He wants the chance to hurt me, thought Osman. I can complain and be attacked, which will make him happy. Or I can say nothing. I will not get any more money whatever I do, but if I say nothing he will not have the satisfaction of making me back down.

"Tomorrow at the same time, chief?" he asked. "How many men?"

"Tomorrow you do what you are good at," replied the enforcer. "You sit on your fat black arse and scratch your balls all day. You can do it the day after, and the day after that too. You can do it all together, talking that bush talk to each other. There is no more work here, even a bush negro can see that. The oil is gone, the clean-up is over. The people who came for the clean-up are gone, and there will be no cleaning, no work and no selling until the summer season starts. And in case you were going to ask, you have half money because you have done only half a job. We planned for a month's work and we have only had work for two weeks. So you get half pay, that's clear."

For a second Osman let the rage build up in him. He felt the blood rushing into his head. He imagined smashing the enforcer to the ground, kicking him until he bled. He knew his friends were behind him. They would help him. We will tear him apart.

He felt his hands lifting and he began to move forwards.

"Better not!" he heard. The words penetrated the mist of rage just as his eyes lifted enough to see that he was looking down the barrel of a pistol. With a massive effort he held himself in check. He turned away. One day, he promised himself, one day you will not be looking. Then we will get you. But he knew they would not, and his fear and humiliation tasted like vomit in his mouth.

CHAPTER THIRTY-NINE

"I, er, I thought you were in Sicily," Yves was stuttering. It sounded banal. He was scrabbling to pull the sheet up and cover his naked body. She could see his erection shrivelling. Beside him on the bed was the English girl. She looked scared.

Simone looked at the girl dispassionately. She has good breasts, she assessed calmly, and she is young. Yves likes that. But soon she will be a little fat.

"And I thought you were a man I wanted, so it seems we were both wrong," she said, speaking clearly and without emotion. "Pack your things, take your friend, and go."

She saw the shock in the face of the English girl. She switched into English.

"Don't worry dear," she said sweetly. "You are welcome to him. By the look of things you have already discovered that sex with Yves is really just Yves making love to himself. There will be more disappointments to come. I can see why he likes you. You should take another look and think why you like him. Probably you can do better for yourself."

Simone felt completely in control. She had found a reservoir of mental strength even though physically she was only just holding herself upright. She was exhausted and she was dying to get into a warm shower then to sleep. I really need to be clean and to sleep, she thought. But first I want to clean my life of this slimy bastard.

She had stripped off beside the car, wiped herself on her dirty clothes, changed into a sweater and jeans from her bag and gone straight to the airport. She had dumped the car in the car park and taken the first flight out of Catania. It took her to London. She had taken the underground into London and then the next Eurostar to Lille, and finally a taxi home to Bergues. It was a long journey, but it was a journey with a destination she wanted to reach. She had slept fitfully on the plane and on the train. She was conscious of people looking at her. She knew she looked awful. Hair a mess, a huge bruise on her neck. But she didn't care. She just wanted to be home. To be safe. To be clean. To see the narrow cobbled streets and the bell tower of Bergues. To know that her neighbours and family cared for her.

Everything was in her bag and she had let herself into the flat. She heard the sounds coming from the bedroom and realised what was happening. She had been going to shout and scream, but something clicked inside her and suddenly she had felt calm. My life has changed for ever, she thought. Yves will have to go, so this will make it easier. So she had put her bag down quietly, drawn herself up tall and looked in the mirror in the hall. She began to push her hair into place then stopped. Fuck them, she said to herself, why should I care what I look like? She had walked to the bedroom and opened the door.

Now she did not move. I won't make this easy for them, she thought.

"Come on," she said. "Get dressed and go. Yves, you will find the rest of your things with the concierge tomorrow. For now just cover that pathetic little cock and go."

She waited for him to speak. He will try to excuse himself. Try to come back and wheedle his way back into my life. But he looked at her again and said nothing. He expected me to be angry, she thought. If I was upset he would have won. But he cannot handle this calm woman.

She watched them all the time while they struggled into their clothes then stood aside to let them out of the bedroom. She followed them down the hallway and out of the apartment door. She closed the door behind them and turned the lock.

A shower, she thought. A hot shower.

****

She could not feel angry any more. She had been angry for too long. Now she just felt sad. A heavy sadness for what could have been. Should have been, thought Bianca, the anger almost coming back.

She looked around at the simple furniture and the small but well-lit living room. It looked empty with her things packed away. There was a patch on the wall where she had taken her favourite picture down. Michiel has so few things, she realised. But we were happy here. We should have our children here now. Well, whatever you are doing I hope it is worth it for you. A week chasing a dream, and another week now without a call or returning my messages. It's enough, it is the last straw. I will not be treated like this. What we had was great, but I need to have my life, not live it waiting for Michiel.

She picked up her mobile phone and tapped the icon to call Michiel. She was not surprised when the phone went straight to voicemail.

"Michiel, I have had enough," she said. Her sadness softened her Rotterdam accent. "You must find what you want, but I cannot do this anymore. I have taken my things. Please don't call me or make this any harder. I shall file for divorce and I do not expect you to contest that. Goodbye."

****

"I should have gone to speak for myself," he said, shaking his head from side to side. "This is unjust. I did everything I could and I saved my crew. They tried to make me confess but I did not. Now I am guilty, and every Captain who comes after me in such a mess will know that jail is waiting. It is not right."

Captain George Anand was talking to his grandson, who helped him with the internet. The signal was poor here in his cottage outside Calcutta, but the boy was clever and for three weeks now he had come every day so that they could follow the news of his trial in the court in Palermo. Today the verdict had been handed down. He had been found guilty *in absentia* of refusing an order from the Coastguard. Guilty of intentional pollution of the coastline. Five years in jail.

"It is a misunderstanding," he went on. "If I had explained myself they would have understood. This is also not fair on the P&I Club. They put up bail of over one million euros for me. Now they will lose that. I finish my career by costing my employer so much. I am in disgrace."

His grandson was brisk but kind. He had packed up his laptop and was on his way out to his scooter.

"Grandfather, you are not in disgrace. You are safe in your house in Calcutta. This money is nothing for them. They themselves told you not to attend the court. You spent one year in jail and one year more having to stay in Sicily before they put up enough money to get your passport back so you could come home. If the seafarers' unions had not campaigned so strongly you would still be there. Do you think the shipowner has not got one million euros he could have paid to have you free and home right at the beginning? Be happy, grandfather. You are still our Captain-gi to all of us, there is no damage to Sicily and you can retire happily. Oh, and my mother says she will be round this evening to cook your favourite prawn curry. She knows how to do it the English way, and you like that."

George Anand loved his grandchildren, but he did not know where they got this attitude from. I am only seventy, he thought. But I am like a dinosaur to them. My life at sea means nothing. He does not know what it means to be Captain of a ship. He wants to work in software development, what on earth is that? They treat me as if I am their child, not the other way round.

He felt the warmth of the sun as he stepped outside to wave the boy off. He shivered slightly. He remembered the cold of the Catania jail. He is so young, he thought. He does not know how I suffered. But honour is honour, and I have let myself and my company down.

CHAPTER FORTY

"Let me get the bill, Dino," said Giuseppe Mammino. "A hundred euros more or less will not make such a difference."

He was smiling.

"In fact, two hundred euros won't make such a difference, so let us enjoy a nice glass of masala before we go," he said. "I know they have the Donnafugata Passito di Pantelleria 2008 here. It has a lovely oily consistency."

He laughed out loud at his own joke and Dino could not stop himself laughing with him. They were sitting at a table outside the Ristorante Largo Vista, on the terrace just above Ortigia's landmark Fountain of Arethusa. The afternoon sun was hot but they were nicely in the shade of the old stone wall and a low awning. In front of them the sun lit up the harbour and they could see right across the bay. Yachts moved slowly in the gathering afternoon sea breeze, their white sails catching the sunlight reflecting from the sparkling sea. Immediately below them tourists thronged the walkway along the cliff top.

"It has been a very pleasant meal, Giuseppe," said Dino. "I thank you for that, although the choice of topic to celebrate might not be to everyone's taste."

"We could have celebrated your promotion, Almirante," said Giuseppe. "But that is still a secret and I imagine you will celebrate that with Maria this weekend. It just seemed right to me to celebrate the end of this whole *Barbara S* business. It has been an expensive business for ENOL, of course. But in the end it has not been so bad for Sicily."

Dino was about to ask how on earth Giuseppe knew of his promotion, which he himself had only heard about that morning. He stopped himself in time. This is Sicily, he remembered.

"You do not know everything, Giuseppe," he replied, with a smile. "Even I do not know yet if I will accept this promotion. So you cannot know. To accept means to go to Rome. That is not a decision for me alone."

"Many people in Sicily will think you would like to leave, Dino," said Giuseppe. "But Sicily has a way of growing on people. And even people from Genova can become someone Sicilians value. I will miss you if you leave."

The waiter had poured two small glasses of the rich, dark dessert wine. They rolled the glasses up against the light, watching the heavy tears of Christ form and coat the sides of the glass. Then they both savoured a sip.

"A rich liquid indeed," said Dino. "About the same price per litre as the oil from the *Barbara S*, if we believe the compensation you and the owners will have to meet. The court in Palermo was not kind to you in its final judgement yesterday, I think."

Giuseppe took another sip and held it in his mouth for a moment before swallowing.

"The court was not kind to ENOL, indeed. A four billion euro claim to pay out will make them sit up in Rome. The American lawyer is very clever, and his Sicilian counterpart, Consentini, has played a brilliantly understated hand. With the funny professor from Savannah we have seen a master class in action. Every municipality in this part of Sicily is rich now. The fishermen are rich, the tourist businesses are rich and look, three years after the spill no-one can remember anything. The beaches and hotels are full, we have just eaten wonderful fish, and now we drink a wonderful wine," he said reflectively. "But not kind to ENOL and not kind to me are not the same thing. ENOL can afford four billion euros, they will get a lot back from the IOPC Funds and the shipowner's P&I Club, and we are selling a lot more fuel now here than we were before the spill, so I rest easily. The best thing is that my bosses are not so keen to be seen here, which suits me fine."

Dino sat back and held up his glass to the light again. You have to see everything through a prism here, he thought.

"Giuseppe," he said, "this is fine sweet wine, made by being very selective with the grapes, which have also to be a little rotten before picking. It has taken me some time, but I taste the essence of Sicily in this glass. *Saluti!*"

****

"Giovanni, did you see the judgement?" Cesare Disario was looking out of the window of his new office. Below his balcony, alongside the dock, he could see cases of food and instruments being loaded onto the slick new oceanographic survey vessel. He watched as the students lined up to lift the cases and carry them one by one up the gangplank.

"Of course I saw the goddam judgement," Giovanni Paci growled into the phone. "Knowing the judgement is my business, and I ain't got my eyes on the mirror the whole day like you, Professor."

Cesare was not put off by Paci's grumpy reply.

"Well, I rang to thank you," he said. "We have funding for years of joint research with the University of Siracusa, and the studies we have done over the last three years have really put us on the map. Even these hung-up literary types here at the university have had to recognise that oceanography can be a profit centre. You did a great job with your uncle-in-law on getting this settlement placed on ENOL and the shipowner."

"You got it, Professor," said Paci. "Now you got years of work and my fees stop when the claim is paid. So remember me when you get wind of another spill, right? Now I godda get back to work, we still got some work to do on BP. The Sicilian courts are a little faster than the ones we have in Louisiana, you understand. Ciao, Disario."

Cesare realised the line had been cut. He shrugged and replaced the receiver. He picked up his new dark blue blazer and slipped it on, buttoning the top gold button.

Well, I might as well go down and check on those students loading the ship, he said to himself. We'll see who is keen on this trip, and then I can decide who will come on the next research supervision trip to Sicily with me.

****

"You are very silent, my Admiral," said Maria. "Even for you."

Dino turned to look at her. His heart gave a little flip. It does that every time, he thought.

They were seated side by side on a rock, high on the hillside above Maria's family village. A light breeze tempered the hot sunshine and flicked the ends of Maria's dark hair. She is so lovely, he thought. He reached out and held her hand.

"I was thinking," he said. "I have not been up here since the night I took the call from that idiot Fraille and found out he had condemned the *Barbara S* to destruction. Three and half years ago, and it could be a lifetime."

"No-one was hurt," said Maria. "And now look, they are so pleased with you that you will be promoted to be an Admiral."

"It was crazy," said Dino seriously. "The accident was my fault, it would not have happened if I had not been here. It was a miracle the crew were saved, and we still have not invited Beppe and his people to a good lunch. The oil disappeared because of the extreme weather, so I had nothing to do with that. It has happened before, off the coast of Spain, and in the Scottish *Braer* spill. The same size ship, and no pollution to see. But everyone insists now that I was some sort of hero and did a great job. I don't feel comfortable."

Maria looked at him teasingly.

"You will look very handsome in an Admiral's uniform," she said. "And I will be a lady you can be proud of at all those functions in Rome. You will be able to afford to buy me a new wardrobe with the Admiral's pay. The local politicians have decided it suits them to make you the hero while they keep the cash. An Admiral's job is what you deserve."

Dino was serious.

"Look, Maria," he said. He felt her flinch slightly, and realised he was gripping her hand too tightly. He relaxed his grip. "I am a career officer. I have always dreamt I would one day become an Admiral. But I do not want to become an Admiral like this. And I do not want to go to Rome. I do not want you to come to Rome and go to functions with me. I want to stay here. In Sicily. With you. But if you want new dresses and functions in Rome I will accept the promotion."

Her eyes seemed so big he feared he would drown. Maria was quiet for what seemed a very long time. Then she leant towards him and kissed him softly on the lips.

"Well then, my Capitano," she said happily. "That is easy because you want what I want. I will go to Rome and make you proud if you want me to. But if you want to stay here, to be in Sicily with me, then that is what I want too. Let us walk down the hill now and see what my mother has prepared for lunch. She has been busy and mysterious all morning. She wanted to celebrate your promotion, and I know my father is in his cellar finding his best wine. Instead we will celebrate a dry old Capitano coming to understand love and deciding to stay here in Sicily."

She paused, just touching his chest with one hand.

"Then after lunch and good wine we can go upstairs for a little siesta. And you will be a very happy Capitano with a very happy wife in a very happy old farmhouse."

She stood up and began to skip down the hill. Dino stood to follow her, and just caught the words over her shoulder.

"We can make a baby," he heard.

CHAPTER FORTY-ONE

The old warden was not sure if children had changed or he had. They seemed so noisy now.

He tried to quieten the group, appealing to the two young teachers with them to keep the noise down.

"You are welcome to the Oasi di Vendicari," he said, projecting his voice but being careful not to shout. "We are privileged here in Sicily to have Europe's most important bird reserve. Every winter thousands of birds come here to escape the harsh weather. There are not so many here now, because most of them have flown north for the summer. But if you are quiet I will take you on a small tour and we will certainly see some herons and other more unusual birds."

I think I will have to retire, he thought to himself. Every day there are school parties. I love children, but in a class like this they become impossible. Noisy children and birds don't mix. The oil spill did not kill many birds in the end, but these visits will do a lot more damage by scaring the birds away.

He felt too tired to get angry. They did not protect us during the oil spill, he recounted to himself. They kept the cash for themselves. Only the Frenchwoman and her helpers came, and even she disappeared without a word. We were saved by the weather, *grazie a Dio*, but the money which followed the oil is a greater curse. The courts gave the Consiglio Nazionale delle Ricerche so much money that they put in place an educational scheme here. So every schoolchild in Sicily is brought to visit our reserve. They are supposed to view the exhibition of how the birds were saved from the oil spill. Somehow the money to build the exhibition never came, but the money for these cursed school trips keeps flowing. So I have children and nothing to show them, and because of the children I will soon have no birds.

"*Silencio!*" he barked, more sharply than he intended. "*Si prega di essere tranquillo.* Try to keep quiet."

He saw the two teachers glance at each other. It's just a day out for them and they laugh at me, he realised. The oil spill means nothing, and the birds mean nothing. Nothing has changed.

Only me, perhaps, he thought.

****

Bianca looked up sharply. She had heard Michiel's name called. She saw only a thin and elegant woman on the next bench talking to her toddler in French.

I'm going mad, she thought. I was crazy to come here on holiday. It's a lovely place, everything is so clean and the beaches are beautiful. Noto is such a nice place, and there are none of those Africans here hassling us to buy handbags and sunglasses. Klaus likes the food too, and the wine. She wriggled happily. The wine makes him more lively, she thought. But I cannot get Michiel out of my head. This is where he disappeared. I cannot tell Klaus that I wanted to come to Sicily to see where I lost my husband, but that is the truth.

She smiled at Klaus and took his arm. She pulled his hand towards the pushchair.

"Look," she said. "Little Ruth loves the sunshine. She has sunshine in her blood. She gets that from me. She is not just a Dutch girl who has rain in her soul."

She saw the look on Klaus's face. He cannot believe this beautiful child is ours, she thought. I cannot believe it myself. I have the steady man I wanted and I have the baby my body was crying out for. Perhaps after this holiday the sunshine and wine will mean we will have another baby. So why am I still thinking about Michiel?

****

"Michiel!" called Simone. "*Viens ici!* Come here. Hold my hand while we cross the road. We will go and see some birds."

She did not notice the couple with the pushchair who were sitting on the next bench, and she did not see that the dark-skinned woman had looked up sharply when she had called her son.

Michiel took her hand trustingly. He is so sweet, she thought. And always so neat and clean. We have just had an ice cream and somehow he eats it without a mess. Not many two-year-olds could do that. It must be genetic.

The early summer sun was fierce and she reached down to adjust Michiel's sun hat.

"We will walk just a little along this lovely beach, my sweetness," she said, "then we will go in the car just a short way. I hope we will see some beautiful birds then. Do you want to see some birds?"

When you are older we will come back here again and I will tell you about your father, she promised herself. I'm not sure what I will say though. That half a day of madness with a man I thought I did not like made me question everything I believed? That you were made in a passion I did not know I could feel? That your father was a brave man who cared about the world?

I can tell you all that, Michiel, she thought. But there are some things I cannot tell you. Like why I have come here on holiday now, just so that I can feel close to your father. I know he is dead, but somehow I feel he is here.

Simone looked around as they walked. They were at the Lido di Noto, the beach resort closest to Noto. It was pristine, the promenade renewed in fine tiles and stone, new benches at regular intervals and a handsome local stone building housing a café and *gelateria*. It too was new.

You were right, thought Simone. She felt a flash of irritation. You were so right, Michiel, this whole coastline is rich now. They got the spoils of the spill. But you did not get your story and you lost your life. It would have been better if you had been a little less right and a little more alive. I wanted you then, and I want you now, to bring up our son with me.

A tug on her hand brought her back to the present.

"*Maman*, birds?" said Michiel.

She smiled. I will tell you that your father changed my life, she thought.

The End

About the author

John Guy served on merchant ships and warships for sixteen years before becoming a ship inspector and then a journalist. He advises companies and organisations working in the global shipping industry on media and crisis management. He has been involved in many oil spill incidents around the world. This is his second novel.

Previous books by John Guy include:

Fiction

The Reluctant Pirate

Non-fiction

Marine Surveying & Consultancy

Effective Writing for the Marine Industry

Follow John's blog on www.johnguybooks.com

If you enjoyed this book then why not read *The Reluctant Pirate*, also by John Guy and available on Amazon as a paperback or in Kindle e book format.

This fast-paced thriller follows Abdi, a Somali boy brought up in the UK, as he is sucked into a pirate gang in Somalia. Tension builds as Islamic militias and the pirates fight over a ship held to ransom while the shipowner and insurer stall over freeing the ship. Abdi faces conflicts between his Western upbringing, his arranged bride in Somalia and his desire for a Norwegian woman who is an officer on the captured ship.

Reading Group Discussion Questions:

1. Everything in this book has actually happened in real life, although not in Sicily. What shocks you most?

2. How did this book challenge your perception of oil spills?

3. Have you ever thought about who pays for cleaning up oil spills and how the money is spent?

4. Were you surprised at the idea of corruption and greed following the compensation?

5. Were you shocked at the way Sicilian politicians were portrayed?

6. Did the international cast of the book make it richer for you?

7. Think about a thirtyish woman you know. Would she have reacted as Simone did to the circumstances she found herself in?

8. Is Simone a bad woman? What would you have done in her place?

9. What most surprised you in the book and why?

10. Oil spills make the news, but shipping doesn't. Did this book make you think more about what happens at sea?

11. The Captain dithered and was part of the reason the accident happened. Did you feel any sympathy for him?

12. Were you offended by any of the stereotype characters in the book?

13. Was the ending a surprise? Did it satisfy you? Why or why not?